Be Mine in Good Hope

Also by Cynthia Rutledge / Cindy Kirk

Harlequin Books by Cynthia Rutledge (2000–2005)

Unforgettable Faith
Undercover Angel
The Marrying Kind
Redeeming Claire
Judging Sara
Trish's Not-So-Little Secret
Wedding Bell Blues
Season for Miracles (online read)
Kiss Me, Kaitlyn
A Love to Keep
The Harvest
Two Hearts
Love Enough for Two
For Love's Sake
Rich, Rugged . . . Royal

Harlequin Books by Cindy Kirk (2007–2016)

Romancing the Nanny
The Tycoon's Son
Claiming the Rancher's Heart
Your Ranch or Mine?
Merry Christmas, Cowboy!
The Doctor's Baby
In Love with John Doe
The Christmas Proposition
If the Ring Fits
Jackson Hole Valentine
The Doctor's Not-So-Little Secret
His Valentine Bride
The Doctor and Mr. Right
Expecting Fortune's Heir
A Jackson Hole Homecoming
One Night with the Doctor
A Sweetheart for Jude Fortune
Her Sister's Boyfriend (online read)
The Husband List
Ready, Set, I Do!
Fortune's Little Heartbreaker
The MD's Unexpected Family
Betting on a Maverick
The Doctor's Valentine Dare
The Doctor's Runaway Fiancée

Harper Collins (Avon) (2007–2008) by Cindy Kirk

When She Was Bad
One Night Stand

Harper Collins Christian (Zondervan) Books by Cindy Kirk

Love at Mistletoe Inn

Amazon Publishing—Montlake Romance

Christmas in Good Hope
Summer in Good Hope

Self-Published

Baby on His Doorstep

Be Mine in Good Hope

CINDY KIRK

This is a work of fiction. Names, characters, organizations, places, events, and incidents are either products of the author's imagination or are used fictitiously.

Text copyright © 2017 Cynthia Rutledge
All rights reserved.

No part of this book may be reproduced, or stored in a retrieval system, or transmitted in any form or by any means, electronic, mechanical, photocopying, recording, or otherwise, without express written permission of the publisher.

Published by Montlake Romance, Seattle

www.apub.com

Amazon, the Amazon logo, and Montlake Romance are trademarks of Amazon.com, Inc., or its affiliates.

ISBN-13: 9781503941731
ISBN-10: 1503941736

Cover design by Damonza

Printed in the United States of America

To editor Lauren Plude for your insightful comments and support. The book wouldn't have been as good without you!

Chapter One

"Marigold."

Her sister's joyful squeal split the air a second before Marigold Bloom found herself enfolded in Prim's arms. She let herself be hugged tight. Only when tears stung the backs of her eyes did she recognize the danger and pull back.

"You look fabulous." Prim's hazel eyes, so like their father's, shone with undisguised delight.

"You're the one who looks fabulous." Marigold held her sister at arm's length. "Simply stunning."

Prim's shimmery green silk flattered her strawberry blonde curls and porcelain complexion. If Marigold had been around prior to the party, she'd have twisted Prim's hair up instead of letting it fall to her shoulders. The updo would have added a touch of elegance, especially with some pearls woven through the silky strands.

"Does Ami know you're here?" Even as she asked the question, Prim surveyed the crowd as if searching for their eldest sister.

"Happy New Year, Marigold." Max Brody, Prim's husband of four months, stepped forward and lightly brushed a welcoming kiss across her cheek.

"Same to you, Max." Marigold liked her new brother-in-law, but the growing concern in his blue eyes said he saw too much. She squeezed her sister's arm. "I'll catch up with you in a bit. Right now I'm off in search of a big glass of champagne and our wonderful hostess."

As Marigold wove her way through the crowd, she was reminded of another party. A party where, like tonight, champagne flowed freely and music and conversation filled the air. She may have started that particular evening alone, but she'd ended it in the arms of a handsome, gray-eyed stranger.

How many times, Marigold wondered, had she revisited that particular interlude over the past eighteen months? *Too many times to count.*

Her life might be unraveling quicker than a row of dropped stitches, but memories of that one perfect night still had the power to buoy her spirits.

Marigold's lips curved as a thought struck her. When she'd left Chicago this afternoon, she'd wondered how she was going to distract a brain that kept reliving the events of the past forty-eight hours ad nauseam. She now had a plan. Instead of ruminating about the mess that was now her life, she'd ruminate on her one and only one-night stand.

Her mood had swung from despairing to almost cheerful when she was stopped by David and Whitney Chapin. She'd once been friends with David's younger sister but hadn't known him all that well. And Whitney? Well, despite the couple's ten-year marriage, Marigold could count on one hand the number of times she'd seen the woman.

"Beck didn't mention you were back in town." David smiled a warm welcome. He was a handsome man with dark hair and eyes that reminded her of gray fog.

"It's a surprise visit." Marigold widened her smile to include his wife, who managed to look both bored and elegant in a shimmery bronze dress that showed off her tanned and toned body to perfection.

The woman reminded Marigold of many of the clients she'd had in Chicago. Whitney's hair, a rich mahogany color with burgundy highlights, was shorter than Marigold remembered from the last time their paths had crossed. The textured razor cut, parted on the side, flattered her angular face and was clearly the work of an expert.

"It's great you could come for the party." David glanced around, his gaze lingering for a second on the pretty tables laden with appetizers and desserts. "Beck and Ami did it up right, and they got a great turnout. I told Whitney I was looking forward to seeing everyone."

"And I told you that all these same people will be at the Valentine dance." Whitney waved a hand adorned with a glittery diamond the size of Texas. "There was no need for us to celebrate New Year's in Good Hope."

Though his pleasant expression never wavered, a muscle in David's jaw jumped before his gaze shifted from his wife back to Marigold.

"I wouldn't have seen you if I hadn't come." David smiled, obviously assuming this was a brief visit and she'd be long gone before next month's festivities.

Dear God, Marigold hoped that was the case. On top of everything else going wrong, the last thing she'd want was to be the third wheel with her sisters and their husbands at the big V-Day dance.

There was not a single doubt in Marigold's mind that a question—or two—about her plans was poised on David's lips. Searching for a way to graciously exit the conversation, she murmured a silent prayer of thanks when she spotted Hadley Newhouse.

"Hadley." Marigold raised her voice to be heard above the din. When the pretty blonde turned, she motioned her over.

Hadley gave Marigold a hug when she reached her, then cast a curious glance in David and Whitney's direction.

"Hi, David." Hadley offered him a polite smile, then extended her hand to Whitney. "I don't believe we've met. I'm Hadley Newhouse. I work at Blooms Bake Shop. Your husband and daughter stop in occasionally. Brynn is adorable."

Whitney's lips lifted in a smile so brief Marigold knew she and Hadley both would have missed it if they hadn't been looking.

"Have you seen Ami, Hadley?" Marigold broke the awkward silence. "I haven't spoken with her yet."

"I know exactly where she is, and she'll definitely want to see you right away." Hadley grabbed the life preserver Marigold tossed her with both hands. "I'll take you to her."

"That'd be fabulous." After saying good-byes to David and Whitney, the two women slipped into the crowd.

"Whitney is a beautiful woman." Marigold kept her tone low. "Too bad she has the personality of a gnat."

Hadley chuckled. "Rumor is she wanted to spend New Year's in New York and isn't happy about being here."

"The best-laid plans . . ." Marigold murmured, thinking of her own.

"Speaking of plans." Hadley's eyes narrowed. "What are you doing back in Good Hope?"

"Long story." Marigold kept her tone light and refused to meet Hadley's scrutinizing gaze. "One best told over chocolate and wine."

"And, I would suspect, with family." Hadley gave her shoulder a supportive squeeze. "Let's find big sister."

With Hadley's help, Ami soon came into view. Marigold's eldest sister stood next to their father and—Marigold barely suppressed a shudder—Anita Fishback, their father's girlfriend.

Ami's husband stood beside his wife, his hand resting supportively on her shoulder.

Marigold was thankful Ami had Beck to lean on. When their mother died eight years ago, Ami had taken over her role as family nurturer. No one in the family could comfort and soothe as well as the eldest Bloom sister.

While Marigold was in desperate need of some mothering, now wasn't the time. Ami had a party to host.

"Thanks for the company, Hadley." Marigold flashed a smile. "Now that I know where Ami is, I'm going to grab a glass of champagne and wait for her to finish speaking with Anita."

"Steering clear of the piranha is always a smart move." Hadley went on to regale her with a recent Anita antic.

Marigold found herself listening with only half an ear. Like a hunting dog spotting its prey, her senses now quivered with anticipation. From past experience she knew this was someone who could keep her happily occupied for hours. Someone who wouldn't ask too many questions.

The man had dark hair and a lean, athletic build. Smoky gray eyes glittered when their gazes locked. Best of all, the man who'd once been a stranger was now headed straight for her.

Cade Rallis spotted Marigold the second she strolled into the parlor. He'd been standing with his back to the wall, lazily surveying the room and debating with Jeremy Rakes which teams would make it to the Super Bowl when he saw her. At that moment Cade knew his conversation with Good Hope's mayor was destined to come to a quick end.

As he and Jeremy continued their spirited discussion, Cade bided his time until Marigold broke free of Hadley.

"Bottom line. The Patriots might make it to the Super Bowl again, but they won't win." Cade handed his empty champagne glass to a male server passing by, clapped Jeremy on the shoulder, and strode off.

He heard someone call his name but didn't turn. When only several feet separated him and Marigold, Cade slowed his pace. With her tumble of blonde hair and pretty, elfin features, Marigold Bloom reminded him of a fairy who might flit away if startled.

Though dressed far more casually than the other partygoers, she still managed to be the most beautiful woman in the room.

"What a nice surprise." He stepped close, let his gaze linger. "I didn't expect to see you here."

"It's my sister's party." Marigold flashed a smile that lifted those luscious ruby lips but didn't quite reach her eyes. "Attending was a last-minute decision."

Which meant she'd hit the blizzard currently raging between Chicago and Good Hope. That explained the lines of strain around her eyes. "How were the roads?"

She lifted one shoulder, let it drop in a careless gesture. "I've seen worse."

"That's a long drive even in the best of conditions." Cade wondered if she'd taken time to eat. He recalled the one evening—and night—they'd spent together. At the wedding reception she'd been so focused on having fun she'd forgotten to fuel up. "I bet you skipped dinner."

"Maybe."

The coy smile lifting the tips of her wide mouth told Cade he'd hit the mark. He placed a palm against her back. "Let's scout up some hors d'oeuvres."

She glanced off to the side, her gaze briefly pausing on where her eldest sister stood before returning to him. "What's tasty?"

Cade rocked back on the heels of the shiny black shoes he'd rented, along with the tux, for tonight's party. Black tie was foreign territory. He'd grown up around soldiers, hung out with fellow cops as an adult. Past New Year's Eves were usually welcomed in with bottles of beer and thick cuts of salami and cheese.

"All the appetizers I've tried have been good," he responded when he realized Marigold was waiting for an answer. He smiled ruefully.

"I'm not certain what's in some of them. Truth is, I'm not sure I want to know."

Because the sparkle in her eyes was so warm and friendly, he leaned close and confided, "I'm a fish out of water here."

"If you are, it doesn't show. You look as if you were born to wear a tux." She reached up and fingered his lapel. "It's an incredibly sexy look."

As her gaze met his and held, Cade felt the same flare of heat he'd experienced when they'd met at his cousin's wedding. Things at the Detroit Police Department had been tense at the time. He'd been ready to kick back and relax. The time spent with Marigold had been the best part of his trip to Door County.

"If we want pizza," he heard himself say, "we won't find it here."

Marigold laughed softly. The sudden flare of heat in her eyes told him she remembered that they'd been naked the last time they shared a pizza.

"We could slip out." He offered an easy smile. "Grab a slice at the new place down by the pier."

She'd been restless that weekend, and he sensed the same edginess now. Cade had no illusions she'd end up in his bed tonight, although that would be nice. Right now, he only hoped for an hour or two alone with her. She was a fascinating woman, one he'd like to get to know better.

"My truck isn't far," he said when she appeared to hesitate. "The pizza will be my treat."

Marigold opened her mouth, but before she could speak, her sister Ami appeared and pulled her close.

"I can't believe you're here. When I saw you across the room, I thought I was hallucinating. But then Beck said he saw you, too. I nearly knocked over a waiter getting to you." Ami paused to take a breath, looped her arm firmly through her sister's, and shot Cade a warning glance. "Marigold is not going anywhere tonight. My baby sister is ringing in the New Year right here."

He lifted his hands in a gesture of surrender. "Simply offering options."

Cade wondered if Ami saw the pain behind Marigold's bright smile. He didn't have a chance to do more than wonder when Beck clapped a hand on his shoulder. "Do you have a moment?"

"Sure. What's up?"

Beckett Cross was a straight shooter and a savvy businessman. In the six months since Cade had arrived in Good Hope, they'd become friends.

"I'm about to rope you into some volunteering." Beck slanted a glance at his wife. "Fashion show. Not-on-Valentine's-Day dance. Or leading a Seedlings troop. Which will it be, Rallis?"

Cade winced. Ever since he'd taken over the role of interim sheriff last summer, he'd been approached weekly about various volunteer "opportunities." While he wanted to give back to the community that had welcomed him so freely, learning the ins and outs of the department responsible for protecting this town was a full-time job.

But seeing the determined gleam in Beck's eyes told Cade that he wasn't going to be able to play the I'm-settling-into-my-job card much longer. Had *fashion show* really been one of the options? Cade took a step back.

"Give him time to digest the options, Beck." Marigold slipped her arm through Cade's. "Right now the sheriff owes me a dance."

"You haven't even told us what you're doing back in Good Hope," Ami protested, concern furrowing her brow.

"Enjoy your guests." In what appeared to be an attempt to mollify her sister, Marigold leaned over and brushed a kiss across Ami's cheek, then wiped off the lipstick with her thumb. "We can chat later."

Ami's jaw jutted out at a stubborn tilt. "Tell me one thing. Are you in trouble?"

If Cade hadn't been a trained observer, and if his gaze hadn't been focused on the woman at his side, he wouldn't have noticed Marigold's barely perceptible hesitation.

"Trouble?" Marigold gave a little laugh and, if possible, smiled even more brightly. She gestured to the crowd with a sweep of one hand. "I'm good. You know me. I'm impulsive. I simply couldn't think of a better place to party in a new year, so here I am."

The tense set to Ami's shoulders eased. Although Cade could tell her sister wasn't completely convinced—*smart woman*—she appeared willing to give Marigold the benefit of the doubt. For now.

"Well, I'm glad you came." Warmth and love laced through Ami's words. "If Fin were here, I'd have all my sisters with me. I can't imagine a more glorious way to ring in another year."

Though Cade couldn't see anything distressing about Ami's comment, Marigold's fingers tightened around his bicep.

"I like this song," he announced as the music changed to a slow, romantic ballad likely popular when his great-grandfather had been in high school. Cade fixed his gaze on Marigold. "Let's dance."

Relief flickered in her eyes. Her sunny smile never wavered. "Let's."

Marigold turned to her sister and brother-in-law. "Mind if I spend the night?"

The request put to rest any hope Cade still harbored of Marigold ringing in the new year in his bed.

Pleasure tinged with relief rippled across Ami's face. "I wouldn't have it any other way."

"You're always welcome," Beck added. "Stay as long as you like."

"Thank you." Marigold's voice wavered slightly, but Cade didn't think Ami or Beck noticed.

Marigold didn't say another word. Instead, with that bright smile still fixed to those pretty red lips, she dragged Cade across the parlor toward the music and dancers in the adjoining room.

Chapter Two

"When are you going to tell me why you're really here?"

Marigold's eyes popped open. After several minutes of swaying with Cade on the dance floor, she'd let her tired eyes drift shut. For the first time since she'd left Chicago, she'd begun to relax.

The way her luck had gone recently, it figured the interlude wouldn't last.

Leaning back slightly in his arms, she glanced up into the smoky gray eyes that had mesmerized her from the moment she'd seen him at her friend Shannon's wedding. He was a good-looking guy, no doubt about it.

He had the trifecta. Tall. Dark. Handsome.

And more. An indefinable something that drew her to him, even when common sense told her to turn tail and run. She could easily get more than she bargained for with this man.

Which meant she should keep her distance. Her life was complicated enough.

"I never believed you could go this long without speaking."

"You haven't been around me all that much." She gave a toss of her head, sending blonde curls rippling down her back like a cascade. "Certainly not enough to know what's considered normal behavior."

"I've observed enough to know that you like to talk, a lot."

Something in that smug smile of his pricked her temper. Marigold embraced the heat coursing through her veins. When Ami had been solicitous, she'd nearly lost it. Yes, anger was better.

"You're an arrogant ass." Though her words were spoken softly, they held a bite.

She was startled when Cade threw back his head and laughed, then twirled her in a spin. When she was once again clasped tightly against his chest, she realized he seemed to be under the impression she'd given him a compliment.

Marigold met his gaze, unblinking. "Ah, just to clarify, that's not a good thing."

The smile that lifted those firm, sensual lips made her insides quiver. "I guess that depends."

She could have asked for clarification of the cryptic remark, but she had a feeling that's exactly what he hoped she'd do.

For several seconds they danced in silence, the music from the ancient Victrola adding an otherworldliness to the evening.

Could this be a dream? Marigold cocked her head. Hope surged as she considered the possibility. She'd been exhausted when she'd returned to Chicago after Christmas.

Perhaps she'd only imagined . . .

Perhaps things weren't as bad . . .

Maybe if she . . .

No. Marigold gave herself a mental slap. She refused to go down that road. She knew too many people who spent their lives wishing for what could have been if only things were different.

Knowing she would survive this bump didn't make this any easier. The thought of all she'd left behind—clients, friends, her cute apartment—had her heart swelling with emotion. Even as tears pushed at her lids, she determinedly blinked them back.

Marigold Bloom never cried in public.

She hadn't cried when she was ten during that horrible parent-teacher conference, nor at Ami's hospital bedside after the car accident. She hadn't shed a single tear at her mother's funeral.

She certainly wouldn't cry now.

Closing her eyes briefly helped her regain her composure. Marigold opened her eyes to find Cade staring.

"Is there anything I can do?" His gaze remained locked on hers, those gray eyes as steady as the man himself.

Oh, how nice it would be if there was something he could do, something *anyone* could do to reverse the events of the past few days. But on the drive to Wisconsin, she'd accepted that part of her life was over.

"I don't know what you mean." She flashed a smile, forced a calm she didn't feel. "I'm dancing in the arms of a handsome man at my sister's New Year's Eve party. Life is good."

That all-seeing gaze didn't waver, but when he grinned, she knew he wouldn't press. She breathed a sigh of relief.

"You think I'm handsome."

She rolled her eyes, even as the intoxicating scent of his musky cologne enveloped her in a warm embrace.

"Do you?" he pressed.

"It may be one of your attributes," she grudgingly conceded but had to add, "although my fav is still arrogant ass."

His now-boyish smile had her stomach doing flip-flops.

"I like your style, Marigold Bloom."

She let her hands slide down his back, wishing it was skin instead of fabric beneath her fingertips. "Since we're on the subject of attributes, I'll add muscular. I adore muscles."

Without warning, that night in his hotel room, her one and only one-night stand, came into sharp focus. Cade had been a perfectly sculpted Adonis with broad shoulders, lean hips, and muscular legs. He'd also been a considerate lover who'd given as much as he took.

All of those factors had allowed her to forgive her indiscretion. Not to mention she'd have had to be dead not to have been swept off her feet that evening, especially with love and romance floating in the summer air.

"I like curves. *Your* curves." His voice dropped low. "I remember how they molded to—"

"Princess."

The male voice stopped Marigold's surge of lust dead in its tracks.

She dropped her hands from where they'd settled on Cade's ass as if it had turned red hot, then turned to embrace her dad. All of this under the watchful eye of Anita Fishback.

She held her father close and breathed in the scent of Polo, a particular favorite of his. This gray-haired man with the pewter-rimmed spectacles had been her rock for as long as she could remember. Steve Bloom was the one man who'd never let her down.

When she finally stepped back, the sorrow kept at bay during her banter with Cade returned. She hated feeling weak and needy, especially with Anita standing there, a speculative glint in her hazel eyes.

Despite the silver dress and dark hair artfully arranged in a twist, the woman reminded Marigold of a vulture ready to swoop.

"I didn't think you'd be able to make it back to Ami's party, but I'm so happy you did." Her father's gentle eyes brimmed with hope behind the silver-framed glasses. "Will you be able to stay for a while?"

"I don't see how." Anita stepped forward, opening her arms wide so Marigold had no choice but to give her a hug. "She's got that big fashion show coming up. Not to mention all her *important* clients."

"Oh, that's right." Her father's proud smile was like a knife to Marigold's heart, but she only smiled back. "I recall you telling me all about the event. Definitely a big deal."

A big deal that had crashed and burned. Marigold had to resist the urge to sigh, which surprised her. She'd never been the sighing sort. Certainly not with Anita's eagle eyes focused on her.

Before Marigold could come up with something that wouldn't quite be a lie but would get her through the evening unscathed, Cade's hand rose to rest on her shoulder.

Anita's watchful gaze sharpened.

"I was telling Marigold how nice it was that she came back to spend New Year's Eve with me." Cade flashed an easy smile.

The comment achieved its purpose.

"You're together?" Anita shot Marigold's dad a questioning look. "You didn't tell me that Marigold and the sheriff were dating."

"Cade and I aren't together." The denial popped out of Marigold's mouth before she could think.

"Actions speak louder than words, Goldilocks." Cade lifted her hand to his lips. "Why else would a woman drive four hours on a snowy night to attend a party?"

Steve's gaze slid from her to Cade. Her father, a brilliant man who taught high school science, appeared to have no trouble sorting out what was really going on. He smiled and turned to the woman at his side.

"I say we let these two young people enjoy their evening together." Steve placed his arm firmly about his date's shoulder, turning her in the direction of the dessert table. "I've got a sudden urge to try those maple-pepper salmon bites you were raving about earlier. While we eat you can finish telling me what you heard about Pastor Schmidt."

"But Marigold said she isn't—"

Anita's protest was lost in the din of conversation and laughter.

Cade pulled Marigold back to him.

When he began to sway to the music, she placed her hands on his shoulders. After a moment, she pressed a kiss against his neck.

He stilled for only a second before he resumed dancing. "I'm surprised you resisted my charms this long."

Ignoring the teasing comment, she let out a breath. "I wanted to thank you."

"For what?"

His innocent tone didn't fool her. The comment he'd made to Anita had been delivered with pinpoint accuracy. "Diverting the vulture."

He smiled. "An apt description."

"My sisters and I actually prefer *piranha*. Or sometimes, if we're feeling particularly charitable, I-Need-a-Man. Whatever you call her, Anita Fishback is a gossip who rejoices in other people's misfortunes."

A dark brow lifted. "What is your misfortune, Marigold?"

"You mean other than dancing with someone who calls me *Goldilocks*?" The light, teasing tone came naturally. For reasons she didn't want to examine too closely, Marigold found it easy to relax around the sheriff.

"Yeah, other than that." His quick grin sent a flash of heat straight to her core.

"It's a long, sad tale of betrayal and loss." She'd intended to toss the words out there with a melodramatic flair, perhaps bring that devastating smile back to his lips.

Unfortunately, the words hit too close to home, and her voice thickened on the last word. She clamped her mouth shut.

Darn. Darn. Darn.

The song from the Victrola changed beats. Marigold found she didn't have the energy—or the desire—to launch into such a high-energy dance. Once again, Cade appeared to sense her desire before she could voice it.

He took her arm, guiding her through a small but enthusiastic group who were swinging their arms and step-kicking to the beat.

"If we're going to dance the Charleston, you need fuel," he said when she found her voice and asked where he was taking her.

"What can you recommend, other than going for pizza?" Feeling infinitely steadier, Marigold slanted a sideways glance. Why did he have to look—and smell—so delicious? "If you remember, Ami put the kibosh on us going out."

"Kibosh? I didn't think anyone under sixty used that word." He tilted his head. "Are you sure you're twenty-eight?"

"Twenty-seven," she corrected, then realized she didn't know his age. "How old are you?"

"Ancient."

"Seriously."

"Thirty-two."

Marigold grimaced. "You *are* old. Thank goodness you've got stamina."

The last part made him grin. "How kind of you to remember."

Oh, she remembered everything about the night they'd spent together. Suddenly warm, she fanned her face with her hand. "Is it hot in here?"

"Blistering."

The twitch of his lips gave him away.

"You're making fun of me."

"Not at all. I'm simply glad to know that I'm not the only one suffering."

She couldn't help it. She dropped her gaze to the front of his trousers but found his jacket covering the area in question.

"If you don't believe me, we could go somewhere private, and I'd be happy to show you."

"I wouldn't be so cocky, mister. I'm the kind who'd call your bluff."

"I'll take a rain check." He gave her arm a squeeze. "Tonight it will be food and family with an enjoyable few hours with me tossed into the mix as a distraction."

He'd nailed it, Marigold thought.

"I don't want to take up all your time. If you want to check out some of the other women in the room, feel free." She paused, then had to hide a grimace when her gaze settled on Eliza Shaw. Though the dark-haired beauty looked stunning in a white-and-silver gown that flattered her model-like figure, Marigold could not recommend her. Not to anyone she liked, anyway.

Eliza might be young, single, and successful, but the executive director of the Cherries was a piranha in the making. Give her another five years and she'd be as insufferable as Anita.

"I expected to see her here with Jeremy." Cade had followed the direction of her gaze, and his now lingered on Eliza. "But they arrived separately."

"You don't miss much."

"It's my job." His tone was matter-of-fact. "I'm a trained observer."

Which likely meant he'd seen through her false bravado. Yet he'd kept quiet. Instead of pushing her to bare her soul, he'd gallantly provided a diversion to keep the questions of others at bay.

"I'll say this once, just so we're clear." He stopped at the edge of a linen-clad table holding a number of silver chafing dishes and lowered his voice. "I'm spending time with you because you're the most interesting, vibrant woman in the room."

A flood of pleasure washed over Marigold even as she cast him a skeptical glance.

"I'm not saying that because I want to get you into bed." He handed her a china plate, took one for himself. "Although that would be a nice side benefit. It's the truth."

When she opened her mouth, he waved away her words before they could leave her lips.

"I know sex isn't happening, at least not tonight. Your sister made that very clear. Not to mention the daggers your father has been shooting me all evening."

"My dad has not—" Marigold stopped when she caught sight of her father. Although he stood halfway across the main parlor, his concerned gaze was indeed focused on Cade. She chuckled and scooped up two bacon-wrapped shrimp. "I'm the baby of the group. It's only natural for my family to be overprotective."

"Understood."

Her hand brushed his when they both reached for the hood of the next dish. A bolt of electricity traveled up her arm.

"I'm going to let you in on a little secret." She kept her voice deliberately low, forcing him to lean close to hear her. "If things were different, I'd have happily gone home with you tonight."

His mouth dropped open. He snapped it shut.

The energy that pulsed between them crackled. Any second Marigold expected to hear a loud boom. While she might not sleep with Cade tonight, by the time midnight rolled around, Marigold saw no reason not to kiss him.

Her body quivered with excitement when the countdown began. Ami and Beck stood in front of the crowd with their glasses raised high. Knowing her sister, Marigold had no doubt the liquid in Ami's glass was some kind of sparkling cider, not champagne.

Prim stood on the other side of Marigold, her husband's arm looped around her shoulder. As the crowd yelled out the numbers, Marigold moistened her lips in anticipation. A kiss was just what she needed to put a shiny star on top of a sucky day.

Out of the corner of her eye, she saw Eliza saunter close. The woman's dark, inverted bob flattered her high cheekbones and slightly slanted eyes. Her makeup had been expertly applied, and the bright red lipstick couldn't help but draw attention to her full lips.

"One," the crowd screamed.

Noisemakers popped and cheers filled the air.

Marigold took a quick gulp of champagne, then turned to Cade, her arms already lifting to wrap around his neck.

But someone was already there. Eliza's slender body wrapped around Cade like a snake, her fingers sliding possessively through his hair.

Fighting a surge of anger and something that felt an awful lot like hurt, Marigold whirled. She had no claim on Cade, but that didn't mean she had to stand there and watch him kiss Eliza.

Seeing red, she didn't notice she'd bumped into Travis Forbes until his body jolted her to a stop.

"Happy New Year, Marigold."

She'd gone to school with Travis. He was one of those guys who was everyone's buddy. Good-looking if you were into the guy-next-door variety.

"Happy New Year, Travis."

She was practically positive that she didn't make the first move. Kissing Travis would be an awful lot like kissing her brother, if she had a brother.

But she also knew she didn't protest when he enfolded her in his arms and pressed his mouth to hers.

Yep, just like kissing a relative.

Marigold was ready to step back when, over Travis's shoulder, she saw Cade approaching, a murderous look in his eyes.

Instead of moving away, she moved in even closer and kissed Travis with all the passion she'd saved up for Cade.

It wasn't her finest moment, but it lessened the sting she felt seeing Cade kiss Eliza. For now, that was good enough.

Cade had plenty of practice keeping his emotions under control. That experience came in handy as he watched his deputy and Marigold exchange spit.

He didn't have any control over the woman—or over Travis—but that didn't mean he had to like what he saw. Or that he had to stay silent. "Deputy."

The intent had been to distract. If the sudden step Travis took back was any indication, he'd startled the man.

All the better.

Marigold tossed back that sexy mane of golden curls, the feline smile on her lips not quite reaching her eyes. "Where's Eliza?"

Ah, his suspicions had been correct. This was payback.

Cade considered his response. He'd honed his analytical skills while in the Marines and during the course of his employment with Detroit PD.

"If I have to hazard a guess, I'd say Eliza is likely kissing every man under fifty." He kept his voice offhand while his gaze remained focused on Marigold's face. "In the post–New Year's Eve haze, for some, any person will do."

Only when he saw a look of shame cross her face did he acknowledge the deputy. Cade extended his hand. "Travis. We haven't had a chance to speak this evening. Happy New Year."

"Happy New Year, sir." Travis gave Cade's hand a shake. The deputy had been with the sheriff's office since graduating five years ago from the University of Wisconsin with a BS in criminal justice.

As one of the trainers and the previous sheriff's right-hand man, it had been assumed—by Travis, anyway—that he'd be appointed interim sheriff when Len Swarts resigned. Cade's application had blown that scenario out of the water.

His leadership experience in the Marines and his background as a ranked officer in a large police force had led to him being offered the position. The offer had come with the caveat that he'd have to win the election in March to keep the position. As of now, Travis was his only opponent on the ballot.

Travis shifted his focus from Cade to Marigold. "I didn't realize the two of you were acquainted."

"We met at Shannon Tracy's wedding." Marigold's expression gave nothing away. "Cade is Shannon's cousin."

"Is that so?" Travis cocked his head. "You never mentioned you were related to Shannon."

"Don't recall it coming up." Cade lifted a shoulder in a careless shrug then sharpened his gaze. "I didn't realize you and Marigold were so intimately acquainted."

Marigold's cheeks pinked slightly, something Cade might have missed if he hadn't been so focused on her.

"We went to high school together." Marigold flashed Travis a smile.

"Old flames reconnecting?" Cade tossed the words out carelessly, trying to get a feel for just how close the two had been.

Marigold opened her mouth to speak but Travis beat her to the punch.

"I wish." Travis winked at Marigold. "This one was way out of my league."

"That's not true—" Marigold protested.

"I was too serious for her." Travis spoke in a matter-of-fact tone. "Marigold is a bright, sparkling star."

"What a nice thing to say."

When Cade saw Marigold warming under the compliment, he decided this particular trip down memory lane had gone far enough. He supposed he could walk away and leave Marigold to reminisce with Travis. But giving up had never been Cade's way.

"If you'll excuse us, our earlier discussion was interrupted by the countdown." The words may have been directed to Travis, but Cade kept his gaze on Marigold.

A look filled those baby blue eyes that he couldn't immediately decipher. His punch of unease didn't relax until she turned to Travis.

"It was good seeing you, Trav."

"We'll have to catch up again soon."

The tenacity that made Travis a good deputy only served to irritate Cade now.

"If you're staying for a few days, we could grab dinner?" Travis's boyish smile held a persuasive edge. "There's a new pizza place down by the pier that's supposed to be good."

Marigold returned his smile with one of her own. "Right now, I'm not sure how long I'll be in Good Hope. But sure, if I do stick, we'll get together."

"Great." The self-satisfied look in the deputy's eyes irritated Cade, but he kept his own face expressionless until the deputy had sauntered away.

"How long will you be staying?" Cade asked in a low tone as he cupped her elbow and maneuvered her through the crowd.

"Your guess is as good as mine." She gave a little laugh. "All I know is it sure isn't going to be long."

Chapter Three

Marigold never did get a kiss from Cade.

Shortly after Travis strode off, Prim and Ami appeared and stuck like glue until the party ended at two in the morning. To his credit, Cade hadn't let himself be run off. The easy way he visited with her sisters' husbands let her know they were friends, not simply acquaintances.

But when the last of the revelers stood at the door, Cade took her hands in his. His gray eyes met hers. "Happy New Year."

When he leaned forward, anticipation surged but was quickly dashed when he merely brushed his lips against her cheek. As far as Marigold was concerned, the tantalizing touch of his mouth barely counted.

"Be seeing you around." He shifted his attention to Beck and Ami. "Great party. I appreciated the invitation."

"Thanks for coming." Ami's tired smile matched the weariness in her eyes.

Then he was gone and it was just family. Other than her father, who'd left shortly before midnight. Apparently someone had stepped on Anita's foot and the resulting gash had needed tending.

"I'm sorry Dad had to leave," Marigold said.

"We'll invite him over for dinner tomorrow," Ami said, then received Beck's nod of confirmation. "We'll pray Anita doesn't come with him."

Over the past two years Marigold and her sisters had tried to like the piranha, truly they had. For so many reasons, the woman was simply not likable.

"We'd love to stay longer, but we told the sitter we'd try not to be too late." Prim gave Marigold a quick hug before holding her back at arm's length. "I'll call in the morning and you can explain why you're here."

"It's a chocolate-and-wine discussion," Marigold told her.

"I assumed." Prim's hazel eyes—so like their father's—softened. "In my mind there's nothing better than wine, chocolate, and conversation before ten a.m."

Marigold's heart swelled with emotion. She kept her voice light. "Give my nephews a hug for me."

Callum and Connor, seven-year-old twins from Prim's first marriage, were feisty and fearless. Marigold adored them.

More hugs were exchanged until Marigold was alone with Ami and Beck.

Marigold slipped her arm around her sister's waist as they made their way to the parlor. They stood in the doorway for a second.

"Looks like a bomb went off in here," Marigold observed.

"Of nuclear proportions." Beck's tone was matter-of-fact. "We have a cleaning crew coming tomorrow. By noon, everything should be back to rights."

"Unfortunately, that means we may have to delay bringing out the wine and chocolate until the afternoon." Ami spoke casually but there was worry in her eyes. "That doesn't mean you and I—"

"No worries. I doubt I'll be out of bed before the cleaning crew leaves." Marigold squeezed her sister's arm. "Conversation and chocolate can wait. Right now, all I care about is getting some sleep."

"I meant it when I said you can stay as long as you like." The sincerity in Beck's tone earned him a smile from his wife. "If your car is unlocked, I'll grab your bags and bring them in."

"Thanks, Beck." In Chicago, everything needed to be locked up tight. Here, well, things were just different in Good Hope.

"Be right back." He brushed a kiss across Ami's cheek, then left the two sisters alone.

"How bad is it?" Ami's soft tone and warm green eyes invited confidences.

Marigold was tempted, oh-so-incredibly tempted to unburden herself, to take the support her sister so unselfishly offered. But her pregnant sister had just hosted a huge party. She had to be exhausted.

The news could wait until tomorrow. God knew nothing was going to change between now and then.

"It's not all that bad," she assured her sister. "I'm alive and healthy. And, while some may have serious doubts, I've still got my wits."

That brought a chuckle as Ami recognized the last as a favorite saying of their grandpa Bloom.

Beck returned just then, a bag in each hand.

Marigold let her gaze linger on the suitcases. Was this all the past eight years amounted to? The thought brought with it a fresh wave of sadness.

Beck's somber brown eyes shifted between her and his wife. "The green room?"

It was the same bedroom she'd stayed in when she was home over Christmas. Never had she imagined she'd be back so soon, and under such depressing circumstances.

Marigold found the strength to flash a smile. "Of course. That one has my name on it."

Ami hugged her so long and hard Marigold thought she might break in two.

"You get some rest." Marigold patted her sister's back, then pulled away as Beck headed upstairs with the suitcases. "We'll chat tomorrow."

Ami reached to shut off the lights, but Marigold stopped her.

"Leave them on for now. Please."

Ami's brows pulled together. "Aren't you coming to bed? After that long drive, you have to be exhausted."

"I am tired, but I thought I'd grab another glass of champagne and just chill for a few minutes." Reading the look of resistance on her sister's face perfectly, Marigold continued, "Unwind a bit. You understand."

Although still not appearing convinced, Ami reluctantly nodded. "If you need anything—"

"I'll ask," Marigold assured her sister. "You know me, I'm not shy."

"No. You're strong and determined." Ami's gaze met hers. "You remember that. And know I'm always here for you."

The lump had barely had a chance to form in her throat when Ami turned toward the stairway.

Once she was alone, Marigold inhaled, then let her breath out slowly. After locating a half-empty bottle of champagne, she found a clean flute and filled it all the way to the top. It was, after all, a brand-new year.

She lifted the glass and offered her own toast . . . to a new start.

Be Mine in Good Hope

Cade wasn't technically on duty New Year's Day, but when he checked in with dispatch and heard there had been some vandalism reported on Market Street, he decided to check out the area.

The house where the damage had occurred sat just down the street from Ami and Beck's home. If the Cross's house or property was similarly affected, he'd have to knock on the door to advise them of the damage. And he just might just get to tell Marigold good morning.

On his stroll down the recently shoveled sidewalk, he gave the house that had reported overturned planters a cursory glance, then moved on down the block to the large three-story Victorian that Beck had purchased even before he'd moved to Good Hope. From what Cade could see, the Cross property appeared undamaged. Likely the party and the constant people coming and going had acted as a barrier to anyone getting too close for mischief.

Still, something may have occurred that might not be immediately visible from the street. It didn't hurt to ask.

Cade stood on the sidewalk in front of the grand old house. It was nearly ten. Several vans advertising a local cleaning service already sat in the driveway. Cade watched several people trudge out with overstuffed garbage bags, laughing and talking.

If Ami and Beck were still sleeping, they had to be deaf.

When Cade reached the sidewalk, he took the porch steps two at a time to hold the front door open for a tiny slip of a woman with two large bags.

"Let me help you with those." He reached out to take the bags from her arms, but she tightened her hold.

"Thanks, Sheriff." She gripped the bags and stepped back. "As I told Mr. Cross, I can manage just fine."

"If you change your mind . . ."

"I'll let you know." In obvious dismissal, the woman slipped past him and made a beeline for one of the vans.

Though the door was ajar, Cade knocked.

Beck appeared moments later. "Hey, Sheriff. Come on in."

Cade didn't know what to make of the fact that Marigold's brother-in-law didn't seem surprised to see him. He cleared his throat. "There have been reports of vandalism in the area. Planters overturned."

"Likely the same kids who've been causing trouble in other parts of Good Hope recently," Beck said mildly. "I just made a pot of coffee. I'm guessing you could use a mug of my strong chicory brew."

"I don't want to intrude—"

"You're not. And, as my wife isn't drinking coffee while she's pregnant, you'll be doing me a favor." Beck slanted a sideways glance in his direction. "We've also got scones, made fresh yesterday."

"I could eat a scone." Though Cade normally preferred cinnamon rolls, if Ami had made the scones, he knew they'd be stellar. He'd been in her bakery—Blooms Bake Shop—many times since moving to Good Hope and had never been disappointed.

Just before they reached the kitchen at the back of the house, sidestepping several more members of the cleaning crew along the way, Cade brought the conversation back to the reason for his visit this morning. "Did you notice any vandalism on your property this morning?"

Beck shook his head. A slight smile lifted the corners of his lips. "Now that we've got that out of the way . . ."

Cade saw Marigold the second he stepped into the kitchen. Sitting at the table, wearing a fluffy pink sweater that made him think of feathers and baby chicks, her curls were pulled back from her face with a sparkly headband that glittered in the overhead light.

Her eyes looked even larger than they had last night, and this morning her pouty lips were bright pink instead of red.

She glanced up from her phone. Her eyes widened and that cotton candy mouth curved. Unlike Beck, it was obvious she hadn't expected to see him this morning. "Hey, Sheriff."

"Hey, hairdresser."

"Hair stylist," she corrected with an easy smile. "What brings you by?"

"There was some vandalism in the neighborhood last night." Beck motioned for Cade to take a seat.

"Vandalism?" Marigold frowned. "In Good Hope?"

"Kid stuff. For now, anyway." Cade dropped into a chair opposite Marigold. He glanced around. "Where's Ami?"

Beck turned from the coffeemaker. His expression softened. "Last I checked, still sleeping."

"We didn't want to wake her." Marigold broke off a piece of the scone on the plate before her. "She's sleeping for two."

Beck set a mug of coffee and a scone before Cade. "I'm going to check on her again."

When he left the room, Marigold smiled after him. "Beck is like a mother hen. He looked in on her barely ten minutes ago."

"Must be love." The mushy words popped out, surprising Cade.

Marigold nodded. "Absolutely."

Cade thought of Alice and their plans to marry. If things had gone as planned, they'd be husband and wife now. But things hadn't gone as planned. He now understood their breakup had been for the best.

He hadn't loved Alice, not the way a man should love the woman he was about to marry. If he had, he'd have fought to rectify the problems that plagued their relationship instead of simply walking away when she told him it was over.

"I'm surprised you're working this morning."

Cade shifted his gaze to find Marigold studying him, an unreadable expression on her pretty face.

He took a big gulp of the strong coffee. "Because of the holiday, we're shorthanded. I'm just helping out."

"Checking on possible vandalism."

"Exactly."

"I hate to say I'm glad something happened in the neighborhood." Marigold's tongue moistened her lips. "But I am."

Heat surged. Cade slowly lowered his mug to the table. "You care to expand on that?"

With great deliberateness, Marigold carefully pushed aside the plate holding her scone even as her eyes remained firmly fixed on his face. "You and me, we have unfinished business."

Cade inclined his head.

"It's time to rectify that situation." Without warning, she rose, leaned across the table, and fastened her mouth to his.

Marigold found Cade's lips as warm and tantalizing as she remembered. The kiss began slowly, as if they had all the time in the world; soothing, caressing . . . arousing. The need bubbling up inside her wanted more than pleasant. When his tongue swept across her lips, she nearly burst into the "Hallelujah Chorus."

As it had that long-ago June night, desire surged hot and demanding. Marigold opened her mouth to his and wound her arms around his neck as the kiss deepened. She cursed the table separating them. The yearning to feel the hard length of his body against her, to revel in the evidence of his need for her, was overwhelming.

She slid her fingers through his hair, the dark strands shorter than she remembered but just as silky.

"What's going on in here?" There was astonishment and a healthy dose of motherly rebuke in Ami's words.

Cade stiffened.

Marigold pushed aside annoyance and reminded herself this wasn't her home. Though she might yearn to take this, ah, *discussion* with Cade upstairs, the double bed with the soft flannel sheets where she'd slept last night wasn't hers, either.

Heaving a dramatic sigh, Marigold reluctantly released her hold on Cade.

"Good morning, dear sister. I hope you slept well." Marigold sat and moved the mug with the now-tepid coffee back in front of her. Though her heart continued to race and her lips tingled, the smile she offered her sister was easy. "You look rested."

Cade stood absolutely still, his face expressionless.

Sit down, she silently urged. The lawman didn't appear to get the message. Or if he received it, he chose not to respond. Marigold was just grateful he didn't apologize.

In her mind, an apology *might* have been necessary if her sister and Beck had come in and found her and Cade naked and having sex on the kitchen table. Unfortunately, they'd been interrupted before that had become a possibility. *Pity.*

Ami opened her mouth. Shut it.

Beck appeared to be hiding a smile.

"Thanks for the coffee, Beck." Cade broke the silence. "I need to check with a few more of your neighbors."

His gaze shifted to Marigold. "Be seeing you."

The slight tilt of Cade's head told her that although he hadn't voiced a question, he had one.

"I'll be around," she told him. "For a while, anyway."

The slow smile that stole over his handsome face was like kerosene on an open fire. When he'd been kissing her, all thoughts of the mess that was now her life had been burned away in the fiery flames of passion. Was it wrong to wish she could have lingered in that place a little while longer?

In minutes Cade was gone and Marigold was left with her sister. And with a brother-in-law who'd given up all attempts to hide his amusement.

"Prim called," Ami told her. "She wondered if we were free for lunch. She'd like to meet us at Muddy Boots."

Marigold took a long sip of the strong chicory blend and tried not to grimace. She loved coffee, but it had to be hot or cold, not lukewarm. "Sounds good to me."

"I'll tell her we'll meet at noon." Ami pulled the phone from her pocket and stepped from the room, leaving Beck alone with Marigold.

She gestured with her head. "Ami is probably telling Prim she walked in on Cade and me kissing."

Beck smiled. "Probably."

Marigold pushed aside the tepid coffee. "Should be an interesting lunch."

Chapter Four

"Too bad Beck doesn't have a liquor license or we could have wine with lunch," Marigold commented as she pulled out a chair and took a seat at the gray Formica table opposite Ami.

Nearly every table in Muddy Boots, the café that Beck had purchased sight unseen, was doing a booming business. Knowing that some of the patrons had likely just stumbled out of bed, for today only, breakfast was being served all day.

"We may not have wine, but we do have chocolate."

Prim's announcement had both sisters swiveling their gazes to her.

"I brought a bag of Doves with me." Primrose grabbed the chair to Marigold's right. "For dessert."

Ami's green eyes glittered. "Or an appetizer?"

"I like the way you think, big sister." Marigold stuck out her hand.

"You two are worse than my boys." Still, Prim smiled as she pulled the paper bag from her purse. With great precision—she was, after all, an accountant—Prim carefully counted out three pieces of the heart-shaped candies wrapped in red foil to each of them.

Marigold had the first of hers unwrapped and in her mouth in less than five seconds. "Ohmigosh these are decadent."

"After all of the sweets I had at the party last night, I shouldn't have any more, but—" Prim paused and carefully unwrapped a piece. Gazing at it for a moment, she sighed before popping it into her mouth. Her lips curved up. "I adore chocolate."

Marigold recognized the dark-haired waitress who sauntered over to take their order as Anita's granddaughter. None of the Bloom sisters held that fact against the college student.

"Hi, Dakota." Ami flashed a smile in the young woman's direction. "My sisters and I decided to get together for a New Year's Day luncheon."

Dakota cast a glance in Marigold's direction and offered a shy smile. "I didn't know you were back."

"You never know where or when I might turn up." Marigold pressed one of the candies into the waitress's hand. "This is for you. Everyone should start the new year with chocolate."

"Thanks." Surprise flickered over Dakota's face before she pocketed the heart-shaped piece of foil. She gazed expectantly at the three sisters. "What can I get you?"

They quickly ordered, and the young girl had barely stepped out of earshot before both Ami and Prim settled their gazes on Marigold. "Tell us what happened. What brought you back to Good Hope?"

As she struggled to know where to begin, Marigold remembered what their mother had always told her daughters when they needed to explain something. *Begin at the beginning.*

"I've mentioned before how stressful it's been at the salon this past year. Steffan's moods have been all over the map." Marigold nibbled on the second piece of candy. "It got so I never knew how he'd be when I walked in the door."

Both sisters murmured sympathies but their eyes remained focused on her. The ball remained in her court.

She received a momentary respite when Dakota returned with their drinks: iced tea for her and Prim, milk for Ami. As business was hopping, Dakota didn't linger.

"Steffan fired me." Although being told her services were no longer needed had knocked her to her knees, Marigold managed to keep her tone matter-of-fact. "The day I returned from Christmas break, he called me into his office and gave me my walking papers. What a lovely Christmas gift."

Sarcasm wove through those last words like a ribbon around a prettily wrapped package.

Though her sisters must have suspected something of the sort had occurred—or else why would she be back in Good Hope so soon?—the astonished looks mixed with outrage on their faces warmed her heart.

"He's been your mentor since you got out of beauty school." Prim's brow furrowed, distress evident in her tone.

"I remember when he first contacted you about working for him." Ami's gaze took on a faraway look. "It was after your success with the mayor's wife. The article in the *Sun-Times* brought you to his attention."

"The chance to work with him, to learn from him, was a dream come true." Eight years ago Marigold had moved to Chicago to attend cosmetology school and had found her niche.

She discovered she had a gift for looking at a person's face and knowing the best cut and color for the bone structure. Her obvious talent had created a buzz.

The mayor's wife, who'd had a rags-to-riches rise when she'd married an up-and-coming politician, visited the school shortly before Marigold's graduation. Marigold had been chosen to do her hair.

It was a publicity stunt designed to show that the mayor and his family hadn't forgotten their working-class roots. The newspaper feature had drawn the attention of Steffan Oliver, an industry legend, who'd recently relocated his popular LA salon to Chicago's Gold Coast.

"I was over the moon when he offered me a job." Marigold's lips curved up. Despite all that had happened, there was pride in her voice. "Steffan is so incredibly talented. I can't tell you how many people fly in just so he can cut their hair. I couldn't believe he wanted *me*."

"I swear we heard you screaming all the way in Good Hope." Ami's face was soft with the memory. "Mom would have been so proud."

The pleasantness of the moment shattered like crystal on tile. Marigold hadn't known how sick her mother had been when she'd left for cosmetology school. By the time she'd graduated and received her job offer, Sarah Bloom had passed away.

A familiar knot of bitterness twisted inside her. She'd never have left Good Hope if she'd known her mother had been so ill.

"You worked for Steffan a long time." Prim lifted her glass of tea to her lips, her eyes never leaving her baby sister's face.

The noise in the café had gone up several decibels since they'd first sat down. It seemed as if everyone had decided at the same time to yell out a greeting to a friend across the dining room or laugh loudly at some joke. Marigold closed her eyes briefly and fought to stay focused.

"Six years." Marigold's voice sounded hollow, even to her own ears. "I considered him a friend as well as a mentor."

"I remember you mentioning last summer he'd been owly," Ami mused.

"Not just with you," Prim reminded her. "You said clients were beginning to notice."

"The trouble between him and his partner was escalating. I knew how much Marc meant to him. He was the reason Steffan relocated his business to Chicago." Marigold sighed. "I thought they were a perfect match. They seemed so happy."

"What does the upheaval in his personal relationship have to do with him firing you?" Ami spoke softly, in deference to the customers seated nearby.

Before she could respond, Dakota arrived with their salads. Marigold waited until the girl stepped away to answer. She'd given the matter a lot of thought on the drive back to Good Hope. "I think when someone's personal life is in turmoil, the unhappiness can't help but spill into their professional life as well."

Her sisters looked at each other and nodded agreement.

"His clients had definitely begun to notice. He was distant, distracted, even snappish at times." Marigold grimaced. "His behavior became a huge concern to everyone in the salon."

"I can imagine," Ami said.

"Clients who patronize the Steffan Oliver Salon expect to be pampered and fawned over from the second they step through the gilt-edged doors. Several of his clients became so upset they asked to be transferred to me."

"Uh-oh." Prim made a face. "I see where this is heading."

"Yeah, uh-oh. Shortly after Thanksgiving, Steffan accused me of stealing his clients, of undermining him." Marigold stabbed a piece of endive with extra vigor. "I assured him I was as shocked as he was by the requests. I don't think he believed me."

Ami's hand closed over hers for a little squeeze. "Why didn't you tell us all this at Christmas?"

"So the guy was stressed and bitchy. That behavior had become the new status quo." Marigold lifted one shoulder, let it drop. "Besides, why dwell on something so negative when we had more important things to discuss, like Prim's new husband."

"Who, by the way, is absolutely wonderful." Ami beamed at her sister. "Our Prim found her prince, not once, but twice."

"I'm a lucky gal. I love being married to Max." Prim's newfound happiness showed, from the face that glowed with happiness to the warmth in her voice each time she spoke her husband's name.

"I'm happy for you." Marigold gave her sister's hand a squeeze.

Prim had endured so much in her young life. She'd become a widow nearly three years ago when her husband had been killed in a climbing accident. She'd reconnected with Max when she'd moved back to Good Hope last year.

Like I reconnected with Cade, Marigold thought, then chided herself. It wasn't the same at all.

Prim and Max had been friends since childhood. She and Cade had only been lovers.

Marigold looked up when Ami squeezed her hand. "I still wish you'd have confided in me, in us."

"We not only had Prim's marriage to discuss, but we had"—Marigold felt her insides soften when she thought of the blessed event that would take place this spring—"to talk about anything and everything to do with Baby Cross."

Her eldest sister had such a nurturing spirit. When the big 3-0 loomed for Ami with no prospects in sight, Marigold had worried she might be single forever. Which would have been a shame for a woman who had so much love to give. "I'm envious of the life you're building with Beck."

Ami's hand dropped to rest protectively on the curve of her barely noticeable baby bump. "My life is like a wonderful dream."

"Mine is like one big nightmare." Marigold regretted uttering the flippant words the instant they left her mouth.

"I'm so sorry—" Ami began.

"Steffan's a jerk." Prim spat the words. "If he ever shows his face in Good Hope, I'll tell him that to his face."

Marigold would have chuckled at her mild-mannered sister uttering such a vehement sentiment if she hadn't been so touched.

"I appreciate the support, more than you'll ever know." She gazed down at the last unwrapped chocolate in her hand. "I believe time will show it was all for the best."

"He just called you in out of the blue and fired you?" Ami apparently was unwilling to drop the subject without gathering more details.

Prim tossed several more chocolates in front of Marigold.

Marigold popped another in her mouth. After letting the taste of chocolate linger on her tongue for several seconds, she washed the rest down with a sip of tea.

She'd convinced herself she had come to grips with what had happened on that horrible day. All the way to Good Hope, Marigold had soothed herself by repeating one of her mother's favorite sayings over and over: when one door closes, another opens.

"I never saw it coming." Now, when her voice trembled and nearly broke, she realized she was still grieving the loss of her life in Chicago. When she was ten, Marigold had vowed to outshine her older sisters. She'd been so close to achieving that goal. Failure, even temporary failure, was a bitter pill to swallow.

The worry blanketing her sisters' faces only made matters worse. Prim and Ami had their own lives, likely their own issues weighing on their minds. She didn't want them worrying about her.

"I still don't understand why he would do such a thing. Why would he get rid of his star employee?"

Lost in her thoughts, Marigold wasn't sure which sister asked the question. Then again, did it really matter?

"I don't know." Marigold glanced out the window, the scene as cold and bleak as her emotions. "Perhaps he simply wanted to make someone—that would be me—as miserable as he was. Like I said, he was jealous some of his clients had scheduled with me. Part of it may have been that I was the one chosen to be the lead hairstylist for Couture Fashion Week. But this is all conjecture. When I pressed for a reason, he refused to give one."

His cold dismissal, as if they'd meant nothing to each other, had hurt the most.

"Despite all his drama the past year, I remained loyal to him. I really believed we were friends." Marigold picked at the edges of her napkin with her fingertips. "I was wrong."

She pushed the salad aside, her stomach as unsettled as her hands.

"Surely there are dozens of other salons in Chicago ready to snap you up. You are, after all, the supremely talented Marigold Bloom."

Even as the knife twisted in her chest, Ami's faith brought a smile to Marigold's lips. "I made a few inquiries. Not one bite. When I called the producer of the fashion show to update my contact information, they told me Steffan had already informed them I was relocating and he'd be taking my position."

"He blackballed you." Prim's voice was low and tight.

Marigold glanced in her normally mild-mannered sister's direction and found hazel eyes as hard as topaz. She nodded. "Appears so."

"You—you should sue," Ami sputtered. "He's obviously defamed your character. I can ask Beck—"

Marigold closed her hand over her Ami's. "The charges would be difficult to prove and wouldn't serve me well professionally in the long run."

Ami's green eyes were incredulous. "Are you telling me you're going to sit back and let him get away with this?"

"Of course not." Marigold's lips curved in a catlike smile. "Haven't you heard the best revenge is massive success? Mark my words. Steffan Oliver will rue the day he showed me the door."

"You're not letting any grass grow under your feet, baby girl." Steve Bloom's smile shone as bright as the overhead sun.

Marigold followed her father's gaze back to the empty storefront.

"You know me. I like to keep busy." Marigold studied the small space on Main Street. Until November the spot had been occupied by

Carly's Cut and Curl, home of the neon dancing scissors sign. Marigold suppressed a shudder. The fact that she was considering operating even temporarily out of this space illustrated just how far she'd fallen. Still, one had to be practical. "Working, even for a month or so, will give me the money I need to relocate."

Marigold saw no need to add that only three days into the new year she was already chafing from too much leisure time. Thankfully, the Wisconsin cosmetology license she'd obtained last year, in order to participate in a Good Hope Cut-A-Thon to raise money for the Giving Tree, gave her options.

When Beck had casually mentioned she could use this commercial space just down the street from Muddy Boots, she'd jumped on the offer with both feet. She'd even dragged her father and sisters into the crisp winter morning to check out the space with her.

"Paint would help." Prim winced at the bright blue door trim. "Those white eyelet curtains at the window definitely have to go."

"What's wrong with the curtains?" Steve asked. "Your mother and I had ones just like those hanging in the kitchen of our first house."

"The fact that you lived in that house over thirty years ago should tell you why they must go." Humor danced in Ami's green eyes.

"It's fine just the way it is." Marigold forced out the lie. "We're not spending any money or time fixing the place up. It's not worth the effort for a few weeks."

"Do we need to discuss this out here? I don't know about the rest of you, but I'm freezing." Beck rubbed his bare hands together. Though he wore a wool jacket over his sweater, her Georgia-born brother-in-law had southern blood flowing through his veins.

Beck might play some pond hockey or go cross-country skiing, but Marigold was fairly certain she'd never see him wearing shorts in fifty-degree weather like a native.

"The temp is over forty, Beck," Prim teased. "Heck, it's practically balmy today."

Her brother-in-law jammed his hands in his pockets. The Bloom family stood clustered together close to the curb. The spot they occupied was far enough away so they could study the frontage with a critical eye yet not disrupt sidewalk traffic.

Now that she'd seen the exterior, Marigold supposed it was time to step inside. She tried to ignore the panic fluttering in her throat by reminding herself this was only temporary. Very temporary.

Suddenly eager to get the rest of the assessment out of the way, Marigold surged forward.

She never saw what hit her.

Clipped in the shoulder and spun around by the first person, Marigold ping-ponged into the second. She fought for balance and heard Ami cry out. Out of the corner of her eye, she saw Beck and her dad rush forward.

An instant later strong hands gripped her arms, giving her the support she needed to steady herself.

"You have quick hands." She glanced up, expecting to see Beck. Instead she found herself face-to-face with Cade.

"How kind of you to notice." There was a wicked gleam in those gray eyes. "Are you okay?"

When she nodded, Cade bellowed several names, then took off running.

By now, her family surrounded her.

"What happened?" Her breath came in little puffs.

"You stepped right in front of them." Ami sounded breathless as she hugged Marigold tight. "I'm so happy you weren't hurt."

"Who did I step in front of?" Marigold pulled back and glanced down the street.

"The boys," Prim told her. "They ran into you."

"Which was unavoidable." Their father's lips formed a hard line. "But there was no excuse for them not to stop and make sure you weren't hurt."

"I think I recognized them." Ami glanced at their father. "Wasn't that—?"

"Yes." Steve didn't wait for Ami to finish. Maybe he didn't see the need, since Beck was already nodding.

"I thought it was them," Prim agreed.

"It appears I'm the only one in the dark here." Marigold glanced at Beck, looking for clarification.

"Kaiden and Braxton Lohmeier, Dakota's younger brothers." Beck's dark eyes turned troubled. "The boys have been on their own a lot since Cassie gave birth last spring. From what I hear the baby is sick a lot, and she has her hands full."

"Anita has tried to help her daughter out." Steve shook his head. "But Cassie refuses to have anything to do with her mother. I can tell you, being estranged from her daughter and grandchildren breaks Anita's heart."

Marigold finally made the connection. The two boys who'd nearly flattened her were Cassie's sons, which made them Anita's grandsons.

Ami worried her bottom lip. "They should have stopped and apologized."

"Not too late." Beck gestured with his head.

Marigold shifted and saw Cade coming down the street with two boys, a hand firmly on each of their shoulders.

"Good man," her father muttered.

Cade and the brothers stopped directly in front of her.

"Marigold, these young men are Braxton and Kaiden Lohmeier. They have something they want to say to you." Underneath Cade's pleasant tone ran an edge of steel.

Though tall and broad-shouldered for their age, from the soft edges to their faces, Marigold pegged the two somewhere in their midteens.

The older one, with pale blue eyes and jet-black hair hanging in them, spoke first. "Sorry."

The kid tossed the word out with the same casual disregard one might flick off a piece of lint.

"Yeah, sorry." His brother was thinner, a couple of inches shorter, with a sulky mouth. Orange streaked his chocolate-brown hair.

Surprisingly, his apology sounded sincere.

"All of a sudden you were there," the boy added in his defense.

"This isn't her fault." Irritation flashed in Cade's eyes and his voice hardened.

The second boy reacted immediately. He pulled back, raising an arm as if anticipating a blow. "I wasn't saying—"

"I stepped in front of them." Marigold offered both boys an apologetic smile. "I'm sorry, too."

"The sheriff is right." The first boy waved a hand as if shoving aside her apology. "My brother and I shouldn't have been running. We should have stopped and made sure you were okay."

The younger boy nodded.

Surprise flicked across Cade's face. Clearly he hadn't expected such sincerity.

"I'm Marigold Bloom." She extended an ungloved hand to the older boy. "I know your mom and sister."

She could have mentioned she also knew their grandmother, but that might make it sound as if she and Anita were friendly.

When the older boy gave her fingers a perfunctory shake, she noticed his jacket edges were dirty and frayed.

"I'm Braxton." He jerked his head toward the younger boy. "That's Kaiden. He goes by K.T."

"It's nice to meet you both." On impulse Marigold reached up and rubbed one of the stringy strands of black between her fingers. "I love your hair. With a little shaping, you'll have the girls flocking. Stop by sometime. I'll make a chick magnet out of you in no time."

Braxton's suspicious gaze lingered on the salon's eyelet curtains before shifting to Marigold. "You want to cut my hair?"

"Shape. Trim." She lifted her shoulders in a nonchalant shrug. "Up to you."

The two boys exchanged glances.

"Thanks." Braxton shifted his gaze to Cade. "Can we go now?"

"Yes, you may go." The words had barely left Cade's mouth when the boys shot off down the sidewalk. He expelled a breath and called after them, "Don't run."

"Well." Ami smiled at Cade and then at Marigold. "You two, together again. The benefits of small-town living."

Chapter Five

"It's not as crowded as I thought it would be." Cade held the door open to the Flying Crane and stepped back to let Katie Ruth enter. He glanced around the bar.

"It's a Thursday night and still early." Though the faintest hint of worry threaded through Katie Ruth Crewes's upbeat tone, the smile she flashed was filled with confidence.

Cade had run into the YMCA's youth activities coordinator on his walk to the bar for tonight's event. Since it benefited a good cause, Cade hoped the evening would be a success. Apparently all money raised from the ten-dollar cover charge to hear the band out of Milwaukee would go toward the Giving Tree.

When Cade had first moved to Good Hope, he'd assumed the Giving Tree was just another charity that helped residents with financial difficulties during the holidays. But he'd since learned this was not a charity, but rather a fund that met the needs of Good Hope residents year-round.

"I'm sure the event will be a hit and raise lots of money." Cade gave Katie Ruth's arm a reassuring squeeze.

The smile she flashed reminded him of the one Marigold had given him on New Year's Eve, bright but edged with worry.

Marigold.

Cade wished the hairstylist was beside him now, enjoying the music.

He'd been in this particular waterfront bar plenty of times. Not only when patrons got rowdy and he was called to break up a scuffle, but socially. Some of his favorite memories from last summer were of sitting on the deck, watching the sun set over the water while enjoying conversation and a cold one with a few of the locals.

"The Bloom family has arrived." Katie Ruth settled a hand on his arm, her voice filled with relief. "We can always count on their support."

Cade's gaze locked with Marigold's. Her slow smile had him taking a step forward.

He knew the second she noticed Katie Ruth's hand on his arm. Marigold gave her hair a toss and turned to Max, her comment making her brother-in-law laugh.

Cade stiffened and fought a surge of jealousy before reminding himself Max was her sister's husband. She'd come with family, not a date.

If Katie Ruth noticed anything amiss, it didn't show. With easy familiarity, she looped her arm through his. "Let's go say hello."

Cade wasn't convinced walking over arm in arm with Katie Ruth was a good idea. Still, he didn't want to keep his distance. He wanted to dance with Marigold like they'd done at the party and catch up on what was new in her life. And, if they could find a private moment, kiss those scorching red lips.

"I'm so happy you could all make it," Katie Ruth gushed, giving Ami a hug and beaming smiles all around.

They were all there. Not only Marigold's two sisters and their spouses, but Steve and Anita, as well.

"We wouldn't miss it," Ami assured Katie Ruth.

"The Giving Tree means a lot to this community." Beck exchanged a glance with his wife. "We'll always support it."

"Look." Prim's gaze shifted, her smile widening. "Cory and Jackie White are here. Those two are the best example of what the Giving Tree is all about."

"I don't get the connection." Cade knew Cory as a thirtysomething high school teacher. He'd heard Jackie had MS, but other than using a cane, she appeared to be doing fine.

"Cory and his wife were helped by the Giving Tree when he was going through treatment for leukemia," Max explained.

"Let's go say hello." Ami took her husband's hand, wiggled her fingers good-bye.

"We'll come with you." Max glanced at Prim and got a nod of agreement.

"I'm so glad you're back." Katie Ruth pulled Marigold in for a quick hug. "How long will you be around?"

"Not long." Marigold's shoulder rose, then dropped in a careless shrug. "No more than a couple of months."

"Some time is better than none," Katie Ruth said cryptically, then leveled those blue eyes on Marigold. "I've been searching for the perfect person to help out with my Seedling project, and here you are, Marigold Bloom."

Marigold held up her hands. "Only here temporarily, remember?"

"Don't you remember how much fun we had when we were Seedlings?" Katie Ruth's face practically glowed. "We had a blast earning badges, having pizza parties, and then, when we were Saplings, going on the big yearly trip to the Dells. We were so proud when we made it all the way to MCTs."

Cade noted Katie Ruth's voice had turned persuasive, the way it did whenever she approached him about volunteering. He admired the woman's passion, and Cade definitely believed in giving back. But, like Marigold, this simply wasn't a good time for him to commit.

"We did have a lot of good times." Marigold's lips curved, and her eyes turned dreamy with memories. "I loved being a Seedling."

"I don't know if you heard, but the organization may have to shut down." Anita expelled a heavy sigh.

A look of horror skittered across Marigold's face. "Why?"

"It's very sad." Anita shook her head. "And frankly, quite puzzling. As a business owner, I have to keep my eye on the bottom line. It's difficult to understand how things could have gotten so out of hand. I'm just sorry it's happening."

Steve's hand rose to rest on Anita's shoulder. "You've got a kind heart, Cookie."

Beside him, Marigold covered her snort of disbelief with a cough.

Though Anita's expression remained one of sympathy and concern, Cade wasn't buying the act.

"The organization has switched financial oversight to Max's accounting firm." Katie Ruth's shoulders were now soldier straight. "I can assure everyone in the community that we won't have these kinds of issues in the future."

"I'll help you, Katie Ruth." Marigold placed her hand on her friend's shoulder. "Just let me know what you need."

"Thank you, Marigold."

The grateful look on Katie Ruth's face had Cade rethinking his earlier refusal to volunteer. Perhaps he could squeeze out some time to help the Seedlings. After all, back in the day, scouting had been a big part of his life. Like his father, he'd made it all the way to Eagle Scout.

"Steven, isn't that Etta Hawley?" Anita pointed to an older woman chatting it up with the bartender.

"What a pleasant surprise." Steve's smile brightened at the sight of his fellow teacher. "When I saw her in the lounge today, she wasn't sure she'd make it tonight."

Katie Ruth's expression softened as her gaze lingered on the woman. "Etta does a lot of volunteer work for me at the Y. If you don't mind, I'm going to wander over and thank her for coming tonight. I know bar noise bothers her, so she probably won't stay long."

"I'll—we'll—go with you." Steve took Anita's arm.

"It'll be wonderful to see her." Anita's comment had Steve squeezing her hand before they headed for the bar.

"She doesn't like Etta," Cade observed.

"Not one bit." Marigold's eyes narrowed as Anita greeted the woman as if they were best friends.

"Appears you're stuck with me, Goldilocks." Cade gave Marigold a wink, knowing he couldn't have orchestrated a better scenario if he'd tried.

"Shouldn't you stick with your date?" Marigold asked in a cool tone.

He angled his head. "I didn't come here with a date."

"What about Katie Ruth?"

"I ran into her on my walk to the bar. We're not together."

Lifting a brow, Marigold cocked her head. "So you expect me to believe you and Katie Ruth aren't dating?"

"Yes. No. It's the truth." Cade stopped and took a breath. Which only made things worse. How could he think with the delectable scent of *her* teasing his nose? Forming a coherent thought was proving impossible. "We're not dating."

Marigold's brows knit together. She was obviously having difficulty following what he was saying. Heck, he was having difficulty himself.

It was all her fault. How could he think when she stood there looking so incredibly sexy in that red dress with black thigh-high boots?

And the sultry scent of her perfume had scrambled what brains cells he had left.

"I know *we're* not dating, Cade." Marigold waved a hand, the fingernails a fire-engine red that matched her dress. "But what about you and Katie Ruth?"

"There is no me and Katie Ruth." Frustration bubbled over into his voice. He raked a hand through his hair. "She and I are not dating. You and I aren't dating. I'm not dating anyone."

Marigold opened her mouth, then shut it. Those luscious red lips twitched. "Got you."

"What?"

She smiled, a full-bodied smile that reached those pretty blue eyes and had them twinkling. "I thought it might be amusing to get you stirred up. It was fun. I enjoyed it."

Cade narrowed his gaze. "You punk'd me."

"Guilty." She flashed a smile, arched a brow. "Are you going to arrest me?"

He snorted out a laugh. He couldn't help it. She looked so doggone pleased with herself.

Marigold ran the tip of her tongue along her top lip in a sensual gesture too practiced not to be deliberate. "I thought maybe you had a thing for blondes."

He reached out and fingered a silky strand of hair. "Only a certain blonde."

"I have a thing for men with dark hair." An impish gleam filled her eyes. "That's all I'm saying."

Cade felt flustered and off balanced, as if he were sixteen again. The cocky self-assurance, which he'd thought was part of his DNA, appeared to have taken the evening off.

Thankfully his brain had resumed normal function. It warned him he needed to make a move. Men had begun to flood the bar, and the way Marigold looked, she wouldn't be alone for long.

"Tomorrow. Seven o'clock. Dinner at Bayside Pizza."

Marigold tilted her head back and offered a coy smile. "Why, Cade Rallis, are you asking me on a date?"

He didn't like the hint of amusement in her tone. Didn't like it one bit.

For a second he was tempted to make a joke of it and walk away. The impulse made him realize the breakup with Alice had affected his confidence more than he thought.

Cade shoved his hands into his pockets. "I thought we could grab some pizza and catch up on what has been going on in our lives since Shannon's wedding. I understand if you're not interested."

Instead of bumbling the words, he sounded as if someone had shoved a red-hot poker up his backside.

"I'll let you in on a little secret." Her eyes twinkled. If she'd been put off by his stiff delivery, it didn't show. "If you hadn't asked me, I'd have asked you."

Relief, as strong as the gale-force winds that brought whitecaps on Green Bay, surged through Cade.

"Good." He nodded, repeated, "Good. I'll stop by Beck and Ami's at seven and pick you up."

"It'll be nice to reconnect while I'm here."

As Cade gazed at Marigold, with her hair shining like spun gold in the bar's fluorescent lighting, he realized he was looking forward to reconnecting with this saucy pixie. Looking forward to it very much.

Cade's thoughts were still focused on a unique display of graffiti when his phone rang Friday morning. Which meant he wasn't thinking clearly. That had to be the reason he was giving Katie Ruth the impression he was actually considering leading a troop of seven-year-olds.

Every other time the Y youth coordinator had called and begged him to be the leader of a group of Seedlings, he'd turned her down without a second thought. But this time he couldn't force the *no* past his lips.

As Katie Ruth continued to talk, Cade's gaze returned to the graffiti. The first thing that had struck him was the "artist" had too much time on his or her hands. The second was the vandal had talent. He found the art surprisingly compelling. Nestled amid bright, flashy swaths of color was a tangle of faces painted starkly in black and white, mouths agape.

The graffiti had him wondering if that boy—or girl—artist might have benefited from early intervention in the form of involvement in a local scouting organization.

"What would be my responsibilities?" he heard himself ask when Katie Ruth paused to take a breath.

For a second there was silence at the other end of the line. Apparently Katie Ruth was as startled as Cade by his response.

She cleared her throat. "You'd have a troop of five to seven kids, most likely a combination of boys and girls."

Boys, Cade could handle. He'd grown up with three brothers. In the Marines and while on Detroit PD, he'd worked primarily alongside men. Girls, little girls, were a different story. He had no idea what they liked or how to best handle them. But a mixture, especially at such a young age, might be manageable.

"You'll meet biweekly, late afternoon or early evening. The children earn merit badges by demonstrating proficiencies in several predefined areas." Katie Ruth sounded as if she were reading from a script. She took a breath and continued, "The children will be eager to earn the badges. We'll also be getting them involved in various Save the Seedlings activities."

Cade brushed aside the second part of Katie Ruth's speech to focus on the first. "Can you give me an example of a predefined area?"

"Certainly." Katie Ruth paused and Cade heard the rustle of papers. "One of the popular badges among this age group is the dog care merit badge."

Dog care seemed relatively innocuous. "Sounds workable."

"Great." Relief threaded through Katie Ruth's voice. "Your first meeting is next Wednesday evening. Five o'clock. Town hall, room 101."

One thing still puzzled Cade. "Why are you just forming troops now? I'd thought that would have been done at the beginning of the school year."

"Usually that's the case," Katie Ruth confirmed. "The children in your troop will be those who, for various reasons, didn't join a troop at the beginning of the year. Once we have enough interest to form a new troop, we set about finding a leader."

"Which would be me."

"Yes, that would be you." Katie Ruth's voice warmed. "Actually we have three new troops being formed. I can't thank you enough for stepping up, Cade. Just so you know, I'll be at the first meeting next week to make sure you get off to a good start."

After another minute of questions Cade clicked off, wondering just what he'd gotten himself into.

Chapter Six

"I'll take it." Marigold glanced around the small apartment where Ami had once lived and gave a decisive nod. "I only brought a couple of bags so getting settled should be a snap."

Marigold punctuated the words with a snap of her fingers. She thought of everything she'd left behind in Chicago. Thankfully, her roommate had not only taken over the lease, she'd bought Marigold's furniture.

"I hope you know I don't want you to move." Ami's protest stopped just short of a whine. "I like having you just down the hall. Beck likes it, too."

As if sensing the rising tension in the room, Prim skirted around her sisters, hands held up. "While you two hash this out, I'll brew some tea."

"I cleared the cupboards when I moved out," Ami told her sister. "There isn't any—"

"I snagged some from downstairs as well as a sack of scones." Prim pointed to her immense purse, a stylish pink-and-black-striped bag. "While you sit and discuss the move, I'll get the kettle going."

The hurt in Ami's eyes had Marigold's heart twisting. She didn't want to distress her sister, but neither did she want to impose on her and Beck's generosity a second longer than necessary. These months before the baby was born were a special time for them as a couple, and she wouldn't intrude.

Marigold took Ami's hand and led her to a cushy sofa. "You and Beck have been so generous. But you both have lots on your plate right now, including getting ready for my niece or nephew."

When Ami opened her mouth, Marigold rushed on, changing the subject so Ami couldn't argue. "You know, if I was the one pregnant, I'd have opted to find out the sex of the baby. That way my sisters could start buying clothes for their new niece or nephew."

Whatever protest Ami had been about to utter appeared to be forgotten as her sister laughed. "Fin told me the same thing at Christmas. Have you two been talking?"

Fin, the second eldest of the Bloom sisters, lived in Los Angeles and had very definite opinions about everything.

"I haven't connected with Fin recently." Marigold fingered the blue crocheted throw accentuated with yellow cabbage roses tossed over the back of the sofa.

"You *have* told her you lost your job." Though said as a statement, there was a question in Ami's voice.

"Not yet." Seeing the look of disapproval in her sister's gaze, Marigold rushed to assure her. "Telling her is definitely in the plans."

"You haven't told Fin?" Shock laced Prim's voice as she returned with a tea tray holding cups and saucers in an art deco floral pattern.

She placed the tray, which also held a plate of scones and linen napkins, on the large trunk that doubled as a coffee table. "Why not?"

Ignoring the question, Marigold lifted a scone from the pretty plate. "These look yummy. Lemon blueberry?"

Ami nodded. "My most popular flavor."

"I've always loved this china pattern." Marigold studied the set that had once belonged to their great-grandmother. "If I were you, I'd have taken these with me when I moved to the big house."

Ami's gaze met hers. "The set is yours for the asking."

"Prim might—" Marigold began.

Prim sat in a nearby chair. "I don't need them. I already have the set from when Rory and I were married."

There had been a time after the accident that had taken her first husband's life that Prim hadn't been able to speak of him without tearing up. While Marigold knew her sister would never forget Rory, Prim had found her zest for life again. Max had brought the light back into her eyes.

"Fin doesn't want the dishes." Ami tossed the comment on the table, obviously thinking that would be Marigold's next rebuttal. "They aren't her style."

Marigold traced the outline of the brightly colored raised flower on the side of the cup with her finger. She wondered how could anyone not love these dishes, not only for their beauty but for the history. Then again, Fin had always gravitated toward the modern.

"It's settled. You'll take them with you," Ami decreed.

Marigold thought of the high risk of breakage when transporting something so fragile any sort of distance. She shook her head. "They're better off right where they are."

"The dishes are yours. Whenever you decide to claim them is up to you." Ami spoke with the authority that went hand in glove with being the eldest sister.

"Now that we've exhausted the scintillating china discussion"—Prim's gaze pinned Marigold—"I want to know why you haven't told Fin you lost your job and are back in Good Hope."

Marigold was considering how to redirect the conversation when Prim shot her a warning glance. "Waste of time."

Prim's comment garnered the attention of both sisters.

"What would be a waste of time?" With nervous fingers, Marigold broke off a small piece of scone.

"You're speaking with the mother of twins." An amused smile lifted Prim's lips. "I know when someone is trying to avoid answering a direct question."

"Is that what Callum and Connor do?" Marigold bit into the scone, found it tasted as good as it looked. "Are my nephews experts at shifting your focus?"

"Why haven't you called Fin?" Prim was like a bull terrier with a bone. But there was concern in her hazel eyes. "She hates being left out of the loop."

Marigold thought of her brash, charismatic older sister, a person who'd likely never had an uncertain moment in her life. A woman everyone agreed led a charmed existence. While she loved Fin to death, Marigold didn't want to be drawn into a discussion of her future plans. Not yet.

"Fin will pressure me to move to Los Angeles." Marigold let the words hang in the air for several heartbeats. "I'm not against living in California. The fact that she is there makes the option incredibly tempting."

"But—" Prim prompted.

Marigold leaned back, took a breath, let it out slowly. "I'm not sure LA is where I'm meant to be."

She paused, expecting her sisters to weigh in. Instead, they sipped their tea.

"Even before I completed my cosmetology courses, I had a job." Marigold recalled the envy in her classmates' eyes. "Being able to work with such a genius was a once-in-a-lifetime opportunity. There was no thought, no decision to be made."

She gazed unseeing at the fireplace's cold hearth.

"The Steffan Oliver Salon." Marigold spoke the name with great reverence. "I thought I'd died and gone to heaven."

"Then, having him fire you over nothing..." Ami's voice trailed off.

"It was brutal." Marigold saw no reason to sugarcoat. Those blasted tears wanted to come, but she blinked them back. "The positive out of all this is I've been given the opportunity to step back and figure out where I'm really meant to be. While I'm deciding, I'll work, so my skills don't get rusty. The money I earn will help with relocation expenses."

"Which is why Carly's Cut and Curl is so perfect." Prim's lips lifted. "You won't have to pay to rent a chair at a salon."

Trust the accountant in her sister to think of the financial bottom line. Which was the only reason Marigold had accepted Beck's offer. Though she knew working in a space with dull, cracked flooring and ugly wallpaper would make her feel even more like a failure, a gal had to be practical. Free space in a prominent location on Main Street had been impossible to resist.

It would also be an impetus, she told herself, a force that would drive her to secure an appropriate new position as soon as possible.

Marigold turned to Ami. "I appreciate you and Beck letting me use the space."

"We'd be happy to do a rent-to-own." Ami's hopeful smile tore at Marigold's heart.

"I'm not staying." Her tone was firm, absolute.

Ami lifted a brow. "I thought you planned to step back and consider *all* possibilities before making any decision."

Marigold rolled her eyes.

"Okay, enough of that for now. You also mentioned wanting to keep busy." Ami paused and her brow furrowed. "Or maybe you didn't say that exactly, but I know you're easily bored. Anyway, Prim and I need a favor."

"Whatever I can do." Marigold relaxed against the back of the sofa, relieved to have the focus off her uncertain future. "I'm happy to help."

"Perfect." Ami flashed a bright smile. "I'll put you down."

"Ah, just exactly what have I agreed to do?" Marigold wondered if she should have asked before agreeing. Yet she couldn't imagine saying no to her sisters, no matter what the request. Not after how kind and supportive they'd both been to her.

"You know that Ami and I are both members of the Cherries." Prim took a sip of tea, giving the comment time to steep.

Marigold felt the first stirrings of unease. She knew all about the Women's Events League, commonly referred to as the Cherries. Everyone in Good Hope was familiar with the group responsible for planning all the holiday events for the community.

"You guys did an outstanding job with the Christmas festivities. Nothing compares to celebrating a holiday in Good Hope."

"Next up is Valentine's Day." Prim's lips lifted in a little smile. "This will be my first one with Max."

"Beck says he's going all out." Ami brushed a strand of hair back from her face. "I'm not sure what that means."

"Whatever Beck has planned is bound to be epic," Prim told her older sister. "Your husband never does anything halfway."

"Neither does Max," Ami teased. "You know he's going to wow you with something special."

Marigold fought a pang of envy as she brought the cup to her lips and took a sip of Earl Grey. "Do you know I've never had a boyfriend on Valentine's Day?"

A startled look crossed Prim's face before she laughed. "Not buying it."

"It's sad but true." Marigold offered a melodramatic sniff, then raised her hand and pretended to brush away a tear.

"Daniel Smithson. Chicago Board of Trade." Prim tossed out the name like she was announcing his pick in the NFL draft. She pointed a finger at Marigold. "Last Valentine's Day."

"I believe you're mistaken, Prim." Ami broke off a piece of scone. "Jason was her valentine last year."

"Well, then, Daniel was her valentine two years ago," Prim insisted.

"Sorry to say, you're both wrong." Marigold realized she'd been so caught up with all the workplace drama that she hadn't thought of either of her former boyfriends in months. "Jason and I began dating after Valentine's Day and broke up before another one had rolled around. It was the same for Daniel."

Marigold remembered with a pang how bright and shiny the hope had been at the beginning of each relationship and how much that hope had tarnished by the time they called it quits and moved on.

Ami's expression remained doubtful.

"I'm still not sure what happened between you and Jason." Prim's teeth caught her upper lip for a second. "I know you weren't eager to start over in New Orleans."

Marigold thought back. Had she really left off a critical detail when she'd told her sisters the story? "It wasn't just the move, although that was definitely a factor. Jason saw his career as being more important than mine."

"I'd forgotten that part." Prim's strawberry-blonde brows pulled together. "Still, I can't imagine if you love someone, not doing whatever is necessary to find common ground."

"The point is we didn't love each other." Marigold lifted the cup of tea to her lips but didn't drink. "Not enough to try to make it work."

"Let's not waste time on the past." Ami's green eyes were steady when they met Marigold's. "This is going to be your year."

Puzzled, Marigold tilted her head. "My year for what?"

Ami smiled broadly. "For having a valentine, of course."

"Cade will be your valentine." Prim punctuated the pronouncement with a decisive nod that sent her strawberry-blonde curls bouncing. "He'll buy you flowers and candy and—"

"—take you to the Valentine's dance," Ami finished her sister's sentence with a note of triumph. "You two will have a glorious time."

Just hearing *Cade* and *valentine* in the same sentence made Marigold smile. "Glorious, huh?"

"Don't be such a cynic." Ami wagged her finger playfully. "Hearts and flowers and love will soon fill the air in Good Hope."

"The Bayshore Hotel is going all out with the decorations for the big event. I'm not sure of all the details, but I know we'll dance under a glittery net of colored balloons to big band love songs." Prim's hazel eyes turned soft. "It will be so romantic."

Marigold wasn't in Good Hope for romance. This was but a temporary stop on her road to the top. Suddenly restless, she set down her cup and stood. She strode to the window and glanced out over the snow-covered trees before turning and resting her back against the sill. "What's the favor?"

"Hearts and Cherries Fashion Show." Ami spoke around a bite of scone, appearing to have expected the change of subject.

Prim gestured expansively. "The event will be bigger and better than ever this year."

Marigold cocked her head. "What's involved?"

"Hearts and Cherries is an effort to showcase creativity and highlight the diverse selection of retail products available in Good Hope." Ami sounded as if she was reciting from a travel brochure.

"The promo materials we've developed emphasize it's a time when local businesses come together for a week of fun, fashionable events," Prim added, smiling, "including the extremely popular fashion show."

The fact that it sounded similar to the Chicago fashion event she'd lost out on intrigued Marigold. "Where do I fit into the picture?"

Ami grinned. "Why, by doing the models' hair, of course."

"Marigold. This is a pleasant surprise."

The masculine voice behind her had Marigold whirling and her heart slamming against her ribs. If she hadn't been lost in her thoughts as she strolled down Main Street, she'd have realized before she got so excited that the timbre was all wrong.

It wasn't Cade smiling back at her, but Travis.

"Hey, Deputy Forbes." Marigold shot him a teasing look. "Out keeping the streets safe for the citizens of Good Hope?"

"Something like that." Travis fell into step beside her.

The brown uniform pants and shirt favored him more than the tux he'd worn on New Year's Eve. Still, he didn't make Marigold's heart beat the slightest bit faster.

His hair was only a shade darker than the pants, and his eyes were a vivid blue. A scattering of freckles gave him a boyish look. The guy-next-door type had always been Prim's thing, not hers. Marigold liked her men a little more edgy.

"I'm surprised you're still in town." When she stopped in front of the general store, Travis held the door open for her, then followed her inside. "I thought for sure you'd be back in Chicago by now."

Like a spirit rising unbidden from the mist, Eliza appeared around a display of power bars. "I was thinking the very same thing."

Though Eliza's voice had a pleasant enough lilt and her lips curved in a semblance of what could pass for a smile, those gray eyes remained cool.

"I like the vest." Marigold waved a casual hand toward Eliza's silver-and-black faux fur vest worn over a dove-gray sweater. Charcoal pants completed the image of a stylish woman who knew how to emphasize her assets.

With an almost imperceptible nod, Eliza accepted the compliment. "Why *are* you back in Good Hope, Marigold?"

Marigold had known this moment was coming, so she wasn't surprised by the question. Not from Travis. And certainly not from Eliza, who she could see was salivating at the thought of digging in her claws.

Marigold kept her tone offhand. "I realized I wasn't living up to my potential in Chicago. The time had come to make a change."

"Change can be good." Travis's voice reverberated with excitement. "Do you plan to—?"

"She won't stay in Good Hope." Eliza cut him off, her eyes glittering. "Just like her sister, Marigold has always been convinced she's too good for our little town."

"I believe I speak for both myself and Fin when I say neither of us ever considered ourselves too good for our hometown." Marigold's voice dripped saccharine. She could do icy. But over the years she'd discovered phony sweet really got Eliza stirred up. "Our careers, our aspirations, simply took us to bigger, but certainly not better, cities."

Travis's gaze shifted from Marigold to Eliza. The continued confusion in his eyes told her he'd assessed the situation and had come up empty. It wasn't surprising he was having such difficulty making the pieces of the puzzle fit. He was, after all, a man.

The radio at his shoulder squawked and a look of relief skittered across his face.

"Duty calls." He gave a brisk nod to both of them. "You ladies have a nice day."

"You, too, Travis," Marigold called out to his retreating back, her gaze focused on Eliza.

Eliza raised a brow. "Don't you have a big fashion show coming up?"

"I do." Marigold smiled brightly, deliberately misunderstanding. "I'm excited to be styling the hair for the Hearts and Cherries Fashion Show."

The startled surprise that crossed Eliza's face brought joy to Marigold's heart. Though she'd only agreed as a favor to her sisters, Eliza's obvious disapproval only strengthened her resolve to be involved.

"The assignment wasn't run by me."

"Sounds to me as if Ami is in charge of the event. No doubt her head would be the one rolling if she hadn't been able to replace Carly with someone competent." Marigold couldn't keep the hint of smug from her voice.

"I instructed Ami to check with Charlotte McCray at Golden Door."

Marigold shrugged. While she was familiar with the upscale salon, she'd yet to meet the owner. Apparently Charlotte spent more time in Chicago than in Good Hope. "You'll have to speak with Ami if you want more details."

"I'll be doing just that." Eliza opened her mouth as if to say more but was stopped by the jangle of bells over the front door.

A sudden softening in Eliza's expression had Marigold turning. Her heart gave a little leap when Cade stepped into the shop. The sheriff appeared deep in conversation with Jeremy, the man Eliza had lusted after since high school.

Marigold smiled. Something told her this quick trip to the store was going to be a whole lot of fun.

Chapter Seven

"The boys and girls in Good Hope need to be challenged." Cade pulled open the door of the general store. "If they aren't, the trouble we've seen lately will only escalate."

"The increase in vandalism is troubling." Jeremy's blue eyes shone with concern. He rubbed his chin, his expression thoughtful. "Especially considering all the community is doing to keep our young people engaged. The middle and high school offer tons of opportunities for involvement. Not to mention all of the YMCA-sponsored activities."

Cade had bumped into the mayor when he'd come from the alley. It had seemed a perfect time to discuss his concerns. "I agree, to a point."

While Jeremy's argument was sound and one Cade had used himself, it had holes. The longer he was in Good Hope the more Cade realized some kids simply needed something different than what was currently offered.

"There's also Big Brothers Big Sisters. The organization is very active in Good—" Jeremy paused just inside the door, his attention drawn to the left.

Cade followed the direction of his companion's gaze. Even though the wind outside held a bite, the sight of the pretty blonde pixie had blood sliding through his veins like warm honey.

Marigold looked as enticing as a slice of homemade cherry pie in her fluffy red sweater. Instead of letting her hair hang loose, she'd pulled it back in some sort of intricately braided tail, leaving little blonde wisps loose around her cheeks.

Eliza stood next to her, a dark force dressed in some sort of furry vest. By their adversarial stances, it was apparent that whatever discussion the two women were having wasn't a friendly one.

If Cade had a little more of an ego, he might have thought they were talking about him, about the New Year's kiss. But he knew even if Eliza's stunt *had* upset Marigold, she'd never have let her feelings show.

He wondered if whatever they were discussing had anything to do with his deputy. Cade and Jeremy had passed Travis on the sidewalk.

Could the deputy have been with Marigold? Based on the kiss the two had exchanged New Year's Eve, it was possible. When he'd seen his deputy with Marigold that night, it had taken all of Cade's willpower not to pull Travis away from her.

He'd had to remind himself that, despite their past fling, he had no hold on the woman. Marigold was free to see whoever she wanted while in Good Hope.

Unfortunately, that fact didn't stop him from fuming.

"I thought it was Eliza's day off," Jeremy muttered under his breath.

It surprised Cade the mayor didn't appear keen on seeing the store's proprietress. The two were a semiregular couple in Good Hope.

"I could put her in a cell." Cade arched a brow. "Lock her up and throw away the key?"

Jeremy's eyes widened slightly. Then he grinned. "Naw. Wouldn't be worth it. Not with the hell she'd raise once she was released."

"Don't say I didn't offer." Chuckling, Cade sauntered in the direction of the two women.

After a second's hesitation, Jeremy followed.

The rough wooden planks creaking under Cade's boots added to the rustic ambience of a business that had been in existence since the early twentieth century. Since the peninsula had a ban on chain stores, this small business with its white clapboard siding and bare-bones interior held everything from fishing lures and bug spray to a full-service pharmacy.

Eliza's eyes flicked over Cade before landing on his companion. "Hello, Jeremy."

The mayor might want to reconsider his offer to put the woman in cuffs and haul her off. Cade's ex had spoken to him in that tone whenever she was pissed. Which had been nearly all the time the last few months they'd been together.

"I was just about to tell Eliza that it was too bad Fin wasn't able to stay to celebrate New Year's Eve with all of us." Marigold smiled sweetly. "Having all of the Bloom sisters together to welcome in the New Year would have been absolutely amazing."

Cade had spoken with Fin at Prim and Max's wedding. Fin Bloom was a beautiful woman and very charming. The way she flirted—easily and effortlessly—told him she was used to men falling all over her. While Cade hadn't been attracted to her, he'd enjoyed the brief conversation they shared.

Marigold's sister had an intelligent mind and strong opinions, two characteristics she shared with Eliza.

"How is Fin?" Jeremy asked when silence descended over the group.

"I don't know if you heard, but she recently switched jobs. That's why she wasn't back for Christmas." Pride filled Marigold's voice and she appeared to be warming to the topic. "Fin—"

"Holding on to a position can be a challenge, especially when ego is involved," Eliza interrupted in a pleasant tone, undoubtedly as sincere as her phony smile. "The Bloom sisters seem to be doing a lot of job hopping. First Prim, then Fin, and now you."

Marigold simply stared at the dark-haired woman for several seconds before shifting to face Cade. "I stopped here to pick up a few things for my new apartment. What brings you by?"

"New apartment?" Cade controlled the urge to break out in a big grin. "You've decided to settle in Good Hope after all?"

"She's not staying." Eliza's chuckle had a finely honed edge. "Some people are never satisfied. It's a 'grass is always greener' thing."

"I'll be around anywhere from a couple of weeks to a couple of months." Marigold kept her gaze on Cade and spoke as if Eliza hadn't spoken. "I'm living in the apartment over the bakery."

"That's a nice space." Jeremy nodded approval. "Great location."

"You can't beat the center of downtown." Marigold smiled. "Not to mention all those wonderful smells I'll be able to inhale every day for free. Best of all, it'll be close to my work."

"You're opening a salon in Good Hope?" Jeremy's expression grew puzzled. "I thought you weren't staying."

"I'm not opening a salon." Marigold spoke firmly, as if to make sure there could be no misunderstanding. "Beck owns the spot where Carly's Cut and Curl was located. I'll use the space while I'm in town."

"Told you she wouldn't stay." Eliza shot Jeremy a pointed glance.

"Another new business in town." Jeremy rubbed his hands together, not bothering to acknowledge Eliza's comment. "Good Hope is definitely a community on the move."

"It's not a new business. It's a *temporary* spot where I can cut hair," Marigold clarified.

Cade heard the note of panic in her tone, but it was so faint he doubted the other two noticed.

Be Mine in Good Hope

"Still, we can use all the fresh blood we can find. I'll have someone call you about getting involved in the rotary." Jeremy's smile only widened at Marigold's groan. "And I'm fairly certain Eliza could use your prowess for some of the Cherries events."

Out of the corner of his eye, Cade saw Eliza jerk upright as if struck by a hot poker.

"Funny you should mention it." Marigold slanted a glance at Eliza. "I was just telling Eliza that Ami has already recruited me to style the hair for the upcoming Hearts and Cherries Fashion Show."

Jeremy gave Eliza the thumbs-up. "Smart move."

Some of the stiffness in the brunette's shoulders eased at Jeremy's approval, but the look she shot Marigold was venomous. "Since Carly bailed on us and it appears Charlotte McCray isn't willing to help . . ."

"It's not like you're scraping the bottom of the barrel." There was a hint of reproach in Jeremy's voice. "Marigold is a top hairstylist. The fact that she'll be lending her talent to the event is something we need to publicize. Having someone of her caliber involved will bring in even more people for the event."

"That's sweet of you to say, Jeremy." Marigold raised herself up and brushed the mayor's cheek with her lips. "You always were my favorite of Fin's high school boyfriends."

Jeremy's brows drew together. "I was her *only* high school boyfriend."

Marigold flashed a grin. "Oh, that's right."

"I'm here to pick up a couple packs of batteries." Cade understood Jeremy and Marigold's easy familiarity. Didn't like it, but understood. He'd heard the stories. Knew Fin Bloom had broken Jeremy Rakes's heart by dumping him right before he left for college.

Though the breakup occurred over ten years ago, the fact that both Jeremy and Fin remained single made the story a point of interest to the Good Hope citizenry. Etta Hawley had sworn to Cade that Jeremy and Fin were *destined* to be together because everyone in the Rakes family married their first love.

Cade had only smiled. *Small-town living at its finest.*

Jeremy never mentioned his failed relationship with Marigold's older sister. Cade never asked about it. Just like Jeremy never asked what had gone wrong between Cade and his former fiancée. Both relationships were done and over and had nothing to do with now.

"I'd be happy to help you carry all this back to the apartment." Cade kept his tone casual, knowing by simply offering he was making his interest in the youngest Bloom clear.

Marigold slipped out a list of twenty items written on a sheet of notebook paper. "Thanks, but I haven't even begun to put a dent in my list. It might take me a while."

"Good thing I know this store like the back of my hand." Cade lifted the list from her hand and quickly scanned it. "I guarantee we'll walk out the door with all these items in ten minutes flat."

As he took Marigold's arm and strolled off down the aisle with her, Cade was aware he was leaving Jeremy to fend for himself. But from what he'd observed, the mayor could handle his own against the woman known for her sharp tongue.

Besides, everyone knew when it came to women, it was every man for himself.

Marigold unlocked the door to the second-story apartment, then turned back to Cade and held out a hand. "Thanks for carrying the bag for me."

Instead of giving her the sack, he closed his free hand over hers and brought it to his lips for a kiss. His gray eyes never left her face. "My pleasure."

"I'd invite you in, but . . ." She paused and searched for what to say. "The place is a mess."

"I'm the sheriff, not the white glove police." His arm remained around the sack.

Marigold had to chuckle even as she knew if she gave in to temptation and let him inside, she and Cade would be alone. *Completely alone.* She shivered at the realization.

With Ami helping Beck at the café and Prim at home enjoying some family time, there was little chance of interruption from her sisters tonight.

Pushing open the door, Marigold stepped back and swept her arm out in a dramatic gesture. "Mi casa es su casa."

Cade sauntered halfway across the living room before stopping. With the sack still cradled in his arms, he turned in a circle. His sharp gray eyes surveyed the cheerful living room and adjoining kitchen with a dinette table for two.

"There isn't a lot of room, but compared to the apartment I shared with a friend in Chicago, it feels incredibly spacious."

"You've got yourself a nice space." He paused, sniffed the air. "And you were right, the place smells like cinnamon and sugar."

"I take no credit for the delectable aroma." Marigold laughed. "That is all courtesy of Ami."

Cade placed the sack on a steamer trunk now doing duty as a coffee table. "Show me the rest."

"There isn't much more to see." Still, she headed down the hall. She gestured to the bathroom with its pink-and-white gingham shower curtain.

Cade studied the space for a moment. "Nice and . . . pink."

She shrugged. "Ami likes pink."

Marigold took a couple more steps and gestured with a careless hand. "The bedroom."

She hadn't expected Cade to walk into the room. When he did, she saw no choice but to follow.

He couldn't have looked more out of place, looming so large and male in a room clearly decorated by someone with female sensibilities.

The four-poster iron bed was covered with a cream-colored, lacy duvet topped with lots of frilly pillows. Though not visible, Marigold remembered beneath all that frill were silk sheets the color of bronze.

The wooden blinds were open, allowing the sunshine to stream in through the single window, which had a nice view of Main Street.

"It's a good space." Cade glanced down at the shiny hardwood floor before his gaze returned to her. "The place is . . ."

He paused, as if searching for the right word. "Homey. Your apartment has a homey feel."

Marigold felt her shoulders relax. She wasn't sure why she felt relief. Perhaps it was because Jason had always been so critical. She shoved aside the memories.

Resting her back against the dresser that had once belonged to her grandmother, she smiled at Cade. "Thanks for carrying my cleaning supplies home and for rescuing me from the wicked witch."

"You didn't need rescuing." Humor danced in his eyes. "From what I observed, you had the situation well under control."

Marigold accepted the compliment with a slight smile. "I know Eliza's hot buttons and how to push. That's a huge advantage."

He raised a brow.

"Mention Fin, especially if you couple her name with Jeremy's in the same sentence, and steam practically rolls out of Eliza's ears."

"She's got the hots for Jeremy." His fingers carelessly stroked one of the brass knobs on the bed's footboard.

Marigold's mouth went dry, remembering how those long fingers had once caressed . . .

"Is that why she gets so upset when she's around the Bloom sisters?" The amusement in his eyes made her suspect he knew the path her mind had been traveling.

"Eliza has always wanted Jeremy for herself." Marigold determinedly pulled her thoughts away from those talented fingers. "For a long time Fin was the only woman Jeremy wanted. I don't think he still feels that way."

She wasn't aware that she'd put a question in her voice until Cade lifted his hands, let them drop. "Jeremy and I are friends, but relatively new ones. He doesn't talk to me about those kinds of things."

"I hope he finds someone." She shifted her gaze out the window. "Jeremy is a good guy. He deserves to be happy."

"Any chance he and Fin might get back together?"

Marigold didn't even need to think before responding. "I can't imagine Fin ever moving back to Good Hope. I can't imagine Jeremy ever leaving."

His gaze lazily searched hers. "You had no plans to return, and yet you're here."

"I'm here temporarily." She stammered as his gaze heated her blood. "I'm not staying forever."

The words barely left her lips when he moved close.

"Well, I guess we better make the most of your time here," he murmured just before his mouth closed over hers.

The taste of Marigold, the smell of her, the feel of her soft curves against his body drove Cade wild. His mouth was greedy and demanding on her lips. She didn't seem to mind. Her fingers raked through his hair, wrapped around his head, pulling him closer as she clung to him.

It was almost as if she worried he might change his mind.

There wasn't a chance in hell of that happening.

"Bed," he finally managed to utter when they came up for air.

"Too many clothes." Marigold's hands stole between them to fumble with his belt buckle.

He brushed her frantic fingers aside. After shutting the blinds with one flick of the wrist, Cade made quick work of shedding his clothes.

Hers hit the floor a second later.

They stood staring at each other for several heartbeats.

Cade let his appreciative gaze linger. Marigold was toned and fit, a petite dynamo with a body designed for long nights of making love.

Her chin lifted, those blue eyes glittering in the light.

Stepping forward, Cade lifted a hand and trailed a finger lightly along that stubborn jaw. "You're every bit as lovely as I remember."

Marigold's gaze dropped. "You're just as impressive."

He grinned, then slanted a glance at the bed, frowned. "It's—"

"Too lovely to mess up?"

"I was about to say 'too froufrou.'"

She laughed as she turned to carefully pull back the duvet.

Cade supposed he could have waited, but the sight of that gorgeous, naked body bent over the bed was much too enticing. He stepped behind her, wrapping his arms around her waist.

Evidence of his arousal pressed against her backside as his hands closed over her breasts.

"Ah." Her breath came out in a shudder. She straightened and arched back against his chest, eyes half-closed.

He nuzzled the sensitive skin behind her ear. When she moaned, he realized this was going to move at warp speed.

Condoms.

He groaned. Swore.

Marigold lifted her head, her breath now coming in little puffs. "Problem?"

"No protection." He started to step away, but she turned, encircled his neck with her arms.

"I'm on the pill." She bit the lobe of his ear. "But I also have condoms. Just picked them up today."

"At the general store?" Cade wasn't sure why he found the thought so horrifying.

Marigold laughed, a full-throated, husky sound that turned Cade's blood to fire. Everything about this woman stirred him, from toes painted a sultry red to that mane of tousled blonde hair.

"No, silly. I swiped them from my sister. She doesn't need them now."

Relieved, Cade tugged her even closer. "Be sure and say thanks next time you see her."

"I'll leave that to you."

The teasing lilt to her voice had him nipping her shoulder.

Her fingers returned to play with his hair. "I put the condoms in the top dresser drawer. Do you want to get them? Or should I?"

"Stay right here." Even though the dresser was mere steps away, he brought his lips to hers for another scorching kiss before retrieving the small box. He tossed it on the nightstand before pulling Marigold to him again. "Miss me?"

"Like you've been gone for years." This time when she lifted her face to his, the kiss was warm and sweet and tender.

A reunion kiss, the kind two lovers might give each other when they'd been apart for a long, long time. As he continued to kiss her, Cade realized just how much he'd missed her. It was as if he'd been waiting for this moment ever since she'd left his bed eighteen months ago.

I was waiting for her.

He found the thought troubling, so he pushed it from his head and concentrated on pleasing the woman in his arms.

Marigold allowed him to lay her on the bed. Looping her arms around Cade's neck, she pulled him down beside her.

For several heartbeats she stared into his eyes. "From the moment I saw you at Ami's house on New Year's Eve, I knew we'd end up here."

His gaze never left hers. "Why did you kiss Travis?"

"Why did you kiss Eliza?"

"She kissed me." That steady gaze never wavered. "It didn't mean anything."

"I'm not sure who kissed who first with Travis. But I kissed him the second time because I knew you were watching and I was pissed about Eliza."

"Fair enough." With one finger, he tucked a strand of hair behind her ear. "You appeared to enjoy it."

"It was like kissing my brother." She wrinkled her nose. "If I had a brother, which I don't."

The tension in his jaw relaxed.

"Now that we've got all that settled." Marigold planted kisses along his jaw. "How about we quit talking?"

He trailed one hand all the way down to her hip, then back up again, his thumbs resting just under her breasts. "Your skin is as soft as these sheets."

"Kiss me." She breathed the words, her eyes dark with desire. "Touch me. I need—for you to touch me."

"Let me compare." He brushed the palm of his hand against the sheets, then returned it to her body, placing it just below her belly. He smiled. "Yep, just as soft."

Marigold groaned. "If I had a gun, I'd point it at your head and tell you to quit joking and get to work."

"Ah, Goldilocks." His hand moved lower. "Your words are music to my ears."

Chapter Eight

"Definitely looks like the business is taking off." Marigold stood with Cade at the bottom of the steps leading up to Bayside Pizza.

Though the building was new, it had a rustic look with weathered wood siding and a deck that encircled the entire building. Heat lamps were strategically positioned, but missing were the tables and chairs that would dot the deck springtime through fall. Winter still held a grip on Good Hope, and even the hardiest of residents wouldn't opt for an outside table with temperatures dipping to the twenties at night.

The windows facing out over the water, triple-paned and large, allowed diners to be comfortable while enjoying a stellar view of Green Bay.

"Now, are you glad we decided to come out?"

"I wasn't averse to leaving the apartment."

Cade shot her a skeptical glance.

"I wasn't," Marigold insisted. "I simply didn't want you to feel obligated to take me out because we had this scheduled for tonight."

"I wanted to take you out on a date." He grinned at the glance she sent him. "Okay, I'd rather have stayed in, but this way we can pick up a take-out menu for future reference."

Marigold liked the sound of *for future reference*. Although their relationship would soon come to an end, that didn't mean she couldn't enjoy the moment. "I can't believe they don't have a menu on their website."

"What website?" He chuckled.

"I know. What business doesn't have a website?" Her smile faded. How could she have forgotten something so basic. "Which reminds me. I need to update mine. It still shows I'm with Steffan."

A blast of wind off the bay had her shivering and climbing the stairs to the restaurant's entrance. Looking forward to getting inside out of the weather, she reached for the door handle. Cade beat her to it.

Marigold stepped inside and simply stood there for a moment, reveling in the air pumping like a steam engine from a heat duct overhead. Once sufficiently warmed, she slowly unwound the black scarf curled like a python around her neck and let it hang loose.

Cade took her coat, stuffed the scarf into one sleeve, then draped it over his arm.

"You have a website?"

"I do." Until this moment, she hadn't given a single thought to all the changes that would need to be made. "I even have a blog incorporated into it, one I've seriously neglected this past week. It's called *Naturally Curlylocks*, and I give advice to clients with—"

He held up a hand, stopping her. "Let me guess. Those with curly hair?"

"Ding. Ding. Ding." She smiled. "We've got a winner."

"What's my prize?" He wiggled his eyebrows suggestively.

"I'll give that some thought and let you know." She stepped into the line that snaked to the reception stand. "In the meantime, I don't suppose you could give me the name of someone who does website updates? I used Steffan's guy before, but . . ."

Marigold let her voice trail off. While she'd been an employee of the Steffan Oliver Salon, Steffan had covered all costs of not only the salon's website but those of the individual stylists, as well. Now that train had left the station and she was on her own.

"I bet your father or your sisters know some tech-savvy kid looking to earn a few bucks." Cade rested his palm against the base of her spine as they moved slowly forward in line.

Marigold's heart performed a series of flutters, and she found herself leaning back slightly, reveling in the touch. Perhaps they should have stayed in bed . . . she shoved the thought aside and refocused. "Did you say you knew someone?"

"No. I said you should ask your family."

"Oh, that's right." Marigold ignored the puzzled look in his eyes. Her mind had been elsewhere, that's all. When she was young, mishearing what she'd been told had been more of an issue. It rarely happened now. "I'll check with the family tomorrow."

Cade was still looking at her oddly when Marigold heard her name. She turned to see Vanessa Eden, stylish as always in a wool jacket the color of ripe plums, striding toward her.

Max's mother gave her a quick hug. "My son mentioned you were back. It's so good to see you."

Though the woman had to be close to fifty, Vanessa could easily pass for forty. Fit and trim, there wasn't a single bag or sag visible. The blunt-cut blonde hair that brushed her shoulders flattered a pretty face, free of lines.

The wrap coat emphasized her slim figure and long legs, encased in black leather boots. From behind thickly mascaraed lashes, she gave

Marigold the once-over, nodded approval. "I hear you're opening a new salon."

Marigold tried not to wince.

"While I'm in town, I'll be seeing clients in the location where"—she swallowed hard and forced out the words—"Carly's Cut and Curl used to be."

"Poor Carly tried. Hair just wasn't her thing. Between those dancing scissors and poodle paper . . ." Vanessa grimaced ever so slightly. "Even if she'd been the best in town, I couldn't get past the ambiance."

Though Marigold heartily agreed, she settled for a simple smile. She'd learned long ago it was best not to say anything negative about another stylist—or her digs—no matter how well-deserved.

An attractive, dark-haired man in his midthirties who'd been weaving his way through tables in the dining area approached Vanessa with a broad smile. "I worried you weren't going to make it."

"Busy day at the Garden." Vanessa sighed, referring to her business, the Garden of Eden, a full-service garden center and nursery at the edge of town. "Paperwork is just not my thing."

"You'd rather stab an ice pick in your eye," the man teased.

"Exactly." Vanessa laughed and slipped her arm through his. "You know me so well."

"I don't believe we've met." Marigold had racked her brain trying to place the attractive man with the broad shoulders and brown eyes but came up empty. He and Vanessa seemed well acquainted. Could he be a friend of Max's? "I'm Marigold Bloom, Max's sister-in-law."

Before she could continue and introduce Cade, the man extended his hand. "Adam Vogele. I farm between Good Hope and Egg Harbor. I grow organic produce."

"I bet those crops include cherries." As red tart cherries were the main crop on the peninsula, Marigold didn't know of a single farmer who didn't set aside some land for orchards.

Adam nodded, his brown eyes warm with good humor.

"Adam and I are here to do some strategizing with Travis Forbes and a group of other Good Hope citizens on what we can do to help get our local boy elected." Vanessa smiled. "You and your friend are welcome to join us."

Only then did Marigold realize that Cade wasn't acquainted with Vanessa. When she glanced in his direction she saw amusement, rather than annoyance, in Cade's gray eyes.

"I don't think so, but I appreciate the invitation." Marigold slipped her arm through Cade's and smiled brightly at Vanessa. "I don't believe you've met our current sheriff, Cade Rallis."

"It didn't take them long to beat a hasty retreat." Marigold spoke quietly to Cade as the hostess showed them to a rustic wooden table that still had bark on the legs.

"They appeared embarrassed, but there's no reason." Once seated, Cade lifted one of the menus and handed it to Marigold before opening his own. "I knew coming in I would likely face an uphill battle in retaining the position. When I met with Len, he told me straight out that one of his deputies desperately wanted the position. In the end, he and Jeremy felt my experience in managing a squad and the wide breadth of my background made me a better choice."

"They made the right decision."

He smiled. "That's kind of you to say."

"I'm rarely kind, but I am honest." Marigold studied his face. "What are you going to do if you lose the election?"

He flipped to the next page in the menu without glancing down. "I'm not going to lose."

"I admire confidence as much as the next gal, but surely you have a contingency plan."

"Welcome to Bayside Pizza." The waitress had dark, curly brown hair and a bright smile. "May I get you something to drink while you look at the menus?"

A flicker of recognition stirred, but Marigold looked to the woman's name tag for confirmation. "Izzie Deshler. How are you?"

A startled look crossed the woman's face before a smile blossomed. "Oh my goodness, Marigold. I didn't expect to see you. I thought you were back in Chicago. What brought you back so soon?"

Marigold ignored the question and turned to Cade. "Izzie and I are part of a crew that serves Christmas dinner at Muddy Boots. She's also the one who did the mural on the café wall."

Surprise skittered across Cade's face. "You're the one who painted the girl in the raincoat splashing up water?"

Izzie flushed. "Yep, that was me."

"It's amazing." Cade's brows pulled together. "You're the one I read about in last week's *Gazette*. You're the one Jeremy appointed to spearhead the alley art project."

"That's right." Pride filled Izzie's voice. "I was honored to be asked."

Apparently noticing Marigold's puzzlement, Cade explained. "The mayor and town board obtained permission from merchants to use the walls of their buildings—the ones facing alleys—as canvases. Izzie here will do some of the art but will also recruit national artists as well as local ones to paint the murals."

"Wow. I'm even more impressed." Marigold sat back in her chair and simply stared.

"It's a fabulous opportunity." Izzie's dark eyes snapped with excitement. "If you know any talented locals who might be interested, send them my way. Beck has my contact information. It was in the article as well."

"I recently came across some really impressive graffiti on one of the alley walls—" Cade began.

"The black-and-white screaming faces?" Izzie interrupted.

Cade nodded.

"If you run across the artist, send him or her to me."

"I'll have to arrest them first."

A startled look crossed Izzie's face.

"Ma'am." A woman at a nearby table lifted her empty glass.

"I'll get you more tea right away." Izzie offered the woman a bright smile before turning back to Cade and Marigold. "It's extra busy tonight because we have a group working on some election stuff that's taking up a number of tables. If you know what you want to drink—"

"Really quick. In terms of the election," Marigold met Izzie's gaze and gestured. "This is Cade Rallis and he's running for sheriff. He has my endorsement and the backing of the entire Bloom family. I hope you'll consider him when it's time to vote."

"Pleased to meet you and I definitely—" Izzie paused, sighed when the woman at the nearby table jiggled the ice in her glass. "Do you know what you'd like to drink?"

While something warm sounded good, Marigold was in the mood to venture on the wild side. Or at least as wild as it got in Good Hope. "I'll try the maple lemonade."

Cade closed his menu. "Make that two."

Marigold's surprise must have shown, because Cade grinned, then shrugged. "Always good to venture out of your comfort zone."

On that they were in total agreement.

After writing down their drink order, Izzie glanced up from her notepad. "I don't want to rush you, but if you know what you want, I can get your order in before the large group. Otherwise it may be a while for your food to come out."

"Appreciate the heads-up." Cade met Marigold's gaze. "Why don't you order for both of us? Anything is fine with me."

"Are you sure?" Marigold's brows drew together. "You might not like what I choose."

"It appears we're both in the mood to live dangerously." He relaxed back in his chair, shot her a warm smile. "As evidenced by the maple lemonade order."

Thirty minutes later, Cade finished the last bite of his goat cheese salad and reached for another piece of the lobster pizza. Instead of cutting off a bite, he simply lifted a slice in his hand.

He let the lobster and asparagus with ricotta linger on his tongue for a moment before swallowing. "I don't know if it's this mix of ingredients or that they bake it in a wood-fired oven, but this pie is tasty."

Marigold considered telling him he should let her order every time they came here but swallowed the words along with another bite of pizza. There was no way of knowing how long she'd be in Good Hope. This might be the only time they'd share a meal.

"Seriously, you hit it out of the ballpark with this selection." Cade smiled as a high-school-aged boy scooped up their empty salad bowls and hurried off as if racing toward first base. "The goat cheese salad was another home run."

"I'm thinking about suggesting Ami add something similar to the Muddy Boots menu." Marigold forked another bite. "It would have been nice to get our salads before the pizza, but they're busy tonight."

Cade shrugged. "I don't mind doing a salad chaser."

"You're easy to please." Marigold reached over and squeezed his hand. She found Cade's attitude a refreshing change from Jason, who liked—or rather demanded—perfection from everyone. Not only waitstaff and work subordinates, but from her as well.

"I appreciated what you said to Izzie about supporting me in the election." His gaze met hers. "I hope you know I don't take your support for granted."

"You're the best person for the job." Marigold spoke in a matter-of-fact tone. "Travis is a good guy. Eventually he'd make a good sheriff somewhere. But he's not ready to lead a department yet. Len and Jeremy made the right call."

"Hearing you say that means a lot to me."

"You can thank me by letting me choose the dessert." Marigold lifted the dessert menu from the table. "Rumor is they have this amazing bread pudding."

Cade grimaced.

"Hey, what happened to Mr. Easy To Please who was in the mood to live dangerously?" Her tone turned teasing. "How can you not like a dessert that contains French bread, dried fruit, vanilla custard, and cream?"

"It does sound good," he admitted. "But I don't know where we're going to put it all."

She motioned for him to lean close, then whispered in his ear. "I can think of several ways to burn off all these calories once we get back to my place."

Before he could reply, Izzie appeared. "Would you like any dessert this evening?"

Cade smiled. "We'll start with the bread pudding."

Marigold discovered that during her time away, Muddy Boots had become *the* place to be on Sunday morning.

When Ami had told her Beck had recently hired extra help to manage the after-church breakfast crowd, she'd assumed her sister was joking. That is, until she'd walked through the door this morning.

Marigold stared in amazement as she watched Katie Ruth flirt with high school principal Clay Chapin, coffee cup in hand. "This scene reminds me of a bar I used to frequent on Friday nights, except for the lack of loud music . . . and the fact that coffee has replaced wine as the drink of choice."

"It's a meat market," Prim confided. "Like a Sunday morning singles club."

"There are married couples here, too," Ami argued.

After surveying the crowd, Marigold concluded her eldest sister was right. There appeared to be an equal numbers of singles versus those attached. While many sat at tables eating, others—like Katie Ruth—roamed from table to table with coffee cup in hand in a strange version of a bar crawl. "I like it. The place has a good vibe."

Ami smiled. "Beck and I love the energy, the camaraderie and—"

"—the constant ring of the cash register?" Marigold gave her sister a wink.

"That, too." Ami laughed.

Prim studied the crowded dining room with the assessing gaze of an accountant. "Now, if we can just find a place to sit."

Relief lit Ami's green eyes. "There's a four-top being cleaned off by the window."

"I saw that one, but there's five of us . . ." Prim, always the accountant, reminded her sister.

"You guys sit." Marigold held up a hand when Ami began to sputter. "I want to mingle."

Ami shook her head. Her chin lifted in a stubborn tilt. "Beck can—"

"Think of it this way. All of these customers are potential clients for me." Marigold lowered her voice. "I need to see and be seen, let people know I'm here and that I'll be cutting hair while I'm in town."

"Katie Ruth already mentioned that fact in the *Open Door*," Prim said, referring to the online newsletter that supplied residents with daily news and gossip. "Trust me, everyone knows you're back in Good Hope."

Prim caught Ami's eyes, and the eldest Bloom sister nodded.

Back in Good Hope.

There was such a finality in the way her sister said the words. Not *back for a visit*, but *back in Good Hope.*

Back, because she'd lost her high-profile position at the Steffan Oliver Salon. Back, because no other top-rated salon in Chicago wanted her. Back and now seeing clients in the former Carly's Cut and Curl location.

Oh, how the mighty fall...

Marigold had seen other stylists crash and burn, most often due to addiction issues. But her slide from grace had occurred through no fault of her own. She forced a smile, gave Ami and Prim a little shove. "Go. Sit down. I'll be fine."

Her sisters had just strolled off when Beck and Max returned from the kitchen. Instead of heading for the table, they moved to her, obviously puzzled to see her standing alone.

"Your wives are over there by the window." Marigold gestured with her head. "I'm preparing to circulate."

Beck glanced in the direction of the table, frowned. "If it's a matter of seating, we can—"

"It's a matter of me wanting to become reacquainted with old friends and meet new ones." She offered Beck and Max a reassuring smile. "Trust me, if I get bored, I have no compunction about booting one of you out of your seat."

Max chuckled.

Beck's gaze searched hers. "May I at least get you a cup of coffee?"

"You're so sweet, but right now I want my hands free."

At her brother-in-law's questioning glance, she winked. "Hugs. Kisses. I'm hoping for a little of both."

Not giving them a chance to argue further, Marigold turned on her heel and stepped into the crowd. While she adored her family and knew they only wanted to be supportive, she needed a little space.

"Hey, stranger."

Marigold turned to find Katie Ruth and her perky smile. Clay was nowhere in sight.

"Quite a crowd," she murmured to the former high school cheerleader.

"It's always like this." Katie Ruth waved to someone by the window who Marigold didn't recognize. "That's why I love coming. It's the best time to connect. You never know who'll be here."

Marigold felt a prickle at the base of her spine. She slowly turned, a smile of welcome already on her lips.

After spending Saturday with her, Cade had left the apartment shortly before dawn on Sunday morning. But not before they'd enjoyed a long—and extremely pleasant—shower together. She could smell her soap and shampoo on him now. Seeing the look in his eyes made her glad she'd decided to wear her favorite cashmere wrap dress to church this morning.

Prim had whispered during the church service that she looked like a sexy siren in red. From the way Cade's eyes kept returning to her chest, Marigold decided red was her new favorite color.

"Don't you both look pretty this morning." His low, husky voice wrapped itself around her spine and caused an inward shudder.

"You don't look so bad yourself." Though dressed simply in jeans and a sweater, he looked yummy enough to eat.

As if sensing the direction of her thoughts, he winked.

Katie Ruth cleared her throat. "I, ah, have your troop list ready. I'll e-mail it to you when I get home."

The comment had Cade angling his body toward the Y director. "That was fast."

Katie Ruth's chuckled and shook her head. "Not really. The first meeting is in three days."

Marigold had spent the first ten years of her life feeling out of step. She'd never liked the feeling. "Troop?"

Both pairs of eyes turned to her.

"Cade has agreed to be the leader of a new Seedlings group we're forming," Katie Ruth explained, her voice filled with satisfaction.

Marigold moved to let a buxom redhead carrying a tray of food pass. The upside of being accommodating was it put her even closer to Cade. The downside was she had to ignore the unsettling flutter his nearness caused in her midsection. It took several erratic heartbeats to find her voice. "I thought troops were formed in the fall."

"We've been short leaders, so those who registered late didn't get in," Katie Ruth informed Marigold before shifting her attention back to Cade. "Brynn Chapin is in your troop. You know David, her father."

Cade nodded.

Marigold wished Katie Ruth had e-mailed her the list so she could peruse the names. "Would I know any of them?"

"I don't think so." Katie Ruth quickly rattled off six names.

None sounded the least bit familiar to Marigold.

"Hold on a minute." Cade's brow furrowed. "Most of those sound like girl names."

"That's because the majority *are* girls." Katie Ruth pulled up the list on her phone. "Yes. Five girls. Two boys."

"I thought the sexes would be evenly mixed."

Was that panic in his voice? Or irritation? Whatever it was, Marigold found her gaze shifting like a ping-pong ball from Katie Ruth to Cade and back again.

"I told you the troops were coed." Katie Ruth's smile vanished. Though her expression gave nothing away, her voice now held the slightest hint of panic. "I've already notified the children's parents of the meeting time and place."

Cade must have heard the panic, too, because he gave the youth activities coordinator a reassuring smile. "I'm not backing out."

"But you wish you could." Marigold's impish smile earned a dark look from Katie Ruth.

Cade didn't deny it. "I don't have any experience with little girls."

"I'll be available the first night to help you get off on the right track," Katie Ruth assured him, settling her hand lightly on the sleeve of his coat.

Cade didn't appear to notice.

Marigold waited for him to brush Katie Ruth's hand away. Irritation surged when he let it linger.

"What she isn't saying is that after that first night, you are on your own." Marigold wasn't sure why she kept trying to stir the pot. Inciting drama wasn't her way, had never been her style. Goodness knows, the past year she'd had enough of Steffan being deliberately provocative to last a lifetime.

But Katie Ruth's hand remained on Cade's sleeve and the woman stood way too close to the sheriff for Marigold's liking.

Mine.

The thought took Marigold by surprise. Despite all those months with Jason, she'd never thought of him as *hers*, had never felt this primal possessiveness.

"Being on my own concerns me." Cade expelled a breath, and a shadow passed over his expression. "I'm concerned I won't do the girls justice."

Katie Ruth's lips tightened. She fixed those cornflower-blue eyes onto Marigold and finally, *finally*, removed her hand from Cade's arm. "I've a fabulous idea. Marigold can help you. She can be a co-leader."

"Ha-ha." Marigold rolled her eyes. "Good one, Katie Ruth."

The blonde didn't crack a smile. "You said you wanted to help. You said I should tell you where you were needed."

Had she really asked Katie Ruth to put her where she was needed? Marigold went blank, unable to recall the exact phrase she'd used. She wished suddenly for a cup of coffee, or really any kind of prop. She didn't know what to do with her hands. They fluttered in the air like a butterfly without direction. "I, ah, assumed you would need help with fundraising. Troop leader is a big commitment. I won't be here for more than a couple months."

When Katie Ruth began to nod as if that was of no concern, Marigold added, "Maybe not even that long. That's at the most. I could be gone way before then."

There was amusement in those blue eyes, even as Katie Ruth waved a dismissive hand. "By the time you pack your bags, Cade will be comfortable leading the troop on his own."

"I like the idea." The tense set to Cade's shoulders visibly eased and he flashed a smile.

Marigold could almost feel the noose tighten around her neck. "It won't work."

"Why not?" Cade and Katie Ruth said in unison.

A doughnut she'd eaten before church formed a leaden weight in the pit of Marigold's stomach. Leading a troop wasn't like helping with a fundraiser or working on a temporary project. Being a troop leader involved forming ties that might prove difficult to break. And being a troop leader with Cade? It would only draw them closer, and they were too close now.

Marigold jerked up her chin. "It just won't work."

"You're not in Chicago anymore, sweetie. In Good Hope everyone is expected to pitch in, do their civic duty." With a stubborn tilt to her jaw, Katie Ruth continued to press. "It's only twice a month. Depending on how long you stay, it may be only a handful of times that you'll have to step in."

"But—"

Katie Ruth arched a brow and her gaze turned speculative. "Unless you have something against working with Cade?"

Chapter Nine

Unless she had something against working with him.

On Sunday, Cade had seen the emotions roll across Marigold's face when Katie Ruth had pinned her down. So many emotions stormed those blue eyes that he couldn't identify them all. In the end, she'd agreed, denying her reluctance had anything to do with him. But something in her eyes told him that fact had played some part in her hesitation.

The thought that she might want to keep her distance from him for *any* reason, no matter how inconsequential, was a knife to the gut.

But he was a Marine in need of backup. He'd assessed the Seedling situation and determined because of various factors, he needed her. Now, three days later, he was happy Katie Ruth had pressed Marigold to agree.

Even with Marigold at his side, he knew he'd rather face a firefight than stand here waiting for seven second graders to burst through the door, five of whom would be of the female persuasion. He slanted a sideways glance. "Ready?"

"Ready as I'll ever be." Marigold fluffed her hair with her fingers, then grabbed a tube of lipstick from a bag the size of a postage stamp and added more red to her lips. "This should be fun."

"You didn't seem all that jazzed Sunday," Cade reminded her. "Katie Ruth practically had to threaten to get you to agree."

"She didn't threaten. I don't respond well to threats." The petite blonde spoke slowly and distinctly, as if to make sure there was no misunderstanding. "I've had a stellar day, and I'm in a glass-half-full mood. If that's a crime—"

She thrust out her wrists. "Cuff me now."

Tempting, he thought. *Oh so very tempting.*

"If you insist." He rubbed his hands together in exaggerated anticipation, then reached into his back pocket for the cuffs.

Marigold rolled her eyes. "Only you, Cade, would go there."

"I'm so glad you're both here." Katie Ruth strolled into the room in the town hall, clipboard in hand. Her gaze settled briefly on Marigold's outstretched wrists, then moved to the cuffs dangling from Cade's fingers. "You might want to put those away. They might scare the children."

Cade shot Marigold a wicked smile and slipped them back into his pocket.

Marigold lowered her hands and stuck out her tongue as soon as Katie Ruth's gaze dropped to the clipboard.

"Before we get down to business." Katie Ruth lifted her gaze and focused on Marigold. "I want the scoop."

Obviously puzzled, Marigold blinked. "What scoop?"

"Don't be coy." Katie Ruth wagged a finger. "It's all over town that you and Travis shared an intimate meal today."

Cade caught the speculative gaze Katie Ruth tossed in his direction. Years of training and self-discipline kept his shock from showing.

"I believe it's a stretch to ever call any lunch at Muddy Boots *intimate*." Marigold's droll tone got a chuckle from Katie Ruth. "But I can recommend the meat loaf to your readers."

For a second Cade didn't follow. Until he recalled Katie Ruth wrote the *Open Door* newsletter, which included a small gossip section. Marigold Bloom having lunch with Travis Forbes was a juicy tidbit residents would find of interest.

This was the first Cade had heard about his deputy and Marigold sharing a meal. He accepted that it wouldn't be the last time someone shoved that bit of intel in his face. When it came to the gossip mill, Good Hope was no different than Trainor, the small Michigan town where Cade had grown up.

Residents loved to speculate, to prevaricate, and if that wasn't juicy enough, to simply make up. It wasn't Cade's favorite part of small-town life, but to his way of thinking you had to take the bad with the good. And there was so much about small-town living to love.

This opinion had not been shared by his former fiancée. As far as Alice was concerned, no town with metropolitan area under a million was worth considering.

"Not good enough."

For a second Cade thought he heard Alice's voice, then realized it was Katie Ruth.

The activities coordinator now stood directly in front of Marigold, her eyes razor sharp. "My readers don't care about meat loaf. They want the down and dirty about you and the deputy."

Marigold hesitated and Cade found himself tempted to step to her rescue. Only the knowledge that she could hold her own against Katie Ruth's bulldoggedness had him staying silent. Marigold's melodramatic sigh made Cade smile.

"If you want the skinny—oh, wait, the down and dirty—I'll give it to you. I ran into Travis on the street. He asked me to lunch. I accepted." Marigold brought a finger to her cherry-red mouth and frowned. "Is it significant I turned down dessert?"

"Depends on what kind of dessert," Cade heard himself say before Katie Ruth could respond.

A smile tugged at the corners of Marigold's lips. "You're right. The kind of dessert does matter."

Katie Ruth stepped closer. "Will you be seeing Travis again?"

Cade found himself holding his breath as he awaited her answer. Before she could respond, the door swung open with a clatter and Prim burst into the room, two redheaded little boys in her wake.

"Aunt Marigold." One of the twins rushed past his mother and flung his arms around his aunt's waist. "Mommy said you'd be here but I didn't believe her."

Prim shook her head, a bemused smile on her lips. "Gee, Callum, thanks."

"I believed you, Mommy," the second twin assured her.

Though the two were identical, something about Callum, the one who'd spoken first, told Cade the boy would need special watching.

"Why didn't I know my nephews were in Cade's troop?" Marigold pinned Katie Ruth with her gaze.

"They weren't assigned to you and Cade until an hour ago." Prim shot them a sheepish smile. "I asked Katie Ruth to do a little finagling and she was able to shift Callum and Connor in and move the other two boys to a different group."

Cade thought of the names on his list. "Were the other parents okay with the last-minute change?"

"Actually, it worked out perfectly," Katie Ruth told him. "The boys are friends and one of the dads was a last-minute add-on as a leader. The son and his friend wanted to be in his troop."

"Fabulous." Marigold fist-bumped her nephews. "Isn't this great, Cade?"

Personally Cade thought it would have been even more wonderful if they'd switched out two girls for the twins. "Yeah. Great."

Callum cast a suspicious glance at the tables and chairs. "Is this going to be like school?"

"I like school." Connor, the other twin, smiled up at his aunt.

Callum rolled his eyes and pinned Cade with bright blue eyes in a freckled face. "Are we going camping?"

His brother's swiveled. "We get to go camping?"

Cade shook his head. "Not tonight."

"Tonight's unit is on proper animal care," Katie Ruth announced after glancing down at her clipboard.

"The group earns a merit badge each time we master a unit," Marigold told the twins.

Cade was impressed. It appeared he wasn't the only one who'd read the materials Katie Ruth had supplied. He only hoped being a troop leader wouldn't have him pretending to be a dog before the meeting concluded. He'd thought about tracking down a dog or a cat earlier, but the day had been a busy one, and he'd forgotten.

"We may need to work on the citizenship in the community unit since we don't have an animal lined up." He shifted his gaze as a group of giggling girls and their parents filed through the door.

Although Cade hadn't been in Good Hope all that long, he recognized all of the parents by face and was personally acquainted with David Chapin.

"Sheriff."

Cade looked down at the twin tugging his sleeve. "Yes, Connor?"

"We have a dog if you need one." The child glanced up at his mother. "We don't live far. Mommy could call Daddy and have him bring Boris."

Prim's lips curved. The soft smile may have been from the polite way her son had offered or the fact that he now called his stepfather *Daddy*.

"Boris is very gentle and loving with children," Prim assured Cade.

He was acquainted with the Russian wolfhound. While the animal was large and could be overenthusiastic at times, from what he'd observed, the dog was gentle and could be trusted around children. "If you don't mind, that'd be great."

Prim had already pulled out her phone to make the call before he finished. "I've got the minivan, so I'll need to run home to transport him. I'll ask Max to have him ready."

"Hey, Cade." David Chapin stepped forward when Prim rushed out. "Thanks for agreeing to do this. Brynn was crushed when we signed her up too late to get into a fall troop."

"Should be a good time." Cade decided Marigold wasn't the only one who could be positive.

David's brow arched. "Over at 6:30?"

Cade nodded. *Ninety minutes*. The way he saw it, a man could tolerate practically anything for an hour and a half. "That's right."

With the confirmation, David crouched down before his daughter, a blonde-haired, blue-eyed girl who didn't appear to resemble either of her parents. "You have fun, kiddo. I'll be back to pick you up when the meeting is over."

He gave Brynn a quick hug, then strolled out. For a second, the little girl looked as if she might cry. Then Marigold grasped one of her hands and began swinging it back and forth like a jump rope.

"We have a special guest on the way." Even as Marigold swung Brynn's hand, she singsonged the announcement to the entire troop.

A little girl with skin the color of café au lait and large brown eyes stepped forward. "Who is it?"

Another child, dressed in all pink, including fancy cowboy boots that glittered, twirled around. "Is it Santa Claus?"

"Geez, everyone knows Santa Claus only comes at Christmas," Callum informed her.

The girl lifted her chin. "He's Santa. He can come anytime he wants."

Cade raked a hand through his hair. "It isn't Santa."

"Who is it then?" a child with two brown pigtails asked.

"Our special guest will be here any minute. You can see for yourself. In the meantime—" Marigold's gaze scanned the group, and she flashed that irresistible smile. "It's time for introductions."

Once the introductions had been completed, Marigold glanced around the circle. As Cade seemed willing to let her take the lead, she rose to the challenge.

"While we wait for our guest of honor to arrive, let's sit." Marigold gestured to a large area rug boasting a turquoise cherry blossom pattern. "I can't wait to tell you about all the fun things Sheriff Cade and I have planned."

She nimbly stepped aside, avoiding the stampede to the rug.

The sound of high-pitched childish conversations and laughter as they sat in a semicircle on the rug brought warmth to Marigold's heart. She loved kids but had spent precious little time with any—including her own nephews—since leaving Good Hope.

An upside to losing her job was, for the next few weeks, she'd be able to spend more time with Callum and Connor. Since Ami wasn't due until May, it was unlikely she'd have the opportunity to rock Ami's firstborn in her arms before heading out for bigger and better.

Cade moved to the rug but remained standing. Impatiently, Marigold motioned him down. He folded his lanky frame encased in blue jeans and a charcoal henley and confiscated the spot beside her.

Unlike his deputies, he didn't wear a uniform. Cade had mentioned he'd gotten out of the habit once he'd gotten his detective's shield. Even without the uniform, she'd have pegged him as a cop. His watchful eyes and keen gaze missed little.

Like when, seconds after taking his place on the rug, Callum gave his twin a hard shove, sending the other boy tumbling from the circle like an off-balanced Weeble. Laugher broke out around the circle as Connor scrambled to right himself. When his twin glared at him, Callum grinned.

Cade opened his mouth to speak, but Marigold shook her head slightly. She had this one. The look she fixed on her sister's eldest son—by two minutes—was the same one she'd seen Prim and Max give him many times. "In this troop we keep our hands to ourselves. Pushing and shoving will not be tolerated. Understand?"

Callum gave a nod, then shifted his gaze to Brynn. Hooking his index fingers in the corners of his mouth, he stretched his lips wide in a crazy face and made her laugh.

Marigold met Cade's gaze and lifted her shoulders. This was the first meeting. Push too hard or be too strict and they risked ruining the fun.

She'd made her point. If Callum continued to bump up against the rules, Marigold would speak to Prim after the meeting. She only wished her sister would hurry and get back with the dog.

There was no need to glance at her phone. Not with the large, round clock on the wall ticking off the minutes. If they were going to get through the unit, they would need to start now, with or without Boris. After introductions were completed, Marigold smiled at the group shifting restlessly on the rug.

"I had so much fun when I was a Seedling. I learned new things and got to do a lot of really cool activities. Not to mention . . ." She paused for dramatic effect and made a great show of surveying the children in the circle. "Who likes pizza?"

Every hand in the circle shot up, including Cade's.

Marigold lifted hers for a second, then lowered it. She put enthusiasm in her voice. "You'll be excited to know that once our group is awarded ten merit badges, we get a pizza party."

The girls clapped.

Callum and Connor made hooting noises normally only heard during ball games.

"Pizza is my favorite food," Brynn announced.

"Mine, too," Callum added, his gaze fixed on Brynn.

"Well, today, if you *all* pay attention and participate, we will get our first merit badge and be on our way to the ten we need for the pizza party." She shifted her gaze to Cade. "Sheriff, would you like to review the seven major dog groups with our Seedlings?"

This time it was Marigold's turn to sit back and listen as Cade gave an entertaining overview that kept the children's attention. His examples of the way various dogs in each group barked had Marigold snorting back laughter.

"I bet many of you have a dog in your home, or maybe in your neighborhood. Who'd like to give me an example of a dog in your home or in the home of a neighbor or friend?" His voice was so persuasive and his smile so engaging, Marigold found herself searching her own brain for an example.

"We have a Dorkie." The little girl with the pink cowboy boots spoke without raising her hand. Hannah had hair the color of fine champagne, big blue eyes, and a missing front tooth. Marigold thought Fin may have been in the same class as her mother. "His name is Chico."

With that kind of name, Marigold would have expected a Chihuahua or perhaps a Mexican hairless. What the heck was a Dorkie? From the puzzled expression on Cade's face, she wasn't the only one confused. "I'm not familiar with the breed."

The girl chewed her lower lip, thought for a second. "Mommy says he's part weenie dog and part Yorkie."

"A dachshund and Yorkshire terrier," Marigold repeated for Cade's benefit when the man still appeared baffled.

Brynn's hand shot up. The girl waited until Cade acknowledged her with a nod before speaking.

"If it's a terrier, it goes in the terrier group." Brynn dropped her hand, her smile triumphant.

Lia, the girl with the gorgeous brown eyes, gave Brynn a high five.

"That's correct." Marigold beamed smiles. "A Yorkshire terrier falls into the terrier group."

"What about the weenie dog?" Connor asked.

"That's a good question, Connor." Cade's slow and deliberate response made Marigold believe he didn't have a clue to the answer.

Marigold only knew the answer because she had a friend back in Chicago who owned a mini dachshund. When reading over the materials in preparation for tonight's meeting, she'd thought of Hamlet.

"The 'dachs' part of the breed's name means 'badgers.' And 'hund' means 'dog.' A dachshund, or weenie dog, is a 'hound' who likes to hunt badgers." Marigold emphasized the word. If she gave the children any additional information she'd be offering up the answer on a silver platter.

"I've never seen a badger, but I think they're like big rats." Callum spoke with an air of authority. "I wanted to get a rat and call him Ratfink, but Mommy said, 'No way, Jose.'"

Her nephew punctuated the pronouncement with a gesture often used by umpires to pronounce someone safe at base.

"Jose isn't my name," Callum clarified when a couple of the girls looked confused. "But that's what she called me."

"She did." Connor gave a vigorous nod. "I heard her. She called him Jose."

Marigold stifled a chuckle.

"I wouldn't want a rat in my house," Brynn declared in a loud voice and received nods of agreement from the other girls.

"I really want a pig," a girl named Sabine blurted. "If I had one, I'd put dresses on her and call her Miss Piggy."

The discussion appeared headed straight down the rabbit hole. With Marigold still wondering how they'd gotten so off course, Cade took the reins.

"Back to the question." Amusement flickered in Cade's gray eyes. "Knowing this *hound* was used for hunting, what category do we think fits?"

"Hound." Lia spoke so softly Marigold doubted the others heard her.

"Lia has the answer." She offered the girl an encouraging smile. "Speak loudly so the others can hear."

"Hound." This time Lia bellowed the answer, ensuring everyone in the entire building—and the next one over—heard her response.

"But that makes Chico a terrier *and* a hound." Hannah's brows pulled together. "How can that be?"

"Good question." Cade shifted his gaze to Marigold. "Would you like to answer that for Hannah and the other Seedlings?"

"My aunt knows everything," Callum boasted. "She's really smart."

"She cuts hair and makes it change color," Connor asserted, offering her a smile.

"I get my hair cut at Golden Door Salon," Brynn announced. "Miss Charlotte is the best in town."

Callum pushed to his knees and his blue eyes flashed. "My aunt is better than creepy ol' Miss Charlotte."

"Boys. Girls. We need to stay on task." Marigold clapped her hands, her heart slamming against her rib cage. How did teachers do this? Barely fifteen minutes in and she was ready for a break.

Shouldn't Boris be here by now? Where was her sister and that blasted wolfhound anyway? Marigold was on the verge of sending out a sisterly SOS when the door eased open.

The children scrambled to their feet as the dog and Prim stepped inside.

"Seedlings. Please remain on the rug." Marigold used every ounce of whatever teacher genes she'd gotten from her father and coupled the command with another firm look.

The dog was even bigger than Marigold remembered. But when her sister told him to sit, he did.

The appearance of the huge animal had the kids mesmerized. When Marigold saw the eager looks on their faces, she felt a surge of relief. She had no doubt the next hour was going to fly by.

She shot a look at Cade, and he gave her a thumbs-up.

Yep, she thought, *we have this handled.*

Chapter Ten

Marigold waited until the last Seedling had disappeared down the hall, chattering happily to their parents, before she collapsed into a metal folding chair. After the events of the past ninety minutes she had a far greater appreciation for what raising two boys alone had been like for her sister. "Children that age have entirely too much energy."

Cade sat in the chair beside hers, an expression that could only be described as shell-shocked on his face. He expelled a breath, shook his head. "All I can say is thank God for Boris."

"I agree." Marigold scooped up a handful of the goldfish crackers Prim had brought back with her for a snack. "I really worried how he'd do, but being around the twins must have desensitized him to shrieking, high-pitched voices and spontaneous hugs."

"I could use some pointers." Cade offered a rueful smile.

"You were a real trooper, as was Boris." Marigold rolled her shoulders to relieve a couple of knots that wanted to settle there. "Though I swear he had a pained expression on his face when the children took turns bandaging his paw."

Cade rose to his feet to stand behind her chair. Before she knew what was happening, his hands were on her shoulders, massaging the knots with strong fingers.

Marigold wanted to weep with relief. Instead she emitted a soft moan.

"You saved the meeting from disaster." He dropped a kiss on the top of her head. "I don't know what I'd have done without you."

"We make a good team. I just kept telling myself that Katie Ruth wouldn't have left us alone with the group if she wasn't certain we could handle them." Marigold didn't want to think what might have happened if she and Cade hadn't read through the materials prior to the meeting and been prepared. It had taken her a whole evening to read through it all, but the effort had paid off. "Future meetings should go okay as long as we follow the outlines."

"I like the sound of 'we.'" His fingers dug just a little deeper into the muscle.

Marigold knew she should remind him she was only helping out for a few weeks, but it wasn't anything he didn't already know. "The kids seem determined to earn those ten merit badges."

"Who knew a pizza party could be such a motivator?" He chuckled, his tone a bit incredulous.

"We may have to start covering two units at a time, or meet more frequently, to get them caught up."

"Works for me."

"This works for me." Marigold let her eyes close, just for a second, as he continued to knead.

"All the talk about pizza tonight has me in the mood for a slice." Cade's tone turned persuasive. "Interested?"

Marigold slowly opened her eyes.

"I thought we could pick one up and take it to your apartment," he continued in a pleasant tone. "Or we can go out. Your choice."

"Aren't you agreeable." She pushed to her feet and began straightening the room in an attempt to corral her wayward thoughts. They'd just made love that morning, yet she found herself wanting him again.

"I'm an agreeable kind of guy." His hands settled on her shoulders, and he turned her around to face him.

She gazed up at him through lowered lashes, and the desire she saw reflected in those smoky depths had her pulse tripping. Anticipation fluttered through her. "Or we could head straight to my place and I could heat up the one I have in the freezer?"

He grinned and shot her a wink. "Even better."

"Are you thinking we'd be dressed while we ate?" She arched a brow, keeping her voice casual and offhand. "Or not?"

"If you're asking me for dress code recommendations, I'd say clothing is optional."

Though it was usually hot and heavy at the beginning of any relationship, something about this *thing* between her and Cade felt different. Every time he looked at her she felt the impact all the way to the tips of her toes. But it was more than sex, though the passion between them was, well, off the charts. No, something about him quieted the clamor in her head. She could fully relax when she was around him.

The thought that in a short time she'd be gone, and what they shared would be over, had her heart stuttering. "Remember, I'm only here temporarily."

"I'm well aware of that fact." He simply stared at her for a long moment, his eyes boring into hers. "Yet I can't think of a single reason not to fully enjoy the time you're here."

The flicker of challenge in his voice had Marigold's pulse going crazy. "Are you suggesting a fling?"

He hesitated, as a man might before a plunge off the side of a mountain. "I'm suggesting we date. Sex may be a part of it . . . or not. Your choice."

Marigold tapped a finger against her lips. "You want to . . . date . . . even knowing I won't be staying?"

"Who knows." His mouth relaxed in a slight smile. "You might—"

"There's no *might*." She stepped back, out of reach. "I will be leaving, more likely sooner than later."

"I'm fine with the here and now, Marigold."

Perhaps it was the firmness in that deep tone or the steadiness of his gaze that reassured her they really did understand each other. Cade wouldn't expect more than she was able to give.

He could have any single woman in town. Look at Katie Ruth. The woman practically salivated whenever Cade stepped into the room. And Marigold would have to have been blind not to have noticed all the women eying him at Ami's party. "Other than I'm fabulous, new in town, and somewhat of a novelty, why me?"

"Who else knows so much about dachshunds?"

Marigold snorted out a laugh.

Cade grasped the hand she'd pulled away and brought it to his lips. With his eyes still locked on hers, he bent his head to brush a kiss against her knuckles. "I realize we both have a lot on our plates, but you know what they say about all work and no play . . ."

"I certainly wouldn't want to be considered a dull dog." Marigold liked Cade's sense of humor and easy manner. For reasons she didn't want to explore too deeply, being around him centered her.

"People will think we're a couple." Marigold thought of Katie Ruth and her gossip column.

"We are a couple." Those cool gray eyes pinned her, daring her to disagree.

The firm ground beneath her feet began to shake. Was he saying he wanted to be exclusive? Though the thought made her uneasy, she was even more uncomfortable with the thought of him dating other women. "Are you willing to forego dates with Katie Ruth?"

"I believe the more relevant question is—are you willing to forego lunches with Travis?"

"You know how much I like dessert."

He nodded, a wary look in his eyes.

She smiled up at him. "I wasn't even tempted."

"Good to know." He brushed his mouth against hers, a brief touch that somehow seemed wildly erotic. "Ready to head to your apartment and fuel up?"

Marigold moistened her lips with the tip of her tongue. "Are we talking pizza or dessert?"

"That's your choice." This time Cade grinned, full-out. "Me, I'm extra fond of dessert."

"This has to stop." Marigold pulled the silk sheet up over her breasts, then flopped back, her head returning to the shared pillow.

"You'll have to be more specific." Cade snaked an arm around her and tugged her close. "The blood in my head is currently occupied elsewhere."

"Seriously?" She arched a brow. "You could do it again?"

"What can I say?" He nuzzled her neck. "I'm a glutton for dessert."

She laughed. "I'm pretty fond of it, myself."

"Then why does it have to stop?" His tone was light, but those smoky gray eyes were puzzled.

"It feels too good."

Those strong fingers that had caused her to cry out only minutes earlier slid up her arm, leaving gooseflesh in their wake. "Are you saying if it feels good, it has to end?"

"Everything good ends." The second the words left her mouth, Marigold wished she could call them back.

She waited for Cade to murmur reassurance, perhaps offer a platitude, the kind of thing her mother used to say when things didn't go as she planned.

Her mother.

A familiar tightness fisted around Marigold's heart, making her eyes sting and breathing difficult. She hadn't been there when her mother had passed, hadn't been able to tell her how much her love and support had meant, hadn't been there to hold her hand and say good-bye.

"Tell me," he urged.

"What?"

"Tell me," he repeated, running his palms lightly up and down her arms.

Marigold supposed she could have shoved his hands away or hopped out of bed. But Cade was so warm, and the gentle stroking on her arm compelled her to pause and reconsider. "I don't understand what you want me to say."

"I want to know who left you." His voice, low and smooth, invited confidences. "Who—or what—made you believe if something feels good, it will end?"

"Everyone knows that." She shifted her eyes from his penetrating gaze. "It's, like, Self-Preservation 101."

"Tell me about your last relationship."

Marigold nearly sighed with relief when she realized he'd assumed she'd been thinking of Jason. Though her pain over the end of that relationship was so miniscule when compared to the loss of her mother, that still didn't mean she wanted to rehash it. It was over and done and played no part in the here and now.

"Tell me," he pressed.

"Maybe I don't feel comfortable sharing my past with you." Only when the words had left her lips did Marigold realize how strange such a remark sounded. Especially taking into account their current positions and the intimacy of the past hour.

"If that's how you really feel, Goldilocks," Cade gave a lock of her hair a tug, "we shouldn't be sharing much of anything, especially dessert."

When he pushed up, she grabbed his arm. Encountering resistance, she tightened her hold.

"That came out wrong. It's not how I feel." She ignored the sudden ache in her chest. "I mean, not exactly. It's hard."

"What's hard?"

"Talking about past failures."

"He hurt you."

She started to deny it, then decided everyone, including the great Marigold Bloom, was allowed one foolish mistake. "Yes."

Cade tapped her arm with his fist. "If he was here, I'd punch him."

"If he was here, I'd punch him myself." Marigold shook off the irritation that always surfaced when she thought of Jason. She'd wasted too much time and energy on the hotshot attorney. She held out a hand and studied the brightly painted nails and smooth skin. "On second thought, he wouldn't be worth the skinned knuckles."

Beside her, Cade chuckled, a low, pleasant, rumbling sound.

"I'm not in the mood for pizza," she announced. "I'll heat up the stew. If you're still curious after we eat, I'll bare my soul."

Before she could rise, Cade leaned over and kissed her with a sweetness that had her heart turning soft and heavy in her chest. When he pulled her close, Marigold rested her head against his chest and let herself relax. Only when her stomach growled did she slip from the bed.

Her sister's ancient chenille robe, soft against her bare skin, provided needed warmth. She snagged a silky man's robe—likely belonging to Beck—and tossed it to Cade.

She supposed they could get dressed, but it would be horribly inconvenient if they decided they wanted another helping of dessert.

While Marigold doubted that would happen, it seemed prudent to leave the option open.

After placing two bowls of leftover beef stew in the microwave, she set the table with two daisy placemats and a couple of napkins. They ate at the dinette table for two in the kitchen with the canary-yellow walls.

Ami likely would have served the dish with some homemade crusty bread or a bowl of pretty, cut-up fruit. Since Marigold didn't have either, she settled for pouring them each a glass of wine.

As if sensing her desire not to get into anything too heavy while they ate, Cade kept the conversation focused on the weather. A quick glance out the window told Marigold the day that had been remarkably sunny had turned dreary. A brisk wind from the north swirled the falling snow into mini cyclones.

Marigold considered brewing a pot of coffee, but before she could rise and pull out the ancient silver percolator Ami had given her, Cade reached across the table.

He turned over her hand, appearing to study the hot-pink nails she'd painted last night.

"You have strong hands." His thumb stroked her palm, making her breath catch. "There's such talent in these fingers."

Marigold recalled how he'd groaned when she touched him. She smiled. "I like the feel of your muscles, the way they ripple under my hands."

"I like that, too." His thumb continued to stroke. "You know, ever since we hooked up at my cousin's wedding, I haven't been able to stop thinking about you."

She swallowed to moisten a mouth that had gone bone-dry. "Really?"

Cade nodded. "I've followed your career. Read all the online articles. You're a force in the industry, Ms. Bloom. A top-notch hairstylist."

The compliment was a balm to her tattered spirit. Deftly, Marigold slipped her hand from his, finding it impossible to think clearly when he was touching her. "Jason didn't think so."

Cade merely raised a brow.

"Though he was proud of the success I'd achieved, he never fully appreciated how important it was for me to reach the top of my field." While all that was true, Marigold also knew she'd held back, never letting him get too close.

"How long were you together?"

"Nearly a year." Marigold thought back to that time, to the months when life held endless possibilities. She was not only making a name for herself, she had a handsome, successful boyfriend. "Jason was a corporate in-house attorney for a multinational corporation. He was a big deal in Chicago legal circles."

"A long time to date and not know someone."

"I knew him," she protested.

"He didn't know you." Cade twisted the stem of the wineglass between his thumb and forefinger, his gaze steady on her face. "He didn't appreciate your talent or realize what your career meant to you."

Marigold shrugged.

"Did you love him?"

"I thought I did." *Be honest*, Marigold told herself. *Don't sugarcoat or gloss.* "Looking back, I think it wasn't each other we loved, but the shine."

At his perplexed look, she smiled. "We looked good together. We loved being seen in each other's company. Loved the spotlight."

Jason had liked showing her off as much as she liked being seen with him. Then why did such a smart and sophisticated arrangement sound rather pathetic when said aloud?

"Did the shine wear off? Is that what happened?"

Marigold blinked.

"Why did you break up?" Cade prompted, his voice low and husky.

"Things came to a head when Jason was approached about making a move to the firm's New Orleans office." Marigold puffed out her cheeks. "He asked me to marry him."

Cade brought the glass to his lips and took a sip. "A proposal does tend to bring things to a head."

"I considered it," she admitted. "I dreaded the thought of rebuilding a client list from the ground up, but New Orleans is a cool city. If I made the sacrifice, I decided he'd have to understand we'd be putting down roots there. I didn't want to relocate only to have to do it all over again in four or five years."

"Sounds fair. What did he say to that?"

"Nothing." Marigold sighed. "I couldn't get in a word. He just kept talking about this fabulous opportunity he'd been given. I assumed he was nervous and wanted to lay it all out first. Long story short, he made it clear that for him to achieve his goal of full partner, my career of 'cutting hair' would have to take a backseat."

"He said that?"

Gray eyes that had been dove soft only moments before were now hard as steel.

Marigold tried to recall if Jason had spoken those exact words. "No, but as he talked, it became obvious he considered his career to be the more important one. In the end, neither of us was willing to compromise."

Cade said nothing.

"The discussion, if you could call it that," Marigold gave a little laugh, "was a watershed moment for me. As Jason continued to stress why the move was such a great thing for him, it hit me that no one will care about my career—or my happiness—as much as I do. I decided that from then on I will go—or I will stay—where it's best for me."

Cade's expression gave nothing away. "Sounds as if you've given the matter a lot of thought."

Marigold nodded. To combat the unexpected wave of sadness washing over her, she smiled broadly and raised her glass in a toast. "Here's to coming to your senses just in time."

Cade lifted his glass. "To happiness."

"Now that you've heard all my deep, dark secrets, tell me about your ex." Marigold set her glass on the table, a speculative gleam in those baby blues.

Cade bought himself a little time by taking another drink of wine. He should have seen this coming, been prepared. It was, after all, a classic case of quid pro quo.

Despite knowing he owed her details, Cade considered several diversionary tactics, including kissing her senseless. While not specifically mentioned in the Marine Corps manual, he thought it stood a good chance of success . . . and he knew he'd enjoy every second of the maneuver.

"I don't know what you're planning, Sheriff, but it won't work." The light, teasing tone was at odds with the determined glint in her eyes. "C'mon. It's time to get down to the nitty-gritty."

Cade preferred not to think about the abrupt end to his two-year relationship. Not simply because he suspected a large part of what went wrong was his fault, but because after the first few months, he hadn't missed Alice. It appeared he and Marigold had something else in common. What they'd each thought was love, wasn't.

He decided if he was required to tell this story, he'd keep it short and sweet. "Alice broke our engagement because of what she ultimately saw as my failure to communicate."

Marigold's blue eyes narrowed. "What did she think you should have communicated but didn't?"

He gave a snort. "Want a laundry list?"

The last time they'd been together, Alice had ranted. He hadn't realized she harbored so much resentment. Even little things, like forgetting to mention his parents' upcoming wedding anniversary, were tossed into the mix.

Marigold waved a slender hand. "I don't need a complete list. Just the incident that pushed her over the edge."

"What makes you think there was an incident?"

She rolled her eyes. "There's always an incident."

Cade considered how much to divulge. Then he realized there was no longer any reason for secrecy. Not for something that had been front-page news.

"I discovered several officers in my unit had failed to log into evidence money and drugs seized during searches of homes. I turned them into Internal Affairs. Alice knew a couple of them pretty well. She felt I should have discussed the situation with her before reporting them." Cade's anger spiked, just as it had when Alice confronted him. Not just anger at her, but at the men—and women—who'd betrayed their badges.

Shoving his chair back, Cade strode to the window and attempted to find calm in the swirling snow outside.

Frustrated, overcome with memories of that ugly time, he whirled and flung out his hands. "For God's sake, what was there to discuss? What could I do but turn them in? I had no choice. They were dirty."

Cade turned back to the window. He didn't move, not even when he heard Marigold's chair slide back, not even when her arms slipped around his waist.

"I agree. You had no choice."

The tension eased from his shoulders but his fingers continued to grip the sill. "A couple of them were friends."

"Which must have made reporting them extra hard." Her voice, smooth as Kentucky bourbon, soothed.

He was silent for a long time, then finally nodded.

She clasped her hands together even as her gaze remained firmly focused on him. "What happened to them?"

"They were indicted for stealing drugs and money obtained in police searches, convicted, and sent to prison." His voice, flat and hollow, seemed to come from far away.

"What about the blue line?"

He grit his teeth. How many times had Alice brought up the blue line? Too many times to count. "It breaks for dirty cops."

"I bet not everyone saw it that way." Her voice remained soft and low.

His unseeing gaze stayed focused on the windowpane.

"So you came here, to Good Hope."

"I wasn't running." He pivoted to face her. "I deliberately sought out the position here. I wanted to live in Good Hope."

"Why?" Marigold appeared genuinely perplexed.

He hesitated, finding it difficult to explain something he didn't fully understand himself. Finding no other options, he leaned back against the sill and went with the truth.

"When I was here for my cousin's wedding, I fell in love with Good Hope, with the people, with the area." He shrugged, looking slightly embarrassed by the admission. "I had friends tell me taking a job as a small-town sheriff was a step down. I don't agree. I believe I'm exactly where I'm meant to be and doing what I'm meant to do."

"I'm happy for you, Cade." Marigold brushed her lips across his mouth, then patted his cheek. "You've found your niche. Me? I'm still searching for that one place that will allow me to soar."

"You can't soar in Good Hope?"

She shook her head, making her hair swing. "Not possible."

Knowing better than to press, he reached out and touched her cheek, one finger trailing slowly along her skin until it reached the line of her jaw. "The good news is we have this time together before you leave. Have you given any thought to my offer?"

She inclined her head, and the sultry scent that was so uniquely hers wrapped around him like a caress. "To enjoy dessert while I'm here?"

"To spend time together." For some reason the distinction seemed important. "To date."

Their eyes met, and he couldn't look away.

"After much consideration . . ." Marigold's blue eyes glittered, and she regarded him intently. Then, without warning, she flung herself into his arms. "I accept."

Chapter Eleven

Yesterday, Marigold had braved a group of seven-year-olds. Today, she faced a more formidable challenge: dealing with Eliza Shaw.

Cade had still been at her apartment last night when the e-mail from the executive director of the Cherries had arrived. Marigold was being summoned to a meeting to discuss the Hearts and Cherries Fashion Show.

"I am so not looking forward to this." She slanted a glance at her sisters.

"I consider a meeting with Eliza on par with a visit to the gynecologist," Prim said dryly.

Ami snorted.

"I don't see what there is to discuss." Marigold paused at the steps leading to historic Hill House, where most of the Cherries' business was conducted.

Ami expelled a heavy sigh. "You know Eliza."

"I wish I didn't," Marigold muttered.

Prim laughed outright. "The woman made my life hell when Max and I were planning the Fourth of July parade. I swear she prayed every night for an epic fail so she could point the finger at me."

"She likes to be in control," Ami said diplomatically.

"That's a kind way of saying Eliza has a dictator sensibility." Prim didn't even bother to lower her voice. She only smiled when her older sister shushed her and continued. "Like most dictators, the woman preys on weakness. Don't let her see you sweat."

Marigold started to laugh, then stopped at the look on Prim's face. "You're kidding, right?"

"She's not." Ami's lips twisted in a rueful smile. "Eliza will be relentless in her attempt to seize control. You can't let her."

"She respects strength." Prim's hazel eyes, so like their father's, were solemn. "Remember, an animal is always more dangerous in their lair, or in this case on her home turf."

"Is there still time to back out?" Marigold realized she was only half joking.

"Having you at the fashion show will be a blast." Ami looped her arm through Marigold's and gave it a squeeze. "The Cherries need you. *I* need you."

"In that case . . ." Marigold looked at the stairs, gave an exaggerated sigh. "I'm ready to enter the inner sanctum. Just give me a sec to gird my loins."

Her sisters' laughter followed her on the climb up the steps.

Fifteen minutes into the conversation Marigold was wondering what the fuss had been about as her sisters and the executive director discussed various Cherrie events, including the upcoming Valentine's dance.

Eliza's gaze settled first on Ami, then on Prim. "Every member of the Cherries is expected to attend."

"We're both planning on being at the dance." Ami's voice held a note of surprise. She turned to Prim. "Is ticket revenue down?"

"According to my records, we're ahead of projections." Prim, the treasurer of the organization, slanted a questioning glance in Eliza's direction. "Is there something going on I don't know?"

"No. You're correct. Ticket sales are on track with last year," Eliza conceded with some reluctance.

"In fact, when I purchased additional tickets for Cade and Marigold yesterday, Lynn made it sound as if we're on track for an early sellout," Prim added.

"You already bought tickets?" Marigold thought back to when she and her sisters had discussed the dance. She was almost positive she hadn't given the green light. "What if I'm not here?"

"No worries." Ami patted her hand. "We can resell them without any problem."

Marigold let herself relax. She grabbed another cookie and munched contentedly until the discussion began to veer into fashion show territory.

"I received a report from Katie Ruth shortly before you arrived on several fundraising efforts under way for the Seedlings and Saplings." Eliza glanced at her laptop. "The avalanche popcorn will be packaged in the stylish treat bags I picked out. The scouts will sell the popcorn in the hotel lobby prior to the fashion show."

Her sisters didn't react to Eliza apparently choosing the bags without input. Marigold surmised this must be one of those pick-your-battles kinds of things.

"You didn't mention the MCTs." Prim's brows drew together, referring to the eleven to twelve age group. "Why aren't they helping? The popcorn sale is a fundraiser for all of the scouts."

"I have the older scouts functioning as gofers during the fashion show. The truth is, people are more likely to buy products from little ones." Eliza's lips lifted in a slight smile. "Who can resist a seven-year-old hawking a prettily wrapped bag of something tasty?"

"What is avalanche popcorn?" Marigold asked, hoping it wasn't a stupid question.

Always one to be exact, Eliza glanced at her notes. "It's popcorn with chocolate, peanut butter, marshmallows, and crispy cereal, drizzled in milk chocolate."

"It's addictive," Ami warned.

"Highly," Prim agreed. "My boys would eat it by the truckload if I let them."

"Sounds yummy." Marigold's stomach stunned her when it growled agreement.

Eliza paused. When those sharp gray eyes leveled on her, Marigold felt the seat beneath her grow hot.

"Enough talk about popcorn. In regard to the fashion show." Eliza tapped the Montblanc lying next to her laptop, and her gaze settled on Marigold. "You'll need to run the hairstyles by me two weeks prior to the event. Some of the styles that are popular in large cities may not be appropriate here."

Marigold laughed, lifted the china cup to her lips. "Yeah, right."

For a second, confusion filled Eliza's almond-shaped eyes. Then they hardened to steel. "I'm serious."

Marigold set down her cup of tea carefully. "Well, I can tell you right now that's not happening."

Out of the corner of her eye, she saw Prim and Ami exchange glances. Her sisters both set down their cups, as if wanting to be prepared in case a hasty retreat became necessary.

Eliza stiffened until her back was ramrod straight. "As executive director, I am in charge of the Cherries. What I say—"

"I am in charge of styling the hair for this event." Marigold's voice remained polite but firm. "I will decide the hairstyles that are appropriate, taking into consideration the model and the clothing they'll be wearing."

Marigold had spent the last six years of her life dealing with difficult people. While she appreciated her sisters' warning, she'd been aware of the type of woman she'd be dealing with when she'd agreed to help Ami with the fashion show.

If Eliza thought she could dominate her, or squish her like a bug under those gorgeous eelskin heels, well, she would soon discover that Marigold Bloom might be small, but she was mighty.

"That is unworkable," Eliza declared.

"But I—" Ami began.

Marigold shook her head ever so slightly, but the barely perceptible movement was enough to have her sister lapsing into silence.

"You are correct, Eliza," Marigold began.

"I'm happy you see it my way." Eliza's lips curved in satisfaction.

"You are correct," Marigold repeated, as if the other woman hadn't spoken, "that it's unworkable to have you interfering in a matter of which you know nothing. I am the expert in the area of hair, and ultimately it is my reputation at stake."

"I am—" Eliza interrupted.

"I'm not finished speaking," Marigold snapped, then offered a conciliatory smile, though she wasn't certain why she bothered. "From what I understand, the goal of this event is to increase the tourism traffic during a traditionally slow time of the year, bolstering revenue for all Good Hope businesses."

"That's correct." Ami spoke before Eliza had a chance.

Prim picked up her cup again, apparently deciding a fast break for the front door was not going to be necessary. She took a sip, her gaze focused on Eliza.

"You are not in charge." The director's words lacked the punch of minutes earlier. "This is a Cherries event."

"I don't wish to be in charge of the entire event." If Eliza could give a little, Marigold figured she could do the same. "But I will retain total autonomy in terms of the hairstyles for the fashion show. Or I won't be involved at all."

The air turned thick, tension humming like electricity from a downed power line.

Marigold picked up her cup, her heart suddenly light. She'd made her feelings clear. The ball was now in Eliza's court.

The only thing Marigold could do now was to wait and see how the game played out.

Cade congratulated himself on a puck well placed as he skated off the ice covering Rakes's Pond. When he'd joined the force in Detroit, he'd thought his days of playing hockey were behind him.

Until this winter, he hadn't given a second thought to the skates gathering dust in his closet. But as soon as the weather turned cold in Good Hope and the ice grew thick, he'd been recruited to join the Ice Holes.

The majority of team members were men in their twenties and thirties. Some, like Jeremy Rakes, were whizzes on the ice. Others, like Beckett Cross, needed to hone their skating skills for a couple more seasons. Beck had grown up in the South, so team members gave him a pass on his less-than-stellar control.

The fact that Cade could skate, had actually played hockey in high school, had been a cause for celebration. Many of the games he'd played this winter were pickup ones. For those scrimmages, teams were chosen by a process known as *drawing sticks* or *sticks in the middle*. Everyone tossed their sticks into a pile, then one of the players divided the sticks into two groups, forming two teams.

In a tournament set for the week before Valentine's Day, Cade would play for the Ice Holes. Being asked to be on a team made him feel part of the community in a way he never had in Detroit.

He sat down on a bench at the side of the pond to unlace his skates, then noticed the other men were making no move to remove their own.

Cade straightened, cocked his head. "Isn't the game over?"

"The extra practice is over," Jeremy clarified, "but there's a community skate every Friday night. Families will start showing up any minute."

"I thought that once the pond froze, other than when the hockey teams practiced, the pond was always open for skating." *So much still to learn*, Cade thought.

"Friday Skate Night is a community event. The lights are turned on, the snack hut opens, and the bonfire is lit. Lots of families come every Friday."

"Sounds nice." As Cade didn't have a family, he once again bent over to untie his laces.

"The Blooms have arrived." Jeremy's announcement had Cade's fingers stilling on the laces. Slowly he straightened.

He spotted Callum and Connor first. As usual, the twins were out in front, followed by Marigold and her sisters. Steve and Anita brought up the rear.

The bag slung over Marigold's shoulder was nearly as large as she was. A hot-pink stocking cap with fuzzy white snowflakes covered much of her hair.

When their gazes locked, Cade lifted a hand. She wiggled her fingers and smiled.

Though tempted to go to her, Cade remained with Jeremy. Yet his gaze on the pretty blonde never wavered. He smiled when he saw Marigold's lips were the same color as her hat.

The mayor shook his head. "It doesn't look right."

"What?"

"Seeing only three Bloom sisters." Jeremy expelled a breath, offered a rueful smile. "In my mind there will always be four."

Cade studied the group, angled his head. "Pretend Anita is Fin."

Jeremy snorted out a laugh. "Delphinium Bloom would cut out your tongue for that comment."

The twins waved wildly when they spotted their father, who'd just strolled up with Beck. Seconds later, two tiny bodies slammed into Max.

"Oof." Max pretended to stumble back, his arms slipping around both boys as if to take them down with him. They shrieked with pleasure.

Cade smiled. There was nothing quite like roughhousing with your dad.

As Max righted himself, Connor's attention shifted to Cade. "Are you here to arrest someone?"

Callum rolled his eyes. "He has skates on, stupid."

Max reacted immediately, clamping a hand on his son's shoulder. "We don't call people names. What do you want to tell your brother?"

It appeared this was familiar territory, because Callum didn't hesitate. "Sorry."

"'s okay." Connor's gaze dropped to Cade's battered skates. "Do you play hockey with my daddy?"

"The sheriff is a clapper," Max told his sons, referring to Cade's powerful slap shot. "He makes me look like a beginner."

Connor's eyes went wide. "Really?"

"Your dad's a fine player," Cade assured the boy but couldn't resist adding, "When he's not falling down."

Max playfully shot out a right jab, a punch Cade easily dodged.

"When you fall down, does it hurt?" Connor gazed at his father, his brows furrowed in concern.

"I'm going to be a clapper," Callum announced loudly.

"You can't even skate backwards," Connor taunted.

"Neither can you." Callum gave his brother a small shove.

Max placed a firm hand on Callum's shoulder, but his voice remained calm. "That's one of the skills we'll be practicing tonight."

Cade turned to Marigold, who'd just walked up. Though it had been less than forty-eight hours since he'd seen her, it felt like an eternity. They'd planned to get together yesterday, but when one of his deputies called in sick, he'd ended up working a double.

He'd called her this morning and hadn't been surprised to hear she'd held her own with Eliza yesterday. "I thought you were busy tonight."

"I am busy." Mischief, along with an unmistakable flash of interest, glittered in Marigold's blue eyes. "I had a date with my family."

"We come every week," Callum told him. "Tonight we get hot chocolate because—"

The boy glanced over his shoulder at his mother for help.

"—because we want to support the Seedlings," Prim added with a smile.

Cade nodded to Steve, who'd just strolled up with Anita clinging to his arm like a leech to a blood source. "Good to see you both."

He shifted his gaze back to Marigold. Even with several feet separating them, he felt the pulse of electricity. He wished he could wrap his arms around her and show her just how much he'd missed her.

But Cade knew how families worked. Heck, he came from one very similar to hers. That's why he would take whatever time necessary to discuss everything from what they planned to eat to the highs and lows of the practice game he and the other Ice Holes had just played.

Once that was done, hopefully he'd snag some alone time with her. Cade wondered if she'd told her family yet they were dating. He didn't have to wait long for the answer.

"I hear you and Marigold are dating." Ami smiled warmly at him. "You don't need my approval, but you have it."

"You have mine as well," Prim added, then swiveled her head and pinned her two young sons with a steely-eyed gaze.

Both jumped back from the bag they'd been riffling through as if the contents had suddenly turned red-hot. Apparently satisfied, Prim refocused on Cade.

He cleared his throat. As a response seemed indicated, he returned their smiles. "Your sister is a fascinating woman."

"I am indeed." She gave him a wink and what could only be described as a come-hither look.

Screw protocol. Cade gestured toward the ice. "Skate with me."

Before Marigold had a chance to respond, Eliza swept up, a black cape coat swirling around her. A red headband held her dark hair back from her face. Her gaze swept over the family like a broom brushing over a dusty floor. "The Blooms are out in full force tonight."

Anita, who stood a few feet away, complaining to Steven about the nitrates in hot dogs, whirled at the sound of Eliza's voice. In seconds, she was hotfooting it in the woman's direction.

"This should be good," Marigold murmured.

Anita pushed Connor and Callum not so gently out of the way in her quest to reach the executive director.

"Eliza, how wonderful to see you," she gushed. "It's been so long. Too long. How have you been?"

"Just fine." As if to ward off a sudden chill, Eliza wrapped her coat more tightly around her. "Thank you for asking."

There was a feline quality to the smile Eliza bestowed on Anita. It might have passed for friendly if Cade hadn't been watching and saw it didn't quite reach her eyes.

With Eliza, things were not always as they seemed. Take her initial approach to the Bloom family. Though it might appear Eliza had come over to greet this group, Cade knew it was Good Hope's mayor, standing on the other side of the family, who was her ultimate target.

Cade had to give the woman props. No matter how much she wanted to be with Jeremy, she knew better than to be too obvious. Which left her stuck—for the moment, anyway—with Anita.

"Do you want to skate?" Cade asked Marigold.

"In a second." Her gaze never left the two women. "I'd like to see how this plays out first."

"How is your dear mother?" Anita exhaled an exaggerated sigh. "I really miss Patty. She and I were once such good friends."

"If that were true, she'd know Patricia never went by Patty," Marigold whispered to Cade, her eyes dancing with barely suppressed amusement.

"Mother is well, thank you. She and Father enjoy life in Palm Springs." Eliza's tone remained polite. "She golfs daily. They entertain frequently."

"Any chance of them moving back to Good Hope?"

"Though they continue to have commercial interests in the area, I doubt they'll ever move back." Eliza shifted in an attempt to keep Jeremy in sight. "They may return for the occasional holiday or if there's business requiring my father's attention."

"I'm surprised he doesn't let you handle those details instead of making a special trip."

A shadow traveled across Eliza's face but was gone so quickly it made Cade wonder if it had been there at all. "If my father couldn't come, he'd likely ask Ethan to fill in for him."

"That makes no sense." Anita's hazel eyes glittered like a shark's, sensing blood. "Why wouldn't he ask you?"

"How is Ethan?" Marigold interrupted.

When Eliza only stared, Marigold smiled brightly.

"Your brother and I were in the same grade in school," she reminded Eliza. "Is he still in Chicago? He and I talked about getting together sometime when I lived there, but it never happened."

"He recently relocated north of the city." Eliza kept her gaze on Marigold, ignoring Anita completely.

Marigold inclined her head. "What's the name of the town?"

"Village Green."

"I've been there." Marigold slanted a glance at Cade. "I swear it's one of the coolest towns in Illinois. It has all these lovely Victorian homes and this gorgeous lake a couple of blocks from downtown. Old-fashioned gas streetlights. A very quaint, artsy community. Fabulous vibe."

"That's what he tells me," Eliza agreed, her smile almost friendly.

"He tells you?" Anita made a disbelieving sound. "You don't know?"

Eliza's gray eyes were cool as she faced Anita. She spoke slowly and deliberately, as if speaking to an especially dull-witted child. "I believe I just mentioned that my brother only recently moved there. I haven't yet had the opportunity to visit him."

"Well, when you see him, be sure and tell him hello." Marigold's tone remained light and friendly.

"Is he dating anyone seriously?" Anita stepped forward, angling herself between the two women. "Ethan was always so smart and personable. And, oh my, what a handsome young man, with those lovely gray eyes and thick brown hair."

"I don't like to judge." Marigold tapped Anita on the shoulder. "But I think he's a little too young for you."

Anita whirled.

"You'd be venturing into cougar territory." Marigold spoke solemnly, somehow managing to keep her expression serious.

The venomous look Anita directed to Marigold had Cade stepping forward.

Marigold gave a subtle shake of her head, and he paused midstep.

Seizing the opportunity she'd been given, Eliza scooted around the women and hurried over to fall casually into step beside Jeremy, who appeared headed toward The Hut.

When Anita finally found her voice, the words she directed at Marigold held an icy chill. "You'll pay for your disrespect."

Marigold batted her lashes, her expression one of innocence and confusion. "I was simply making an observation. Are you saying you don't think he's too young for you?"

Anita hissed her displeasure. With her jaw set in a hard line, her gaze swept the immediate area. "Steven, did you hear what your daughter said to me?"

Several feet away, Steven held a laughing Callum upside down. He turned his head. "Which one?"

"Which one what?" Anita snapped, not bothering to mask her irritation.

"Which daughter?" Steve had to speak loudly to be heard over his grandson's laughter.

Eliza wasn't the only one who could seize an opportunity. Cade had waited long enough. He held out a hand to Marigold. "Skate with me?"

Her fingers curved around his. "Yes."

"Finally." He expelled a relieved breath as they headed for the ice.

Chapter Twelve

"About Anita," Cade began once I-Need-a-Man was merely another person at the pond's edge. "I didn't like the way she—"

"Let's not waste one second more on the Wicked Witch." Marigold shot Cade a mischievous smile. "If we're lucky, while we're skating, Callum will toss a bucket of water on her and she'll melt away."

Cade's laugher was so infectious Marigold had to join in.

By the time they'd made a complete circle on the ice, Anita had been relegated to Marigold's mental garbage can, leaving her free to focus on the beautiful evening and the handsome man skating at her side. "My sisters think it's wonderful that I'm dating you."

He grinned. "Ami and Prim are smart women."

"I made it clear, of course, that it's only temporary."

Cade merely slipped an arm around her waist and skated faster. As they glided across the ice, Marigold lost herself in the pleasure of the moment.

The lights draped around the perimeter of the pond bathed the area in a bright white glow. The piped-in music kicked on, the perfect accompaniment to the laughter and conversation filling the cool air.

"I used to skate at Millennium Park when I lived in Chicago." Marigold visualized the scene in her head. "It's especially lovely at night, with the skyscrapers lit up all around you."

"Campus Martius is like that in Detroit." Cade took her into his arms for an ice dancing move that left her breathless. "You skate until midnight surrounded by the city's tallest buildings. While they aren't nearly as grand as the ones in Chicago, it's still impressive."

She thought of him and his former fiancée. What was her name? Ah, yes, Alice. The one who thought Cade shouldn't turn in dirty cops. "Did Alice like to skate?"

"Not much." He laughed. "She wasn't overly fond of cold weather, either. What about Jason?"

"Skating was a means to an end for him. 'See and be seen' was his motto." Marigold kept her tone light, realizing that had also been her mantra for many years. "I don't fault him for it. Being visible was also part of my business plan."

Cade's gloved hand tightened around hers. "You're getting plenty of visibility tonight."

"Tonight isn't about visibility." She breathed in air and her nose tingled from the tangy scent of pine.

"What is it about then?"

Marigold shot him a coquettish smile.

Cade cocked his head.

"Tonight is about you," she said, then added, "and about me. It's about us having fun together."

If his arm tightening about her was any indication, he understood. Marigold leaned her head against him as they skated and let herself simply enjoy the moment. She'd given her sisters the impression this was a simple fling. Though the Bloom sisters had no secrets, she hadn't chosen to elaborate on all the confusing feelings tugging at her.

None of those emotions mattered anyway. No matter how much she enjoyed spending time with Cade, she wouldn't be staying in Good Hope.

The kind of success she sought couldn't be found here. Everyone agreed she was on her way to the top. Then her world had collapsed around her. She'd been stupid not to see . . .

No. Marigold stopped the thought in its tracks. She wasn't stupid. Not stupid. Never stupid. God, how she hated that word.

She'd simply had—she struggled to find the right word—blinders, yes, she'd had *blinders* on when it came to Steffan. Having misplaced loyalty didn't make her stupid. Marigold calmed herself with thoughts of the future. A successful future.

While she was enjoying this interlude in Good Hope, it was time she came up with a solid plan for her return to the fast lane. When she got back to the apartment, she'd dig a little deeper into several of the salons on her dream list, then bullet point her next steps.

"I didn't know K.T. and Braxton could skate so well."

Marigold glanced around and saw her entire family was now on the ice, with the exception of Anita, who thankfully wasn't family. Not yet, anyway. The brunette sat on one of the benches encircling the pond. Her gloved hands were cupped around a steaming cup of cocoa, undoubtedly bought by Steve to support the Seedlings.

Anita's gaze remained fixed on Marigold's father, who was currently circling the pond with his grandsons. The proprietary way the brunette watched him struck a harsh chord.

"This is the first time I've seen Anita's grandsons on the ice."

Following the direction of his gaze, Marigold spotted the Lohmeier boys. Their black skates were even more battered than hers, but she had to give the boys props. "They've got mad skills."

As Marigold watched, Braxton turned and skated backward with an ease Marigold envied. She noticed his gaze—as well as his brother's—kept darting to the side of the pond. "Who are they looking at?"

Cade jerked his head in the direction of a bench near where Marigold had left her skating bag. "They're out to impress her."

Marigold narrowed her gaze in that direction, expecting to see a pretty young girl in her midteens. Instead, she stifled a grimace. "Why would they try to impress Anita?"

"Because she's their grandmother."

"In name only." Marigold's heart twisted. "I don't believe Anita wants anything to do with either of them."

"That's my take, too." Cade's tone was grim.

"I don't understand it. Those two might be a bit rough around the edges, but they seem like nice boys." When Cade had brought the brothers to her for an apology, Marigold had expected to see a defiant toughness in their eyes. Instead there'd been a shyness, a vulnerability that had touched her heart. "They need their grandmother. And, while we're wishing on a star, they need a father as well."

"Clint Gourley lived with their mother for a number of years."

"Clint is a douche bag." Marigold saw no need to pull punches. "He may have lived with Cassie, but he was no father to her sons. The best thing that happened to those kids was when Clint moved out."

"I was involved in the investigation of that string of burglaries last summer." Cade's gaze kept straying to the boys. "While I wasn't the officer who ultimately arrested Clint, I concur with your assessment of his character."

Cade's gaze had turned brooding by the time they circled the pond again.

"What are you thinking?"

"Nothing," he murmured, but those gray eyes told a different story.

An instant later he jerked back. His dark brows slammed together. "Hey, why'd you pinch me?"

She offered a sweet smile. "You're cooking up something. I want in on the action."

Cade chuckled and shook his head. "I've never known anyone quite like you."

Marigold lifted her hand and let her pincher finger and thumb snap open and closed.

"Okay, okay." He lifted both hands in surrender, and his expression turned serious. "A boy needs a dad. Or at least, a solid father figure. Someone to give guidance. Those kids are no exception."

A memory stirred as Marigold watched her dad clap Max on the shoulder before joining Anita on the sidelines. "Did Max ever mention that my dad was his Big Brother when he was growing up?"

The surprise in Cade's eyes answered her question.

"Max's father died when he was a little guy." Marigold paused to call out a greeting to Greer Chapin, who was currently skating with Travis. "His mother remarried a couple of times, but the guys didn't stick. Max was in middle school when he and my father were paired up."

"Does your dad still volunteer?"

She and Cade now skated hand in hand, crossing the ice at a leisurely pace that favored conversation. She loved it when his beautiful gray eyes turned from teasing to serious. Loved it when his lips quirked up in humor. Loved talking with him.

So many things to love about this man.

Marigold's heart began to beat against her ribs like a closed fist. Panic wrapped around her throat and squeezed tight.

No reason to worry. No reason to worry. No reason to worry. By the time she mentally repeated the words a third time, the tightness around her throat eased and she could breathe again.

"Does he?"

"Does who what?"

"Does your father still mentor kids?"

"Yes. No. Wait." Marigold blew out an exasperated breath as she fought to focus. She hated days like this, days when she had difficulty filtering out background noise, days when the perfect word refused to pop into her head. "I don't know for sure if he still volunteers, but I think he does. My father is very civic minded."

"Let's ask him." Cade guided them to the edge of the pond. Marigold hadn't noticed the chill in the air until Cade turned as if to walk away.

Then he paused and extended his hand. "Come with me."

"Why?" She expected him to say that Steve was her father. Or perhaps laugh and say he'd be a fool to leave a woman as pretty as her alone.

"We're a team."

"In what world?" she said laughingly.

"In the Good Hope world." His strong face remained sober as those gray eyes met hers. "As long as you're here, we're together. Being together makes you and me partners."

His expression relaxed, and the smile he shot her sent warmth flooding all the way to her toes.

Basking in the glow, Marigold considered whether she'd ever been anyone's partner. It didn't take her long to conclude this was something new. She'd always asserted she liked to fly solo. Even during her time with Jason, they'd never been a team.

Marigold wasn't sure she was comfortable being Cade's wingman, or partner, or whatever the heck else he wanted to call her. Still, she went with him to where her father now sat laughing with Anita.

Anita's gaze immediately honed in on Marigold's hand, nestled firmly in Cade's.

Marigold fought the urge to pull her hand free, as if she were a child caught with her hand in the cookie jar instead of a grown woman holding the hand of the man she was dating.

Temporarily dating.

"You two were doing a smash-up job out there on the ice." Steve's stocking cap proclaimed him as the World's Best Grandpa. The cap completely covered his wiry hair, except for one recalcitrant gray strand peeking out midforehead.

Marigold's heart swelled with love for this kind, gentle man who'd been her rock for as long as she could remember. "It's easy to look good when you have a talented partner."

There was that word again. *Partner.*

"Your crossover maneuvers are top-notch." Steve cast an admiring look at Cade. "I can see why the Ice Holes recruited you."

Anita's eyes took on a faraway glow and a smile tugged at the corners of her lips. "That name is about as bad as the one you and Richard chose for your team."

"The Lucky Pucks." Steve grinned. "Those were good times. After a game we'd always go for pizza afterwards with the kids."

"The pizza place in Egg Harbor," Anita supplied. "The one with all those vintage pinball machines in the back."

Marigold had only vague memories of those outings. She'd always wondered what tied her father and Anita together. It was easy to forget the history they shared.

Because the last thing she wanted was to stroll down memory lane with her dad and Anita, Marigold glanced around. "Any idea where I can find Ami and Prim?"

"Last I knew they were up at the house." Steve gestured toward the three-story home at the top of the hill. "Jeremy got a new train set, and he wanted to show the boys."

Jeremy fit perfectly in the fabric of the Bloom family. Marigold knew she wasn't the only one in the family who wished things had worked out between him and Fin.

She wondered if Fin's career in LA made her happy. Wondered if her sister's current boyfriend, Xander Tillman, would be The One.

Marigold didn't feel as if she could properly assess the relationship, as she'd never met the guy. The producer had always been "too busy" to come with Fin to Good Hope at holiday time.

"From what you're saying, Big Brothers sounds like a wonderful program," Cade told her father.

"I strongly believe every boy can benefit from a positive role model in this life." Steve's eyes darkened with emotion. "The relationship isn't one-sided. The Big Brother gains so much, too."

Marigold realized while she'd been assessing Fin's life, the conversation had veered into Big Brother territory. Had her father brought up the topic? Or had Cade?

"Are you interested in participating in the program?" Steve's voice shook with an eagerness he didn't bother to disguise. "I can give you a contact name and phone number if you're ready to apply and get started."

"I'd prefer to wait until after the election."

"That would be a mistake."

Cade turned in response to the soft, southern drawl to find Beck shaking his head.

"Max and I have been doing some strategizing." Beck jerked a thumb in his brother-in-law's direction. "We feel it's important for you to show the citizens of Good Hope you've made this community your home."

"Let them see you've settled in." Max's gaze was thoughtful. "That you're involved and committed to living here."

Settled. Committed. Marigold shifted uneasily. Definitely not her type of conversation.

"Are you still living in that boarding house?" Anita drew everyone's attention with the unexpected question.

Cade nodded. "Temporarily."

"While I hate to disagree with Beck and Max, I think you're being smart hedging your bets." Anita took Steve's hand and gave it a squeeze.

"While Steve and I, and I daresay the rest of the Bloom family, are behind you one hundred percent, there's no guarantee you'll win the election in March."

Concern that appeared quite genuine blanketed Anita's features. "To tell you the truth, I'm a little worried. I've heard quite a few people say they're planning on voting for Travis."

"Travis doesn't have near the experience—" Marigold began, but Cade's fingers tightening around hers had her defense dying in her throat.

"That's the thing about elections." Cade spoke easily, confidently, as if he'd been through dozens. "You never know who will win until the votes are counted."

"So true." Anita nodded. "Yet I've spoken with many people who believe Travis should have been appointed. Hometown boy and all that."

"Like Anita said, we'll do whatever we can to support you." Steve patted her hand.

"Back to Big Brothers." Cade shifted his stance and faced Steve directly, effectively ending the campaign discussion. "Have you ever considered becoming a Big Brother to K.T. and Braxton Lohmeier?"

Marigold found satisfaction in Anita's gasp, although she was found herself equally startled by Cade's suggestion. She was even more surprised when Cade slanted a glance at her, a clear request for backup.

Partners, he'd said.

"I think it's a fabulous idea, Dad." Marigold forced enthusiasm into her voice. It wasn't hard. She did think it'd be a great match. "The two are at the age you work with best, and you know the family. It would be a perfect all around."

"I hadn't really thought about being matched again." Steve rubbed his chin, his hazel eyes thoughtful. "What you're saying makes sense. I—"

"You can't mentor them." Anita's words sliced the chilled air. "It's not a good idea."

Her father glanced at his girlfriend. He appeared genuinely puzzled by her vehemence. "Why not?"

Marigold could almost see the wheels churning in Anita's brain. The woman had to know she stood on unsteady ground. Steve valued family, and these were her grandsons.

The brunette gave Steve's arm a mollifying pat. "We'll chat about this later."

Steve cocked his head. "What's wrong with now?"

Anita's gaze shifted to Marigold. "Because now is the perfect time to discuss the fact that your daughter has been in town less than two weeks and is already sleeping with the sheriff."

Because his palm rested against Marigold's back, Cade felt her jerk as Anita's blow connected.

The unexpected offensive maneuver held the added benefit of diverting Steve's attention from her. A double win for Anita.

"Is it true?" Steve glanced from Cade to Marigold, then back to Cade.

Marigold's mouth opened, closed. Two bright spots of color that had nothing to do with the weather dotted her cheeks.

Keeping his gaze on Steve's face, Cade took Marigold's hand firmly in his.

From everything Cade had observed, Steve Bloom appeared to be a social liberal who rarely meddled in his daughters' affairs. But Marigold *was* the baby of the Bloom family. That fact undoubtedly made her father even more protective.

Marigold opened her mouth again to say, well, Cade wasn't exactly sure what she planned to say. It didn't matter. Anita was his dragon to slay. Marigold, his princess to protect.

"I first met Marigold at my cousin Shannon's wedding the summer before last." When Marigold attempted to pull her hand away, Cade only tightened his hold. "Your daughter made quite an impression on me."

Cade turned to Marigold and smiled. He wasn't surprised to see her gorgeous blue eyes, normally as clear as the sky, held storm clouds.

"I couldn't forget her." Cade spoke directly to Steve, keeping his gaze focused on the older man's eyes, willing him to see he spoke from the heart. "Although we lived in different cities, we remained connected. Apart, but not really apart, if that makes sense to you."

"Sarah and I had that connection." Steve's smile turned wistful. "Even now, I—"

"You said you weren't with him." Apparently sensing control of the conversation slipping from her grasp, Anita pinned Marigold with her gaze. "At the New Year's Eve party I specifically asked if you were together—"

"Sometimes, Anita, you ask questions that are really none of your business." Despite the tight set to her jaw, Marigold's tone managed to remain calm. "You bring up matters that are personal and private. Such as my relationship with Cade."

Though she'd directed her comments to Anita, red crept up Steven's neck.

"You make an excellent point." Regret was written all over the man's face. "Your relationship with Cade is not my—nor Anita's—business."

Marigold's father slanted a pointed look at his girlfriend.

"I was simply inquiring—" Anita began.

"You were asking about, commenting on, something that was none of your concern." Steve's tone held a note of apology. "I'm ashamed to admit I got caught up in the asking. I'm sorry for it."

Cade met the schoolteacher's gaze. "I have feelings for your daughter. I won't hurt her."

"When you care about someone, hurt and pain are often part of the bargain. You're a good man, Cade. I'm happy you and my daughter are together."

"Now that we have that settled"—Marigold pinned Anita with her blue eyes—"you never did say why you object to my father being Braxton and K.T.'s Big Brother."

Marigold's innocent expression and sweet smile didn't fool Cade. From the controlled steam seeping out of Anita's ears, it didn't fool her, either.

Only Steve appeared to take the shift back to the question as a normal progression of the conversation.

As the silence lengthened, Anita's fingers tightened around the cup she still held. If the woman could have gotten away with it, Cade had no doubt she'd have flung the cocoa into Marigold's face.

"I'm afraid my reasons are," Anita paused to clear her throat, "deeply personal."

Deeply personal, my ass, Cade thought.

Yet he had to admire the way Anita delivered the words. And the sheen of tears she'd conjured up was the mark of a real pro. It was no wonder Steve had been taken in by her.

"Deeply personal?" Marigold laughed. "Seriously, Anita? We're talking Big Brothers here."

Before the woman could respond, Ami and Prim ambled over.

"I'm sorry to interrupt." Prim offered an apologetic smile to the group before turning to her husband. "You know how we promised to teach the twins how to skate backwards? Well, Ami and I tried but—"

"We botched it badly." Ami stepped to her husband and gave a little smile. "Would you and Max mind giving it a shot?"

"I'm not sure how much help Beck will be." Max gave his brother-in-law a wink. "But I'll bring him along for pickup duty. Where are the twins now?"

Prim pointed to where Callum and Connor stood at the edge of the pond. The boys appeared to be trying to chop a hole in the ice with a hockey stick.

Beck cocked his head. "Whose stick are they using?"

"Mine," Max roared and took off running with Beck at his heels.

"We didn't mean to interrupt your discussion." Prim's gaze swept the group, and her expression showed genuine regret. "But it's getting late and we'd promised the boys. I—"

"It's okay, sweetheart." Steve reached over and squeezed Prim's hand.

"What's going on here?" Bypassing Anita, Ami's gaze shifted to Marigold.

"Dad is considering doing the Big Brother thing with Braxton and K.T. Lohmeier." Marigold smiled brightly. "I think it's a good idea."

"It's a fabulous one." Prim's voice rose. "You only have to ask Max. He'll tell you what having Dad mentor him meant."

"Why just considering?" Ami inclined her head. "Are the boys unwilling to participate in the program?"

Beck always said Ami was sharp. The way she zeroed in on the nuance of the statement told Cade the man knew his wife well.

"They haven't been approached yet." Marigold slanted a glance at Anita, whose lips were pressed together in a tight, firm line. "Anita doesn't approve."

Prim shifted to face Anita, her expression genuinely puzzled. "What possible reservations could you have? It's such a great program."

"She said her reasons are *deeply personal*." Marigold drawled the last words.

"Okay. I'm clearly missing something." Ami focused on her father. "Do you understand?"

Steve crossed his arms, shook his head.

All eyes shifted to Anita.

"If I must air my family's dirty laundry . . ." Anita drew in a deep breath and let it out with theatrical slowness. Once she had command of center stage, she fixed her amber eyes on Steve. "I'm trying to dissuade you because I see approaching Cassie as pointless. She won't agree to you being involved with the boys. She knows you and I are involved."

Ami raised a hand. "I don't understand what you and my father dating has to do with him being a Big Brother to Braxton and K.T."

"Any attempts I've made over the years to counsel Cassie about her lifestyle, about doing better by herself and her children, has been taken as criticism. After the baby was born, I thought we were making progress. But when I told her she needed to get Clint out of the house and bring Dakota back home, she once again cut me out of her life." Two perfect tears slipped down Anita's cheeks. She paused to clear her throat. "It breaks my heart not to have a place in my grandchildren's lives."

Steve gave her shoulders a squeeze. "She'll come around, Cookie."

Marigold arched a brow. "Because of this breech in your family, you expect my father to step away from them, too."

"Of course not." Anita dabbed at her eyes with a tissue pulled from her pocket. She gave Steve a watery smile. "I simply don't want him to get his hopes up. And frankly, I'm afraid if Big Brothers put forth Steve as a possible mentor, Cassie will say no to the program. Not because she doesn't see value in what they're offering, but as a way of thumbing her nose at me."

"That makes sense." Steve gave a reluctant nod.

"Does this mean you're not going to even try?" Marigold asked.

"It means," Steve's gaze slid from Anita to Cade before settling on Marigold, "I'm going to give everything that has happened this evening more thought. Then I'll decide where to go from here."

Chapter Thirteen

"This hot chocolate is pretty good." Marigold wrapped her fingers around the cup they'd purchased on their way to the parking lot. After the incident with Anita, Marigold had been ready to leave. Still, she'd stuck around another hour.

After opening the passenger door for her, Cade rounded the front of the Jeep and slipped behind the wheel.

Marigold knew he'd been puzzled when she'd insisted on stopping to pick up a drink as they were leaving. He didn't understand the side trip did double duty. She not only showed her support for the Seedlings, she gave the impression of being at not all bothered by Anita's remarks.

"Having the Seedlings sell cocoa on Friday nights was a brilliant idea." Cade started the engine but kept the vehicle in park. "Though it appeared parents were doing most of the work."

"I can't imagine Callum and Connor serving hot cocoa, even with Prim and Max there." Like Cade, Marigold kept her tone pleasant and conversational.

Keep it together, she told herself when a watchful waiting filled the interior of the vehicle. Didn't Cade realize she wouldn't ruin what was left of the evening by bringing up Anita? Still, seeing her father take the woman's arm shortly before she and Cade left had stung. How could her dad be nice to such an awful woman?

"Anita is a hard one."

Marigold whipped around to face Cade, the quick movement sending the cocoa sloshing to the rim of her cup. "Hard?"

"Difficult to figure." Cade drummed his fingers against the steering wheel. "I thought I had her pegged. That remark about us sleeping together confirmed my initial assessment. But when she was talking about the past she and your father shared and her family troubles, she seemed almost . . . human."

Marigold reluctantly nodded agreement.

"I assume Richard was her first husband?"

"That's right." Marigold took a sip of cocoa. "Richard died of a heart attack almost twenty years ago. I don't remember much about him, but everyone says he was a nice guy."

Silence filled the cab for several heartbeats.

"That tie to the past likely explains why your father has cut Anita so much slack." Cade slanted a sideways glance. "But I guarantee the woman is going to have some explaining to do tonight."

"About the Big Brother thing?"

"No." Cade reached over and brushed a strand of hair back from her face with a gentle hand. "About the remark she made concerning our relationship. Your father was seriously pissed."

"I was caught off guard. Normally I give as good as I get. But occasionally I have trouble finding the right words." Marigold flushed. "Your response was perfect."

For a long moment, he said nothing. "I meant every word."

Marigold recalled what he'd said about connections, about bonds that could hold two people close despite time and distance. Before she'd returned to Good Hope, before Cade, she wouldn't have understood the concept. Now she did.

In the dim light, their gazes locked. Time seemed to stretch and extend. He opened his mouth as if to say more, but pressed his lips together and backed out of the stall.

"There's a piece of property I'm considering." Cade turned toward town. "I'd like to show it to you and get your opinion."

While Marigold welcomed the change in topic, she wondered if he was serious. Was this really a good time for him to buy a house? "Is this because Beck and Max said you should put down roots?"

"I run my own life and I make my own decisions." A muscle in Cade's jaw jumped. "Actually I've had my eye on this particular property since I moved here. The owners plan to list it with a realtor next week but are willing to give me first rights of refusal."

Cade turned off the highway at the next corner. This road was paved but barely wide enough for two cars to pass.

When he made another turn and Marigold realized where they were headed, she didn't bother to hide her surprise. "You're looking at property in *this* area?"

He flashed a grin. "Go big or go home."

This particular stretch of waterfront, known locally as Millionaire's Row, contained some of the most expensive homes in the area. If Marigold wasn't mistaken, David and Whitney Chapin lived just down the road.

"You've been holding out on me, Rallis." Marigold kept her tone light. "What did you do? Win the lottery? Rob a bank?"

Cade's lips twitched as he made one last turn. "Neither."

He didn't elaborate and Marigold didn't push. There would be plenty of time to grill him once she saw the house. She gazed out the window, enjoying the drive.

"My sisters and I loved hiking this area. Back then, the cottages were small and our parents knew all the owners." The memories of those childhood days wrapped around her like a comforting blanket, sending warmth coursing through her blood. "We always came home with buckets of wild blackberries and thimbleberries."

"Thimbleberry?" Cade's tone was skeptical. "Are you making that up?"

Marigold laughed softly, understanding his puzzlement. "Some people call them blackcap raspberries, but around here you'll hear them called thimbleberries."

"I'm not familiar with either term."

"Tart but delicious." Marigold ran her tongue across her lips, remembering the taste. "Ami makes loads of jam every summer. I'll see you get a jar."

The Jeep slowed to a crawl. "You put it on bread? Like any other jelly or jam?"

"Just like any other jam." If this drive and conversation were his way of trying to distract and soothe her, it was working. "But Ami does this dessert thing with the berries, pound cake, chocolate bars, and marshmallows that everyone should experience at least once in their lifetime."

"Sounds intriguing." He slanted her a sideways glance and grinned. "I'll ask her to make it for us sometime."

Us. Marigold's heart twisted. She'd be long gone before the berries were at their peak.

Cade pulled the Jeep to the side of the road. Seconds later they stood, with snow crunching under their boots, at the edge of the freshly plowed road.

Marigold gazed over the plot of ground blanketed in white. Tall pines stood like green sentinels at the northernmost edge of the lot.

"Home sweet home." Cade offered a sardonic smile. "What do you think?"

"I think the temperature must have dropped twenty degrees since we left the pond." Marigold hunched her shoulders against the stiff breeze off the bay. "Ah, there's no house here."

"A house?" Cade chuckled. "I can barely afford the ground."

When he named the figure the owners were asking, she whistled, although she wasn't surprised. "How are you going to afford it?"

"My grandma Gwen died last year." Cade's tone might be light, but Marigold saw the sorrow in his eyes.

"I'm sorry." Marigold squeezed his arm. "Losing someone you love is never easy."

"Yes, well." Cade took a breath, let it out slowly. "Instead of leaving her estate to her children—my father and his brother—she opted to divide it between her five grandkids."

Marigold tapped a gloved finger against her lips. "Are you saying I've been dating a rich guy?"

He chuckled. "A rich guy who will soon be land poor."

"Are you really going to buy this lot?"

He shoved his hands into his pockets, rocked back on his heels. "Seriously considering it."

Marigold didn't want to be a naysayer like Anita, but the woman *had* brought up a few valid points. "What about the election?"

His gaze had returned to the property. A slight smile now lifted his lips. "What about it?"

"First, I'm sure you'll win." Marigold wanted that on the table. She certainly didn't want Cade thinking she'd lost faith in him. "But what if something crazy happens and you lose? Do you plan to stay and work under Travis?"

A muscle in Cade's jaw jumped and the smile disappeared. "Going from being in charge to being a subordinate would never work."

Marigold opened her mouth, prepared to argue the point, then realized he was right.

"Would you stick around and look for another position in Good Hope?" Marigold had no doubt with all his leadership experience, Jeremy could find him something.

"For me, being in law enforcement—protecting and serving the public—isn't simply a job." Cade shrugged. "It's who I am."

It didn't take a puzzle master like Prim to put together these pieces. "You'd relocate."

He pulled his hands from his pockets, lifted them, and let them fall. "I'd have no choice."

Marigold chewed on her bottom lip. Just when you thought the puzzle was nearly solved, a piece refused to fit. "Then why sink your money into property here before you know whether or not you're staying?"

Instead of answering, he slung an arm around her shoulders, gave her a squeeze. "You're starting to look like Rudolph with that red nose. Let's get you out of the wind."

Before slipping into the vehicle, Marigold paused to give the property—with its amazing view of Green Bay—one last glance. "The sunrises will be spectacular."

"You like it." Cade sounded pleased.

"There isn't a better spot on the entire peninsula."

Something flickered in his eyes. "I'm going to call the owner in the morning and have the papers drawn up."

The first thing Marigold did when she was inside the Jeep was to turn the heater on high. Only when she was properly thawed out and could feel her nose again did she repeat the question he'd yet to answer. "Why buy land in a community where you might not stay?"

He hesitated for so long she was forced to give him a poke in the ribs.

"Have you seen the interest rate on CDs lately?" Cade fiddled with the air flow before continuing. "If I decide to sell, I'll more than recoup the money I've paid."

Logical, Marigold thought, but not the whole story. "Why else?"

"You think there's more?"

Her gaze locked on his. "Spill."

Cade flashed a smile. "You know me so well."

It was true, but the realization troubled her, so Marigold simply motioned for him to start talking.

"Because my dad was in the military, we moved a lot. It seemed that just when I got used to a place, he'd get new orders and we'd pack up again." Cade's voice remained low, almost as if he was talking to himself. "At first I liked meeting new kids and seeing new places, but as I got older, not so much. I vowed that once I was on my own, I'd find a place that felt like home and settle there. I found everything I was looking for here. Even if I have to move, one day I'll be back. While I may not have been born here, this is my home."

Marigold understood the lure of Good Hope. Even now she had to fight the pull. Though the vow she'd made when she was ten would keep her far away, this town would always have her heart.

For a long moment Marigold was silent. Then she made another vow. She would do whatever it took to help him win the upcoming election.

Because if she couldn't make this place her home, she'd darn well see that he could.

Marigold considered asking Cade to sleep over but knew tomorrow would be a full day. Blooms Bake Shop would be open for business and Marigold had promised to help Hadley with the counter sales. After a hectic holiday season, she wanted her eldest sister to be able to sleep in and have a relaxing day with her husband.

"I'd like to stay." Cade brushed a lock of hair back from her cheek with one finger.

His closeness, the feel of his body against hers, nearly undid her resolve. Because it seemed the thing to do, and because she couldn't help herself, Marigold looped her arms around his neck, held him tight for several seconds. "Thank you."

"You're welcome." His breath was warm against her ear. "For what?"

"For being you." She pulled back and laughed softly. "I really want you to stay, but I have to be up before dawn."

"Damn." He gave her a halfhearted smile.

"There's always a good night kiss." Her hands rested on his shoulders. "What kind of girlfriend would I be if I let you walk away without one?"

"Your family seems okay with us dating."

"They like you." It was a bit disconcerting just how easily they'd accepted her and Cade's relationship.

"I like them, too." His hands touched the hair that now tumbled in a disheveled mess about her shoulders. "Beautiful. Simply beautiful."

Marigold's chest turned gooey soft. Things were so easy with Cade. Unlike Jason, it didn't seem important that his girlfriend always look camera ready.

She'd miss Cade. A lot. Just how much was a disturbing realization, but not disturbing enough to stop her from holding him tight when his mouth closed over hers in a long, soul-shattering kiss.

Several kisses later, her heart raced like she was headed for the checkered flag. Marigold was ready to say no to sleep and yes to Cade when he abruptly released her.

"Get some sleep, Goldilocks." His voice might be ragged, but it held a determined edge. "I'll wait outside until I hear the locks click."

Knowing this was the sensible solution didn't make it any easier. When the lock slid into place, Marigold shrugged off the sadness that wanted to settle and headed straight for the bedroom. Thoughts of Cade lingered as she pulled on flannel pajamas and slippers.

Not very sexy, but she didn't have a handsome man ready to keep her warm. The down-filled comforter gracing the bed couldn't come close to the heat she and Cade generated. Glancing at the clock on the wall, Marigold realized if she called it a night now, she could get several hours of sleep in before the alarm sounded.

The trouble was, after his kisses, she felt more revved than sleepy.

Marigold turned on the television, winced at the sitcom's jarring laugh track, and clicked it off. After tossing the remote back on the table, she briefly considered powering up her laptop but didn't see the point.

Her gaze settled on her art journal. She'd pulled the book—along with various supplies—out from one of the boxes she'd unpacked earlier.

Flipping open the journal, Marigold glanced at several of the last entries. It was like picturing herself at the top of a mountain peak one minute then hitting the ground with a solid thud the next.

The last page she'd worked on had been done the day Steffan fired her. Marigold remembered that night well. She'd longed to escape into sleep but, because of the emotions churning inside her, had found it impossible to settle.

The journal had provided an avenue for the rage. The writing, the painting, the pasting, had been cathartic.

With her heart thumping, Marigold read the words she'd written less than a month earlier. One phrase in particular caught and held her attention.

My life, as I know it, is over.

Dark colors of paint slashed across several pages in bold, angry strokes. Bright blue tears fell from eyes in a face she'd painted ghostly white, the bright red lips turned downward like a sad clown.

At any other time, the melodramatic style might have made her smile. But there was no humor in the memory. Reading snippets of words pasted on the page brought fresh pain.

Steffan's betrayal of their friendship had ripped her heart in two. Though she'd tried to find the positive in the action, she'd been crushed. Some women might have gone out and gotten drunk. That had never been her style. Instead she'd channeled her anger into art, the pain and fury evident in the journal entry.

It was unbelievable that, after over five very successful years, she found herself now back at square one.

No, she set her jaw, not back to square one. She had skills and a business savvy honed from years of working so closely with Steffan. She'd been given a gift, an opportunity to make choices about her future from a position of strength.

Impulsively Marigold picked up her favorite calligraphy pen and wrote in bold letters across the top of a new page: *Know What You Want!*

The script stood in sharp contrast to the words she added next using various colored Sharpie pens: prepare, discover, courage, confidence, bold, faith, innovative, and spectacular.

Marigold papered the pages with pictures of hairstyles and successful salons. Once she was satisfied, she cut out the word LIFE from a magazine cover and glued it to the page.

These next pages would be her nod to the here and now. Marigold felt her heart lighten as she cut and pasted words like: happiness, joy, fun, friendship, and laughter.

Her brushstrokes on the page captured the bright blue skies of Good Hope and the oranges and pinks of the amazing sunsets. Everything was bright colors and a little cheesy. She laughed when her gaze lingered on a picture of a unicorn in the stack of magazine photos she'd brought with her. She barely resisted the urge to add it to the page.

Once she was satisfied, she left the page to dry.

As it had that dark night weeks ago, the simple act of putting her emotions on the page had steadied her. While she might be closer to sleep than she'd been an hour earlier, the night still felt incomplete.

She stood at the window overlooking Main Street for several long moments. It was a clear night and the full moon was bright. Marigold could almost believe she could see the boarding house Cade called home. Was he asleep?

Giving in to impulse, she picked up her phone and formulated a quick text.

Think of me.

After a brief mental tussle, she added, **I'm thinking of you.**

Before she could erase the text, she hit Send.

"I got your text." Cade held the phone against his ear. He'd been surprised—and pleased—when his phone had dinged and he saw the text from Marigold. He nearly replied, but the fact she'd reached out to him with a message that felt oddly intimate seemed to demand more. "I was thinking of you, too."

Silence filled the connection. Had he made a mistake by being honest? Though he had to be careful, as she was skittish about anything smacking of serious romance, if this relationship had a chance of working, he had to be himself.

If this relationship had a chance of working...

Cade nearly laughed, though he didn't feel much like laughing. Marigold had made it clear she'd be gone long before summer. Likely long before the election in March, she'd be living in some big city working in a fancy salon. Far from Good Hope. Far from him.

The knowledge formed a hard knot in the ball of his stomach.

"I'm wearing that silk nightie," she purred. "The one you enjoy taking off."

Cade had just plopped down in the chair to pull off his boots when her words slapped him in the face. He was very familiar with the paper-thin garment in soft blue. His body went instantly hard.

It didn't take a detective's shield to know she assumed he'd called for phone sex. Or—and he thought this an equally likely possibility—his response had hit her on an emotional level. Keeping any interaction on the sexual level was her way of keeping distance between them.

He wouldn't let that happen.

"It's cold out tonight." Still aroused, Cade shifted uncomfortably in the chair. Despite the strain, he managed to keep his voice easy. "If I was with you now, we'd build a fire. We'd sit on the sofa and enjoy a glass of wine."

"Or we could go to bed and find other ways to keep warm."

Dear God, give me strength.

Cade closed his eyes and plucked the first nonsexual thought from a brain floundering from loss of blood. "My dad and I aren't much for talking."

"Your father?" The sultry purr disappeared.

He understood the surprise. Cade wasn't sure where that thought had come from, either. But now that it was out there, he went with it.

"He's a great guy and all. But it was difficult talking with him about stuff going on in my life, things that bugged me. He wasn't much for talking about feelings." Cade's laugh held a touch of desperation. "You know those articles that say parents should spend quality time with their kids?"

"I've read them."

Instead of elaborating as he'd hoped, she let the words hang in the air. The conversation was at critical mass. Normally Cade would have gladly let it die. But Marigold reaching out to him tonight felt too important.

His gut told him this could be one of those moments he could easily end up regretting. A time he would look back on and see he'd had the opportunity to take their relationship to another level but had backed off.

He rubbed his chin. "It seems to me a parent has to be around enough so there's the opportunity for the child to bring up what's on their mind."

"I'm not following." Marigold sounded more perplexed than irritated by the direction of the conversation.

Cade wasn't sure where he was going with this, either. He pulled off a boot and tossed it to the floor. It landed with a loud thud on the hardwood.

Alice had been right. He sucked at communicating. But he'd started down this road and saw no choice but to plow ahead.

"Let's say a parent wants to spend quality hours with their kid. The mom or dad schedules that quality time when it works for them, not for the child. I don't know about you, but talking never happened on a schedule for me. Our best conversations usually occurred when my dad and I were in the driveway, washing the car or shooting some hoops."

Marigold took a moment—one that felt like an eternity—to respond.

"It was like that at my house, too," she finally admitted. "All the serious talks with my mother happened when we were baking cookies."

Lurching ahead, he thought, though the conversation reminded him of an easily stalled engine you had to keep infusing with fuel.

"How about your father? Was he around much?" Cade hoped Marigold would pick up this ball and run with it. Or at least take it a few steps.

"My dad was always someone we could go to if we had a problem or concern." Marigold paused. "The only time he was out of reach was when my mother was first diagnosed with leukemia."

Cade heard the hitch in her voice. He didn't have to be in the same room with her to know the pain of that time was written across her face. "How old were you?"

"Twelve. The doctors gave her a ten percent chance to live to the weekend." This time Marigold's voice broke. She cleared her throat.

"I'd just finished up my first year of middle school. The diagnosis—and the horrible prognosis—took us all by surprise. She'd always been so healthy."

He knew Marigold's mother hadn't died all that long ago, so she'd obviously beaten those odds. "She survived."

"The doctors were amazed. They called Sarah Bloom their ninja warrior." Despite the thickness in her voice, pride seeped through. "She fought hard. My dad's entire focus was supporting her in her battle with cancer."

"What about you and your sisters?"

"We took over the household chores. We did all we could to make her life, his life, easier." Marigold sighed. "The solid foundation they'd built for us all those years—and our faith—helped us cope. But our world, the one we'd known, no longer existed. The two people we depended on for support and guidance now needed us."

"It must have been difficult." His heart ached for that young girl of twelve. "At least you and your sisters had each other."

"You'd think." Marigold gave a humorless chuckle. "Actually, we all struggled. Ami, who until that summer had never given my folks a second's worth of trouble, got a little wild."

"Ami?"

The surprise in his voice had her laughing.

"Difficult to believe, but true." Her voice turned serious. "She began staying out late and partying. One night she hit a tree with her car. Her friend was seriously injured. It was a very scary time for my parents."

Not only for the parents, Cade thought, but for a young sister watching a revered older sibling spiral out of control.

"How did Fin react to your mother's illness?"

The silence returned for a long moment.

"Fin changed. At first she and Jeremy grew even closer. He was such a comfort to her. But within weeks, something happened."

Cade waited for her to continue.

"Fin began spending more time in her room, which wasn't like her at all. Then I watched her begin to distance herself from Jeremy."

"How did she do that?"

"She took me on dates with them." Marigold gave a little laugh. "I didn't want to go, but she insisted."

Cade thought back to his senior year and the girls he'd dated. "Didn't Jeremy find it odd his girlfriend was bringing her little sister along?"

"She always had some reason that made sense. And he was preoccupied with getting ready to go away to college. Then she ended it. Everyone was shocked. No one more than Jeremy."

The detective in Cade thought Fin's actions sounded like someone with a guilty conscience. But that didn't much matter now. He was simply grateful the conversation was finally flowing smoothly. "What about Prim?"

"Prim stayed steady." The tension in Marigold's voice eased. "She and her first husband, Rory, were dating back then. He gave her a lot of support."

Who gave you support? Cade wanted to ask Marigold.

As if she sensed the question, Marigold exhaled a ragged breath. "Me, I muddled through. Sometimes I think I'm still muddling."

"During the time I spent in the Marines, I lost several good friends in battle." Cade glanced out the window of his room at the falling snow. "Losing people you care about changes you. The experience can cause you to close in, to not let yourself care, or if you do, to not care too much. It's a protective thing. If I don't care, I won't feel pain when that person is gone."

"Self-preservation," Marigold agreed.

"True. The problem is, unless we let ourselves care, unless we open our hearts completely, we run the risk of missing out on the best life has to offer."

Chapter Fourteen

"I don't know how Ami gets up this early," Marigold grumbled as she took her place behind the bakery counter. "It about killed me."

"Poor Marigold. My heart breaks." Hadley grinned. "You really didn't have to show up until right before we opened."

"I know, but other than when I'm back at Christmas, I don't get to do a lot of baking. Helping you was fun." Knowing they wouldn't unlock the doors for another fifteen minutes, Marigold relaxed and took another sip of the strong chicory blend her sister now stocked.

"I'm glad you enjoyed it. It was fun for me, too." Hadley leaned her back against the spotless stainless steel counters, keeping one eye on the ovens. "I appreciate you handling the counter today. I've got some special orders being picked up this afternoon that will keep me busy in the back."

"We close at four today, right?" Marigold thought she had the winter hours down but knew Ami and Hadley had been playing around with them.

"Nine until four. Fridays through Mondays." Glancing at the clock, Hadley drained her cup, then straightened. "Looks like it's go time."

"Think we'll be busy?" From the amount of bakery goods, it seemed as if Hadley was expecting hordes of customers today.

"Oh, my." Hadley gave a little laugh. "Just wait and see."

By three o'clock, Marigold was regretting her choice of footwear. While her ankle boots were absolutely adorable, they weren't meant for hours of standing.

Thankfully, she'd been able to wear jeans. Even better, Ami didn't make her employees wear white frilly aprons like the kind Anita forced on her Crumb and Cake staff. Instead, her sister had presented her with a pink, long-sleeved tee with "Baking Up Some Love," the slogan of Blooms Bake Shop, emblazoned across the front.

Taking advantage of a break in the crowds, Marigold was wiping down the tables when the bells over the door jingled. She looked up in time to see Lindsay Lohmeier stride into the shop.

Lindsay had been Ami's friend since childhood. None of the Bloom sisters held the fact she was also Anita's daughter against her.

A warm smile lifted Lindsay's lips when she spotted Marigold. "I wondered how long it'd take before our paths would cross."

The blonde crossed the shop in several long strides to give Marigold a hug. "When you left after Christmas I was certain I wouldn't see you again until Ami and Beck's baby was born."

"Things change." Marigold forced a casual tone. "I'm just in Good Hope temporarily."

"Still, I'm glad. And did I hear you might be doing some—?" Lindsay made snipping motions with her fingers.

"That's right." Though the thought of working under the dancing scissors sign still made her cringe, she reminded herself it was temporary means to an end. "I'll be working out of the old Carly's Cut and Curl location. By appointment only."

"I'll be calling." Lindsay lifted a strand of blonde hair going dull. "I desperately need highlights for spring."

Lindsay let the piece of hair drop and turned her attention to the bake case.

Everyone who walked into the bakery displayed that same look of awe when seeing the extensive pastry selection. After giving Lindsay a few seconds to drool, Marigold smiled. "You know you can't go wrong, no matter what you choose."

Lindsay continued to hesitate, tapping a finger against her coral-colored mouth. "I'm tempted to go with my fav, the lemon-blueberry scone. I absolutely adore Ami's scones. But I'm feeling adventurous today, so give me a kouign amann and a medium vanilla latte."

"Whole or skim milk?"

"Whole." Lindsay laughed. "Told you I was feeling adventurous."

Slipping behind the counter, Marigold winked. "In that case I'll even add extra whipped cream."

Instead of taking a seat, Lindsay remained by the counter, breaking off tiny caramelized pieces of the kouign amann that Marigold had plated for her.

"I'll count the indulgence as my reward for going above and beyond this morning."

"What did you do?" Marigold knew Lindsay worked as a floral designer at the Enchanted Florist down the block but wasn't sure all that job involved.

"Our Internet had issues this morning. Shirley, who has absolutely zero technical skills, kept insisting I fix it." Lindsay opened her mouth, mimicking a silent scream while her hands pulsed in the air. "I was on the phone all morning with technical support. We finally determined it was a router problem. They're bringing out a new one this afternoon."

"I'm impressed." Marigold wondered if Lindsay might be able to help her. "Do you know a lot about computers?"

Lindsay's lips lifted in a wry smile. "I'd say I know just enough to be dangerous."

"The reason I ask is I'm looking for someone with good web skills. I need to make some changes to my website." Marigold poured the frothy milk from the small stainless pitcher into the cup already containing the espresso. "The salon I'm planning to contact will check me out on all social media sites, so I'd like someone to get right on it and do a good job."

"That definitely wouldn't be me." Lindsay's gaze turned thoughtful. Then she snapped her fingers. "Braxton."

Marigold handed Lindsay the latte. "Your nephew?"

"The kid is a whiz with computers." Lindsay took a sip, sighed. "Whole milk makes such a difference. How much do I owe you?"

She rang up the purchase while Lindsay settled on one of the stools by the counter.

As they were alone in the shop, Marigold dropped on the stool next to Lindsay. "Tell me about Braxton."

Lindsay angled her head. "Have you met him?"

"I ran into him recently on the sidewalk." Marigold knew that wasn't quite accurate. Braxton had run into *her*. "He seemed nice."

"His appearance turns some adults off, especially the judgmental types. But Brax is very responsible. If you hire him, he'll do the job and do it right. And he can really use the money." Concern darkened Lindsay's eyes. "Cassie struggles financially. The boys are on their own for everything that isn't an absolute necessity."

Marigold could sympathize. With four children and a schoolteacher breadwinner, there hadn't been a lot of cash for extras in the Bloom household, either. But Cassie and her children's situation sounded especially dire. "I understand your mom and Cassie are estranged."

"They're both incredibly stubborn." Lindsay sighed. "My mother has amazing grandkids, but because of their feud, Cassie won't allow her to have contact with them. Dakota is a wonderful girl, so smart and personable. Braxton is a whiz with computers, and K.T. is an amazing painter."

Marigold couldn't hide her surprise. "He paints houses?"

"No." Lindsay laughed. "He's an artist."

"That's impressive."

"K.T. is very talented." Lindsay lifted her cup and took another sip. "His stuff is a bit abstract for my tastes, but really compelling."

Marigold tapped a fingernail against the counter. "Izzie Deshler, the one who did the mural in Muddy Boots, is looking for local artists for an alley art project. K.T. might want to contact her. Beck will have Izzie's contact information."

"I'll mention it to him. Thanks." Lindsay stood. "I better head back before my boss starts screaming my name up and down Main Street."

Before Lindsay could take a step, the bells jingled and Steve stepped into the shop.

Marigold's welcoming smile faltered. After plastering it firmly back in place, she hurried across the dining area to greet her dad. "What a nice surprise. I thought you'd be at the high school."

"It's Saturday." He shot her a teasing smile, though his eyes remained watchful. "Even teachers need a break now and then."

Marigold might have mentioned something about last night, but when Steve turned and greeted Lindsay, it reminded her they weren't alone.

"It's good to see you again, Mr. Bloom." To Marigold's surprise, Lindsay stepped forward to give Steve a quick hug. "I understand you and Mom went skating last night."

"We did." Steve shot a quick sideways glance at Marigold. "Though I'm not sure Anita ever got on the ice."

"Let me guess." Lindsay cocked her head and pressed one finger against her lips. "She sat on a bench the entire time drinking coffee and complaining about the cold."

"Close." Steve gave a little chuckle. "Only it was hot cocoa. The Seedlings were selling it as a fundraiser."

"It's nice to see her getting out, even if she's not fully participating." Lindsay's cheery expression sobered. "After she and Bernie split, she threw herself into her work. I'm glad to see her having fun. I know she's really looking forward to the Valentine's dance. She and I went shopping last week in Milwaukee for a dress."

"I bet that was fun," Marigold drawled.

Lindsay chuckled. "She's so picky that shopping with her can be a chore. But five minutes after walking into her favorite store, we found 'the one.' Wait until you see the red dress, Mr. Bloom. It looks amazing on her."

Steve shifted from foot to foot as if his favorite Rockports had suddenly turned uncomfortable. "Anita looks nice in whatever she wears."

"Lindsay was telling me Braxton is not only a great skater, he's good with computers. I'm going to see if he's interested in updating my personal website." Marigold was determined to get the subject off Anita before the conversation became any more awkward. "And did you know K.T. is an up-and-coming artist?"

"Lila Nordstrom, the art teacher, may have mentioned that fact once in passing." Steve spoke absently, his glance straying to the clock on the wall proclaiming It's Cupcake Time. "Any chance I can get a cherry Danish and a coffee?"

The clock began to chime, and Lindsay gave a little yelp. "I need to scoot."

Her father stepped to the door and opened it for the young woman. "It was good to see you."

"Keep my mother in line." With a cheery wave, Lindsay hurried through the door. "Though I'm not sure that's possible."

The words, tossed over Lindsay's shoulder, hung in the air long after she'd disappeared from sight.

Marigold turned toward the counter. "Coffee and Danish coming right up."

But when she stepped past her father, his fingers closed around her arm. Her first impulse was to jerk back. She went with the second.

Marigold froze, turning her head slowly to meet his gaze. She offered a polite smile, the kind you'd give a stranger. "Would you like to change your order?"

"Forget the order." He released his hold on her arm, a look of abject weariness on his face. "I'd like it if we could talk."

She lifted a brow. "Isn't that what we're doing?"

"Oh, sweetheart." He sighed the endearment, and Marigold saw pain in those familiar hazel eyes. The love mixing with the pain in those amber depths had her feeling like a brat.

"I'll get you the coffee and Danish, and some for myself, as well." Going with instinct, Marigold stepped to him. Wrapping her arms around his lean frame, she rested her cheek against his chest as she'd done so many times when she was young and in need of comfort. "I love you, Dad."

"Love you, too, baby."

The quiver in his voice had Marigold closing her eyes and tightening her hold. After a long moment, she stepped back.

"Have a seat." Marigold gestured to a table in a corner. She turned the sign on the door to closed before slipping behind the counter.

By the time she sat across from her father, pastries and coffee mugs between them on the cobalt-blue table, Marigold felt steadier. Still, she took a gulp of the steaming brew as one might toss back a whiskey before heading into battle.

This wasn't a battle, she reminded herself. This was a Danish and conversation with her father.

"I'm sorry about last night," Steve began. "I—"

"It's over." Marigold covered his hand with hers. "Let's not rehash the past."

"We need to talk." His firm tone brooked no argument. "When Anita said that about you, ah, sleeping with Cade, I was shocked. You're my daughter, my baby girl."

Heat crept up her neck. Was there anything more awkward than having your *father* bring up your sex life? "You don't have—"

"Cade explained it perfectly. I understand because the connection you two share is the same as what I had with your mother." His lips lifted in a lopsided grin. "We couldn't keep our hands off each other."

Yes, Marigold thought. *Having your father allude to his sex life was worse. Much worse.*

"But I digress." Her father's expression sobered and she saw the lines of strain on his face. "Anita had no right to say what she did. I had no right to press the issue."

Silence settled over the table.

Marigold's fingers began to shred the napkin in her lap. What did he expect her to say? She searched for the right words, ones that would assuage his guilt but not prolong the discussion. Her brain refused to cooperate.

Steve cleared his throat. "I came here today to ask your forgiveness. I hurt you. That's something I never want to do, and I'm sorry."

"It's not you who should be asking for forgiveness." The words popped out before Marigold could stop them. "It's her. I don't even know why you're with her. None of us do. She's an evil, vile woman who delights in bringing pain to others with her words."

Her father flinched as if he'd been struck, then took off his glasses and wiped a hand across his eyes. "I didn't realize you felt so strongly . . ."

"Why are you with her?" Marigold shoved back her chair with a clatter and flung out her hands. "Just tell me that. Because I don't understand."

"Sit down, sweetheart." Steve gestured to the chair she'd nearly toppled. "And I'll tell you."

Marigold didn't want to talk. She wanted her father to eat his Danish, drink his coffee, and leave her alone. Sometime during the conversation her heart had swelled to near bursting, and the ache was making her weepy. Besides, what did it matter what she thought of Anita?

He didn't tell her who to date.

She didn't have the right to tell him.

Marigold massaged the back of her tight neck with one hand, wishing she'd gotten more sleep last night. Thinking clearly was always more difficult without a good night's rest. She would tell her father to go, that she needed time to work through this in her head, that they would talk later.

Then she looked into his eyes and saw the bald hope.

She sat down.

Steve took a sip of coffee. He reached out a hand as if to close over the one she'd rested on the table, but pulled back at the last second and wrapped his fingers around the mug instead.

"I've known Anita for years. Sarah and I socialized often with her and her husband. After Richard passed away, your mother and Anita continued to go shopping and get together for coffee." Steve sat back, his eyes turning distant with memories. "After she married Bernie, neither of us saw much of her. Then they divorced and Sarah died . . ."

Her father's gaze dropped to the pastry. Instead of simply lifting it to his lips, he made a big show of cutting a precise slice out of the piece. When he finally looked up, his eyes held a sheen. "I was lonely. All of you girls were grown and busy with your own lives. I have friends and colleagues in Good Hope, but I felt alone and so very lonely. I don't know if you can understand what that's like but—"

"I know what it's like to be lonely." Marigold thought of her life in Chicago. Such a busy city. Everyone so intent on making their mark.

Like her father, she'd had friends and colleagues but no one to fill the empty place in her heart.

Jason had been so focused on building his career they'd ended up seeing each other only on weekends. It was no wonder they hadn't formed a true connection. Even as the thought struck, she realized they could have seen each other every day and never had the connection she'd formed with Cade in only a few weeks.

"Being with Anita has been nice. We know many of the same people, and we both enjoy having a partner for social activities." A shadow passed over his expression. "She and I had a heart-to-heart last night. I told her I can't be with someone who isn't good to my girls."

Though hope surged, Marigold kept her voice level. "Are you telling me you broke up with her?"

"That was my intent. She broke down and cried. She begged me to give her a second chance." Her father took off his glasses and scrubbed a hand over his face. "She told me she would change, promised she would change. I told her I needed to think about it."

He didn't say it, but Marigold knew she had only to say the word and Anita would be history. As tempted as she was to do just that, this wasn't her decision to make.

"Everyone deserves a second chance." Marigold wasn't sure where the words came from, but the voice sounded very much like her own.

Her father's eyes widened. "You think so?"

Marigold reached across the table. She took his hand in hers. It was a strong hand, just like the man himself. Strong with a deep sense of fairness and honor. He wasn't perfect, but then who was? "A wise man once told me everyone deserves a second chance."

The relief that surged across his face told her he hadn't been ready, not yet anyway, to sever that link with Anita. Marigold understood. She'd been there with Jason. She'd hung on to a relationship that no longer worked, reluctant to cut that last tie. The good news was, once she *had* been ready, she'd been able to move on with no regrets, no wondering what might have been.

"I wanted to wait to discuss the matter with your sisters until I'd gotten your thoughts." He pushed to his feet. "I'm going to speak with Ami now. Then Prim. I'll call Fin this evening. She likes to be kept in the loop."

Her sisters, Marigold thought, were going to kick her to the curb when they heard she'd given her blessing to their father continuing to date I-Need-a-Man. She only hoped he understood she hadn't given him her blessing to *marry* the woman. "Dad."

He turned, a question in his gaze.

"What Cade said about connections, well, it was profound." She stepped close. Despite the seriousness of what she was about to say, Marigold nearly smiled when she caught a whiff of Polo, his signature scent. "You don't marry someone just because you're lonely and hope to fill a void in your life. You only marry them if there's a strong connection, a love for the ages, like the one you had with Mom. Otherwise, you end up being alone, even if you do marry."

Her father pondered the words for a moment. "That's why you didn't marry Jason."

Marigold found herself nodding, though she knew the issues between her and the attorney went much deeper than a lack of connection.

"And," Steve moved to the door and opened it, then looked back at her, "that's why you're with Cade."

He was out the door and gone before she could utter a single word.

Chapter Fifteen

The next morning, instead of attending church and meeting her family at Muddy Boots for breakfast, Marigold stayed home and focused on getting the wording perfect on several e-mail queries to the salons in New York City that seemed a good fit. She'd follow up with a personal call, but accomplishing the task made her feel as if she was making progress.

Seeing movement in the right direction was especially important today. This afternoon she and her family were scheduled to meet at Carly's Cut and Curl. As the place had been empty for several months, some general cleaning was necessary before she opened for business tomorrow.

Though she needed the money, just the thought of picking up her scissors at such a place made her stomach churn. Heck, she'd been able to cut hair better than Carly when she'd been in high school. The cash she'd gotten from her friends for styling their hair had kept her in designer jeans.

No designer jeans today. Marigold glanced down. For today's fun adventure she'd pulled out an old pair of Levi's and coupled them with a long-sleeved tee she should have gotten rid of years ago. She slowed her steps down the stairs, in no hurry to reach the salon.

Marigold couldn't help but wonder what she'd done to deserve such misfortune. She'd been a superb stylist and a loyal friend to Steffan. She hadn't deserved to be fired and then blackballed.

It was almost as if the fates had come together and conspired to bring her down a notch—or ten—in order to teach her some kind of lesson. Force her back to where she'd started to show her she wasn't such hot stuff? Make her see she would never be as smart and accomplished as her sisters? That her dreams were foolish and success would never be hers?

"No."

She hadn't realized she'd spoken aloud until the shouted word echoed in the empty stairwell.

Marigold paused and took a deep, steadying breath. She lifted her chin, squared her shoulders. While she might be down at the moment, this dip was a mere bump in the road of life. Maybe she was here to learn some lesson. She'd always believed no experience was wasted as long as you learned and grew from it.

This might also be a lesson in perseverance, in staying a course. Working out of this salon would also be a lesson in humility. Her lips quirked upward. A *huge* lesson in humility.

By the time she reached the Cut and Curl, she'd nearly convinced herself that working in such a setting was no big deal. A means to an end. The fact that no lights were on told her she was the first of her family to arrive.

That was good. Very good.

When she'd been inside before, it was only for a minute. Just long enough to see there was a shampoo bowl and chair and to tell Beck the space would work. That day, she hadn't thought of the place as hers.

No matter how much she mentally prepared herself, she had the feeling that accepting that this was where she'd be working for the next few weeks was likely to be a jolt. She wanted to experience that jolt without witnesses.

As she turned the heavy copper key in the lock and stepped inside, Marigold realized she hadn't been prepared. Not for this. It was as if all her worst fears were here, taunting her. She barely heard the ugly blue door shutting behind her.

Taking a ragged breath, Marigold took in the dusty white eyelet curtains at the window, the dull and scratched hardwood floor, and the wall mirror with a crack in the lower right corner. And the wallpaper . . .

Marigold shuddered. That long-ago day in the principal's office when her father had looked sick and her mother had cried, she'd promised herself just "getting by" would never be her lot in life.

This was worse than any "getting by" she could have imagined . . .

Walking to the mirror behind the blue shampoo bowl, Marigold stared at her reflection. Though dressing up to do heavy cleaning made no sense, as she gazed at herself now and saw the hair twisted in a messy mass on the top of her head, she wished she'd made the effort. All she needed was a pink smock with her name embroidered on it to make the image of a small-town failure complete.

Hot tears stung the backs of her eyes.

"Sorry I'm late." The door that she'd failed to lock behind her creaked open and Cade pushed inside, his hands balancing several pizza boxes. "I stopped to grab a couple of pies. Since it's close to dinnertime, I figured we might get hungry."

Marigold turned from the mirror. Gazing down, she blinked rapidly and pretended to be consumed with unfastening the buttons of her coat. When she released the last one, she had her emotions back under control. "That was nice of you."

Cade flashed a smile. After shrugging off his jacket, he set the boxes on a countertop topped with a blue faux-marble pattern. "I'm a nice guy."

Marigold knew he was probably expecting a pithy retort, but at the moment she didn't have a single ounce of pithy in her.

"I missed you, Goldilocks."

She didn't protest when he pulled her into his arms but rested her head against his broad chest, finding comfort in the steady beat of his heart against her ear.

He rubbed his hands up and down her back in long, soothing strokes. "Bad day?"

"You mean other than the fact I'm going to be working out of this shit hole?"

Her mother would have washed her mouth out with soap for using such language. Cade only chuckled. "It's not so bad."

She jerked back and made a sweeping gesture with one hand. "Take a good look, Mr. Trained Observer, and say that again with a straight face."

Cade did as she requested, inspecting the interior with the same care he'd give a crime scene. His lips twitched when his gaze settled on the prancing poodle wallpaper.

He shot her a quizzical look. "What do poodles in rhinestone collars have to do with a hair salon? Did Carly operate a dog grooming business out of here as well?"

Marigold couldn't help it. The image his words conjured up, coupled with the light blue wallpaper with the frolicking white poodles, was so ridiculous she had to laugh. Either that or cry.

Everyone said laughter was good for the soul, and it must be true, because she felt her mood lift enough to snag a piece of pizza.

By the time Ami and Prim and the rest of her family strolled through the door, Marigold felt centered again.

"Where's Max?" Beck asked, taking one of the caddies filled with cleaning supplies Prim offered him.

"He's home with the boys." Prim's smile was rueful. "The twins' idea of cleaning is to get a sponge soaking wet and toss it at each other."

"Will you look at that wallpaper." Beck gave a chuckle and shifted his gaze to his wife. "What does that remind you of?"

"The wallpaper in Muddy Boots when you bought it." Ami must have noticed Marigold's confusion because she turned to her sister. "It had little coffeepots all over it."

"Mud-brown and mustard-yellow coffeepots." Beck shook his head. "Unbelievable."

"I thought it was kind of cute," Ami teased.

"No one thought that wallpaper was cute." Beck slipped an arm around his wife's waist and pulled her to him. "Not even you, darlin'."

"Okay, maybe it was a little ugly." Ami brushed a quick kiss across Beck's cheek. "But look at Muddy Boots now. It's gorgeous. Sometimes when something starts off . . ."

"Ugly." Prim supplied.

"Yes, ugly. Well, it makes you appreciate the changes even more."

Pollyanna has nothing on Ami, Marigold thought.

Their mother had loved the movie *Pollyanna*, and she and her girls had watched the Hayley Mills version at least once a year. They'd even played the glad game.

"Well, I'm *glad* the place isn't any larger," Marigold heard herself say. "Because then there would be even more poodles staring at me."

"I'm glad the eyelet curtains aren't something you wanted to save." Ami jumped into the game that was second nature to her. "Because no curtains will allow natural sunlight to brighten the room."

Prim gazed from one sister to the other, then a smile slowly spread across her face. "I'm glad we had a mother who taught us to always look on the bright side, to make the best of any situation."

"I wish I could have known her," Beck said simply.

"You would have liked her." Marigold sighed. "Everyone did."

For a moment no one spoke, then Prim handed a caddy to Ami. "These are all green, pregnancy-approved products."

"Do I get pregnancy-approved products, too?" Cade joked.

"We all get them," Prim said, her expression serious. "The way I see it, none of us should be exposed to harsh chemicals."

The door creaked open once again and everyone turned.

"Sorry we're late." Steve hesitated, his gaze going to Marigold. "I swung by and picked up Anita. She wanted to help."

Marigold hadn't seen Anita since Friday night at the pond and would have been happy never to see her again. But she *had* given her dad the green light on the second chance. And Anita had shown up dressed to work.

"Thanks for coming." Marigold put a note of warmth in her tone and was rewarded by the flash of pleasure in her father's eyes.

Her sisters scattered as if fearful the piranha might want to start up a conversation with them. Anita didn't seem to notice as her gaze remained fixed on Marigold.

The older woman took several steps, closing the distance between them.

"I'm very sorry about what I said Friday night. There's no excuse for my actions. I want to assure you that type of behavior won't happen again." Anita's voice trembled slightly. "I gave your father my word. Now I'm giving you mine. I hope you can forgive me and we can start over."

When Anita held out her hand, Marigold took it.

Second chances.

New opportunities.

Forgiveness.

Was one of these the lesson she was in Good Hope to learn?

"I find it strange," Marigold mused as she turned to lock the door of the salon, "the connection I see between this place and some of the people I knew in Chicago."

Cade pulled his brows together. "I don't follow."

"Sometimes the shine only goes so deep." For several heartbeats her gaze remained focused on the door's peeling blue paint. "Sometimes it isn't there at all."

Cade still wasn't certain he understood, but he was happy her mood had shifted from sad to philosophic. When he'd first arrived at the salon, he'd seen the distress in her eyes. All he'd wanted to do was hold her tight and let her lean on him. But then her sisters had arrived and she'd put on her strong face.

The wallpaper talk had lightened the mood. And when Ami and Prim had mentioned being *glad* about different things, Marigold had seemed to settle.

"What was all that *glad* talk about?"

As the night was unusually warm, they decided to take a walk instead of heading straight back to her apartment.

Marigold's hand, nestled in the crook of his elbow, tightened around his bicep. "It's a game we used to play growing up. At my mother's instigation."

"We don't have to talk about it." He spoke quickly. "I was just curious."

"It's okay. It's a good memory." She gave a little laugh. "The purpose of the glad game is to look for the good in any situation."

She continued without giving him a chance to respond. "For example, you have to win an election to keep your job. What about the situation makes that a good thing?"

Cade thought for a moment.

But when he opened his mouth, she added, "Oh, and start the sentence with 'I'm glad.'"

"I'm glad," Cade paused and grinned, "that you're so bossy."

She bumped her hip into his with enough force to send them both skidding on a stray patch of ice. "I know sarcasm when I hear it, buster. If you want to get lucky tonight . . ."

He laughed and steadied her, knowing he'd get lucky either way. They couldn't seem to keep their hands off each other.

"I'm waiting." Her voice, now tinged with impatience, broke through his thoughts.

Cade moved his arm so her hand slid down. He gently locked their fingers together. "I'm glad I have to run because the experience has shown me how many friends I've made and the support I've gained in my short time in Good Hope."

"That's good." She squeezed his hand and nodded approval. "Excellent, in fact."

"What about you? What good has come from you losing your job?" The second the words left his mouth, Cade wished he could snatch them back. Spending time in Carly's Cut and Curl this evening had to have been a kick in the gut. He didn't need to keep adding to her pain with his thoughtless questions. "Forget it. Let's focus on the beautiful weather. Can you believe how warm it got today?"

Though it was only January, the balmy night and mild breeze from the bay made it feel almost like spring. He thought how nice it would be when it was warm enough to take Marigold to the Flying Crane. They'd sit on the large deck overlooking the water, a plate of nachos and a couple of beers between them. Maybe she'd have one of their fancy margaritas. They'd laugh and talk and . . .

Cade reined in the fanciful thoughts, reminding himself that by the time the weather cooperated enough to eat on the deck, Marigold would be long gone.

"You don't have to coddle me." Her eyes turned soft and she gave his arm a squeeze. "I'll play the game."

The night sky was clear with only a sliver of a moon overhead, a perfect backdrop to showcase the twinkling stars to full advantage.

But Cade wasn't looking at the sky. He was looking at Marigold, with her curly crop of blonde hair spilling out from a simple black hat, brows now furrowed in concentration.

"I'm glad I lost my job because it gave me the opportunity to spend time with my family . . . and with you." A gentle heat filled the air between them. "If I hadn't returned to Good Hope, I'd never have gotten to know you. That would have been my loss."

Hope rose inside him, and the force was so strong, the words he'd been keeping under tight control spilled out. "What can I do to convince you to stay?"

The question dangled naked in the still night air.

Marigold stopped walking. With a slow, calculated movement, she turned and faced him.

"I'd like you to consider staying. See if you could find success here." Despite his efforts to keep his tone casual, Cade heard the tension. He could bullet point all the positives for her to stay in Good Hope, but they wouldn't be any she didn't already know. That left speaking from the heart. "What we have is—"

He hesitated. Would the word *magical* sound lame? And what if the connection was only on his side? Maybe what he considered special wasn't special at all, at least not to her.

His momentary pause gave her the opening he hadn't wanted to give.

"We agreed going in our relationship would be temporary." Her voice reminded him of piano wire, wound a little too tight. "If what we have now isn't enough or isn't working for you, just tell me and we can end this now."

Panic flared, but he ruthlessly stomped it down. In the Marine Corps, he'd learned to keep his emotions under control, especially in difficult situations. When he spoke, his tone was easy. "I'd like you to stay. That's all. I don't expect that to happen."

He must have sounded convincing, because she relaxed and resumed walking. She even took his arm.

"I don't know if I told you I e-mailed a couple of salons in New York City. There's one in the West Village I really like. It has a great rep. Not only is it color based, I've heard from several of my connections that Angelo is actively seeking someone who has a special interest in clients with curly hair. If I could pick any salon to restart my climb to the top—it would be there." The words tumbled out on a single breath. Though outwardly she appeared relaxed, there was a tension in her grip that hadn't been there before. "On the other hand, Fin is still pushing me to move to LA."

"Are any salons in California on your short list?" Wherever Marigold chose to settle, Cade wanted her happy.

"Several possibilities *might* work." Doubt shimmered in her voice. "Fin also has contacts at various studios. She's confident she can get me studio work. Marigold Bloom. Hairstylist to the stars."

Her laugh held a brittle edge.

"Is that what you want?"

"It's what Fin wants." A shadow passed over her face. "She's pushing hard."

"She wants you close." Cade told himself he shouldn't resent Fin's efforts. After all, hadn't he tried to do the same?

"Yes." Marigold's unhappy tone had his heart lurching. "She's used to getting what she wants."

"Not this time." His tone was a gruff rasp.

She angled her head.

"I'm certain at the end of the day, what matters to her is that you're happy."

The doubtful expression on Marigold's pretty face told him she wasn't convinced.

Cade leaned over and kissed her, finding her mouth warm and sweet. "Trust me on this. When you love someone, it's their happiness that matters, not your own."

Chapter Sixteen

Marigold planned to ditch Cade once they reached her apartment. On their walk down to the waterfront, she'd received a text from Fin. Apparently her contact at the studio had told her they were "very interested." Marigold could almost feel the noose tightening about her neck.

The knowledge that Fin's roommate had moved out a couple of months earlier, leaving space in her apartment for Marigold, only added to the pressure. She needed to decompress, to center herself.

Yes, she had a lot on her plate.

As if he sensed her stress, Cade kept the conversation light on the way home. They climbed the steps to her apartment in silence.

Tell him good night and shut the door.

Cade leaned against the doorjamb and the musky scent of his cologne teased her nostrils. As desire pooled low in her belly, the coldness that had wrapped around her like an icy glove began to thaw. She remembered how good it felt to have his arms were around her. When he was holding her close, she didn't have to think. All she had to do was feel.

"I'm not ready for the evening to end." His low voice held a sexy huskiness and a question.

Logic said to turn him away. Somehow, despite her best efforts to keep him at arm's length, he'd managed to creep under her skin. The burgeoning closeness posed a danger.

Not if it was only about sex.

Before her brain could counter the point, Marigold jerked him inside and kicked the door shut. She fastened her mouth to his in a ferocious kiss.

He answered in kind, raking his fingers through her hair and pulling her so close she felt his arousal.

"I want it fast and hard," she ordered when they came up for air.

"Hard is never a problem when I'm around you." Cade gave a half laugh as he fumbled with her clothes.

She pushed his hands away. "You take yours. I'll take mine. Faster that way."

Though the race had only started, Marigold's breath already came in short puffs.

There had been too much talk of family and love this evening. What she and Cade shared was all sex and passion, the here and now.

A woman didn't need to think, only had to feel, when the sex was hard and fast. That's the way she wanted it, not slow and dreamy.

Seconds after their clothes hit the floor, her mouth was hot on his. They wouldn't make it to the bed. Fine with her. They tumbled onto the sofa, all mouths and tongues and groping hands. Her world became a kaleidoscope of pleasure, driving all thoughts from her mind.

Yet, with him, the whirling spiral of emotions and sensations seemed profoundly different. There was chemistry between them, an intimacy and a spark she'd never experienced before with anyone else.

Marigold rode the building pressure until their bodies were damp and sweaty, and still she clung to him. And when the combination of emotion and physical sensation sent her crashing over the edge, it seemed right to be in his arms when the world exploded.

Afterward, Marigold simply lay there, sated and slightly dazed, naked except for the socks she hadn't taken time to pull off. Cade's warm body blanketed hers. When she finally opened her eyes, it was to the feel of his lips against her neck and to the murmur of words she couldn't quite make out. Somehow, they still managed to make her uneasy.

Pressing her hands flat against his chest, she pushed. "You're squishing me."

Brushing a quick kiss across her mouth, he lifted himself up to his forearms and studied her, gray eyes boring into blue.

She shifted her gaze, worried what he might see if he looked too closely. "That was fun, but—"

"Grab your clothes and get out?"

Marigold felt her face heat. "I've got a busy day tomorrow."

"Understood."

He rolled off her with the ease of an athlete.

When he began pulling on clothes, she sat up and wrapped the cotton throw from the back of the sofa around her. "I'm not tossing you out."

Cade looked up from lacing his boots.

Marigold surged to her feet.

"I'm not tossing you out." She repeated the words, but this time her voice cracked.

"Hey." Cade moved to her, then cupped her face in his hand. "You're shaking. What's wrong?"

Marigold realized with sudden horror it was true. Worse yet, she couldn't seem to stop.

Ignoring her protests, he wrapped his strong arms around her and held her, simply held her close against him until the trembling subsided.

"I won't ask for more than you're willing to give." His hands moved slowly up and down her back in gentle, soothing strokes.

The only light in the room came from the streetlamps down below and from the moon, casting its golden glow though the slats of the blinds.

Marigold knew she should push him away. Now that her brain was firing on all circuits, she realized that's what she'd tried—and failed—to do tonight with sex.

Tears stung the backs of her eyes. This time, instead of pushing him away, she buried her face against his chest and held tight.

She could no longer deny the obvious.

She'd fallen in love with Cade Rallis.

Marigold's head jerked up at the sound of the bells over the doors ringing. Business this Tuesday morning had been brisk.

Sticking her phone in her pocket, Marigold stood. "You boys hold down the fort."

Slouched in a chair in the back room of the salon, K.T. didn't even glance up from his drawing pad. The brothers were out of school this week for semester break. She'd discovered them outside her front door when she arrived to open the shop.

K.T. had arrived with his brother, bringing a sketch pad with him. Apparently Izzie wanted to see some samples of his work. Though he'd taken pictures of a few previous projects, he was determined to show her a couple of new ideas.

Currently in the process of refining her web page, Braxton remained totally focused on her laptop screen. It hadn't taken Marigold long to discover the boy was a perfectionist. Only after grilling her for several minutes had he started the updates.

"Do you need anything from me?" Marigold paused at the door separating the back office from the salon.

Braxton waved a dismissive hand and changed the color of the header, then frowned and promptly changed it back.

K.T. lifted his head from his sketch pad. "Okay if I get another soda?"

"Help yourself." Marigold straightened her black tunic and stepped from the office into the main salon, pulling the door closed behind her.

She hoped this was another walk-in, like the woman she'd finished only fifteen minutes earlier, rather than a friend wanting to chat.

The first thing she noticed was the beautiful brunette appeared dressed for a big-city shopping-and-lunch day. Thigh-high eelskin boots showed from under a plum-colored boiled-wool coat. The second was just how very out of place Whitney Chapin looked in this environment.

"Hi, Whitney." Marigold forced a bright smile. "How nice of you to stop by."

Instead of immediately returning the greeting, Whitney's assessing gaze slowly perused the interior of the shop. When her eyes finally returned to Marigold, she saw shock and dismay in the blue depths.

Somehow Marigold managed to keep her smile from slipping. "What can I do for you today?"

Whitney's gaze shifted to the poodle wallpaper, then back to Marigold.

"I need my brows shaped." Whitney waved a hand that held a diamond the size of Texas in the air. "Charlotte isn't in this week. I don't trust anyone else at Golden Door."

Marigold inclined her head. "Yet you'd trust me?"

Whitney sighed. "You worked for one of the top salons in Chicago. Besides, I'm leaving for Boca in the morning and I'm desperate. I refuse to show up with shaggy brows."

In no universe could the woman's brows be considered shaggy, though they could benefit from some fine-tuning.

"I believe I can fit you in." Marigold gestured to the chair the color of a blueberry snow cone. "Does this mean Brynn won't be at Seedlings tomorrow?"

"Why wouldn't she be there?" Whitney looked puzzled, then gave a little laugh. "Oh, now I see. You thought my daughter was coming with me."

"I assumed it was a quick family trip." Marigold should have realized there wouldn't be time for the child to go all the way to Boca and back during the rest of semester break. "But it's also nice for parents to have some alone time."

"David isn't coming." Whitney's mouth, covered in bronze sparkly lipstick, curved. Amusement filled her gaze. "This is a girls' trip. I plan to do some serious basking in the sun. I'm sick to death of this horrid snow."

Marigold kept her expression carefully blank.

She thought of Prim and Max, whose life revolved around the twins and doing things as a family. It would be no different, she knew, for Ami and Beck once the baby arrived.

But she wasn't in the judging business. She was here to provide a service and earn money.

Whitney was on her way out the door when Hadley dropped by. The two women exchanged polite smiles.

Once the door had shut, Hadley turned to Marigold, a look of surprise on her pretty face. "I thought she only saw Charlotte."

"She was desperate." Marigold's lips twisted in a wry smile. "Charlotte is out of town and Whitney needed her brows shaped before a trip to Boca."

Inclining her head, Hadley frowned. "The Chapins are headed to Boca?"

"No. Just her. Girls' trip." Marigold smiled thinly. "I'm all for people having their alone time, but I have to wonder how often she sees her child and her husband."

Hadley expelled a heavy sigh, her blue eyes resembling stormy seas. "Hardly ever."

Marigold thought of the years Prim had spent as a single parent. "At least Brynn has a good dad."

"I wanted her to have a mother, too."

Marigold, in the process of tidying up the station, frowned. "What did you say?"

Hadley leaned over to organize some magazines, her hair swinging forward, hiding her face. When she straightened, her gaze was thoughtful, her tone matter-of-fact. "What I meant to say is I believe every child deserves not only a loving father, but a mother as well. Brynn is no exception. She's been in the bakery numerous times with her dad. She seems like such a sweet little girl."

"She's a great addition to our Seedling troop." *Our.* Marigold realized with a start she'd just tied herself to Cade. *Again.*

The door to the back flung open with a clatter.

"Hey, we got—" Braxton stopped so abruptly that K.T. bumped into him.

"I believe you boys know Hadley Newhouse from the bakery."

Braxton gave a jerky nod.

"We've seen her." K.T. shoved his hands into his pockets. "How you doin'?"

"Stellar." Hadley slanted a glance at Marigold. "I know Braxton and K.T. very well. Braxton likes bear claws. K.T. prefers anything jelly filled."

"Wish I had one now." Braxton turned to Marigold. "The changes are done, if you want to see them."

"Of course I want to see." Marigold motioned to Hadley. "Come and see. Braxton is updating my website."

As they stepped into the small office area in the back, Marigold's gaze was immediately drawn to her laptop. The website he'd updated filled the screen. Only he hadn't simply updated it, he'd changed it.

As Marigold stared at the warm yet elegant—there was no other word for it—design, tears filled her eyes.

"You don't like it." Braxton's voice was flat.

"I love it." She whirled and wrapped her arms around his skinny frame, giving him a hug. "You're a genius."

His face turned red as his brother hooted.

"You did this?" Hadley turned to Braxton. "All by yourself?"

"He helped a little with the colors." Braxton jerked a thumb in his brother's direction. "He's the artist. I'm the computer genius."

"In your dreams." K.T. gave his brother a shove.

Marigold put her hands on both of the boys' shoulders, just as she'd seen her sister do countless times when the twins got rowdy. "Both of you are extremely talented."

"This is really nice." Hadley lifted her gaze from the screen. "You should show this to Ami and Beck. Their sites could use more punch."

Marigold turned to Braxton. "If they're interested, do you think you'd have time?"

She had no idea how much time Braxton's studies and other activities took up.

"I like earning money." Braxton spoke with the honesty of youth. "Heck, yeah, I'm interested."

"I'll speak with them," Marigold promised.

"Show them your site. They'll be blown away." Braxton's arrogant tone had her hiding a grin. "For now I've set up a whole new area so it won't interfere with your current website. Let me know if you want any final adjustments."

"Thank you, Braxton." Marigold met his gaze, held it. "I appreciate it."

He lifted a skinny shoulder, let it drop. "No prob."

"Your hair looks good." Hadley tossed out the compliment when the boys began gathering up their stuff.

"She did it." K.T. gestured with his head to Marigold. "We gotta go."

"Wait." Marigold scrambled for her purse. "I need to pay you." She pressed a hundred-dollar bill into the boy's hand.

Braxton's gaze dropped. His palm remained open and he simply stared.

"Is it enough? Your aunt told me what you charged but I think she must have gotten the price wrong. It was hardly anything."

K.T.'s eyes went wide at the sight of the bill sitting in his brother's outstretched hand. "You can get those shoes you've been wanting, Brax."

Braxton's hand closed convulsively over the bill. "With this much money, we can both get a pair."

For the first time Marigold notice their shoes: torn, tattered, and more suitable for summer than a Wisconsin winter. Her heart gave a lurch. "When can you finish up?"

The brothers exchanged glances. "What about Wednesday?"

Marigold shook her head. "That won't work. Do you have any other night free?"

"Mom has a new job and we have to watch the baby." Braxton spoke in a matter-of-fact tone. "How about next Saturday?"

"I need it done before then." Marigold already knew what Angelo would think if he pulled up her site and found it filled with references to the Steffan Oliver Salon.

"If you're sure you don't want any changes, I can stay and do it now." His unexpected smile startled her. "If you decide you want something changed later, you know where to find me."

"Great. Let's go with that plan."

When the boys sat back down in front of the laptop, she and Hadley returned to the salon. Hadley brushed the strands around her face back with the palm of her hand. "Charlotte didn't layer these enough for me."

"I'm not turning down business." Marigold gestured to the shampoo bowl.

Hadley shook her head. "Just cut it dry."

While Marigold preferred to cut damp hair, she draped a smock around Hadley and picked up the scissors.

"You're a good person." Hadley reached over and gave Marigold's arm a squeeze. "And you did a terrific job with their hair."

Back in Chicago Marigold had received more than her share of compliments and accolades. But this one felt more personal and sincere. "I'd never have been able to do it in Chicago. Cut their hair, I mean."

"Why not?"

"Steffan didn't allow us to comp cuts, even on our own time. The boys would never have been able to afford my prices." Marigold glanced around the tiny shop. "I guess there are some benefits to being on your own, even if you're working out of a place that looks more like a poodle parlor than a salon."

Hadley appeared to be hiding a smile. "Do you have big plans for Wednesday?"

"Not really."

"You couldn't meet the boys that night."

As she ran a comb through the strands framing Hadley's face, Marigold assessed the cut. Hadley was right. It could benefit from a little fine-tuning. "Wednesday is the Seedlings' meeting. Our goal is to get the kids caught up on badges by Valentine's Day. They're doing all this extra fundraising at various events and will be earning badges for civic involvement, so that helps."

"Do you have your dress?"

Marigold blinked. "What dress?"

Hadley rolled her eyes. "The one for the Valentine's dance at the Bayshore."

For one brief moment, Marigold considered telling Hadley she'd never been a big fan of the holiday and didn't intend to start now. But that kind of heresy might prompt a lengthy debate.

"No dress yet." Marigold waved an airy hand. "There's no rush. The dance is over a month away."

Hadley pointed to the calendar on the wall. "Less than a month."

"Anyway, back to the Seedlings." Marigold snipped a few ends, sighed. "I'd hoped Whitney was coming because we're going to need all the extra hands we can get for our unit on rock climbing."

"Did she know you wanted parents there?"

"We sent an e-mail alert out last week." Marigold paused. "I'm pretty sure David will stay."

"Sounds like a fun unit."

"If you're available, I'd love it if you'd stop by and help." Marigold offered her most beguiling smile and her tone turned persuasive. "If you do, this trim is on me."

Hadley thought for a moment, then grinned. "In that case, how can I refuse?"

Chapter Seventeen

Marigold glanced at the YMCA rock wall and felt sweat pool at the base of her spine. A knot of fear took up residence in the pit of her stomach. Because of the nature of the event, instead of holding the Seedlings' meeting at the town hall, Katie Ruth had arranged for them to meet at the Y.

The youth coordinator had also kindly solicited several of the most experienced rock climbing instructors to be on hand. But when one of them suggested Marigold go first to show how easily it could be done when you followed instructions, she'd been struck dumb.

How could she tell the kids she was terrified of heights without casting a pall over the evening's adventure? Especially when most—heck, all—of the children seemed eager and excited.

Marigold thought she'd done her part by reviewing the climbing etiquette that was the safety part of the presentation. While she was talking, her nephews had inched on their bottoms closer and closer to the climbing wall.

Apparently the part about taking turns had the twins worried they wouldn't be first. Never, ever, had Marigold thought she'd be tossed to the front of the line.

"It will be easy." Lars, a tall, blond man with a toothy grin, patted her on the shoulder. "We're going to have you use an auto belay device. The one thing to keep in mind is that when you lean back and let go, you'll briefly free fall before the device engages."

"That brief free fall is usually a favorite of the children," Anissa, the other instructor, equally blonde and smiley, confided.

Free fall?

The blood that had been slugging through Marigold's veins froze. When Lars held out the harness, perspiration dotted her brow.

She couldn't speak, she knew she couldn't, at least not without her teeth chattering, so she didn't even try. Her gaze went instinctually to Cade.

Though his face remained impassive, concern filled his eyes.

"Lars." Cade spoke in an easy, confident tone. "Before we do the demonstration, could you pass around the ropes you brought? Let's see if the Seedlings can pick out the ones showing signs of wear or damage."

Cade turned to the group of children and their parents. "The adults can help the children inspect each rope."

If Lars appeared puzzled by the request, it didn't show. He and Anissa pulled out short segments of rope from a bin and gave one to each of the children.

"Each rope segment is marked with a letter. Once you've inspected yours, please pass it to the person on your right. Make a mental note of the letter of ones you consider damaged or worn." Anissa smiled. "I'll give you a few minutes, and then we'll discuss."

While the ropes were being passed out, Cade pulled Marigold aside. "What's wrong?"

You are strong. You are mighty.

She'd been saying the words over and over in her head, but this time the mantra wasn't working.

"You can tell me," he said softly. "Anything."

Looking into those soft, gray eyes, she realized she could. She moistened her dry lips with the tip of her tongue.

"I'm afraid of heights." Shame flooded her. "So much for being strong and mighty."

A puzzled look crept into his eyes.

She gave a little laugh that held no humor. "Never mind that. I've been terrified of heights since I fell out of our backyard tree when I was five. I broke my arm."

Marigold wasn't sure what she expected Cade to say or do. Perhaps tell her to *buck up* as Jason had when he'd wanted to eat at the Michelin-starred French restaurant high above the financial district. Simply looking out the panels of glass over the city below had made her nauseous.

Or maybe Cade would encourage her to face her fears. Marigold knew that's what she should do. But she also knew there was an excellent possibility she'd humiliate herself in front of a group of second graders.

"I'll climb." He spoke gently, taking both of her hands in his, his gaze never leaving her face.

"They'll know."

"Who will know?" His voice was soft as a caress.

"The kids. Their parents. Everyone."

"It doesn't matter."

But it did, at least to her. She'd always fostered an aura of invincibility. If she tried to climb and failed, that facade would come crashing down.

"Marigold," Lars asked, "are you ready?"

Cade grabbed her arm when she turned. "You don't have to do this."

"I do." Like a condemned prisoner on her way to face the gallows, Marigold turned toward the wall. She looked up, then down, clenched her hands together to still their trembling.

Cade's jaw set in a hard line. "I'm going to—"

"I realize this is probably out of line."

Marigold shifted her gaze to Hadley. The blonde, who'd been helping David and Brynn study the ropes, stepped forward.

"I used to do a lot of climbing. It was so much fun and I've missed it terribly." The look on her pretty face was one of calculated supplication. "Would you mind terribly if I took your place? The adults won't get a chance on the wall tonight, and I'd really like to see if those old skills are still there."

Marigold gazed at the pretty blonde and knew, without a single doubt, that Hadley was her friend. Somehow she'd sensed Marigold's fear and had come riding to the rescue.

A sudden thought struck Marigold with the force of a sledgehammer. Had the terror she'd tried so hard to hide been that obvious? Marigold glanced around the room but didn't see a single pitying look.

Even Lars appeared unconcerned. "I don't care who does it, but we need to get started so each child will have time on the wall."

"Sure, Hadley." Marigold smiled, hoping her relief didn't show. "You can have my turn."

As the blonde took the harness from Lars, Cade took Marigold's hand in his. The ice in her veins began to thaw.

Hadley shot her a wink as Lars began discussing proper procedure with the Seedlings. Marigold grinned back, then glanced up at Cade.

Friends. Lovers.

Marigold had forgotten that in Good Hope you were never alone. Someone always had your back.

Sometimes the help came from the familiar and sometimes from the unexpected.

But one thing you could count on, the support would always be there.

Cade glanced over at Marigold as the children began filing from the room. "How does dinner at Muddy Boots sound?"

Marigold did a quick internal assessment. The stomach that had been twisty-tied during the meeting was now relaxed and growling. "Sounds great."

Her sister and Max had already left with the twins or she'd have asked them to join them.

Marigold spotted Hadley with David and Brynn. The blonde had been in her element on the wall. Her enthusiasm had put all the children—and parents—at ease.

"It was a good meeting." David's hand rested on his daughter's shoulder. "Brynn really enjoyed herself."

"Hadley says I have po—" Brynn's brow furrowed.

"Potential," Hadley supplied. "You were like a little monkey on that wall."

"Sure surprised me." David shook his head. "Brynn has never been one for sports."

"You just have to find the right one." Hadley and Brynn exchanged a smile.

There was something about the two of them, about the three of them, Marigold mentally corrected. They seemed more of a family unit than when Whitney was in the picture. Of course, from what Marigold had observed in her short time back, Whitney rarely was in the picture.

"Would you like to join us for dinner at Muddy Boots?" Marigold asked.

"I like Muddy Boots." Brynn looked imploringly up at her father. "I'm hungry, too."

"Honey, I think Marigold was asking Hadley to join them." David's voice was gentle, holding no reproach.

"Actually, I was asking all three of you," Marigold clarified.

"I could eat." Hadley's casual tone was at odds with her watchful eyes.

"We'd love to join you." The words had barely left David's lips when Brynn squealed. He grinned. "It appears that was the correct answer."

Although Muddy Boots was crowded, they got one of the last open tables, a rectangular six-top by the window.

"You do a good job with the children." David's gaze shifted from Cade to Marigold. "Both of you."

"I like kids." Cade's lips lifted in a wry smile. "Though with three brothers, I know boys better than girls."

"Have you thought about starting a family of your own?" Hadley asked.

"I have to have a wife first." Cade smiled. "I'm kind of a traditional guy that way."

"I'm not even going to ask you." Hadley turned to Marigold. "You're all about your career."

"You say that as if it's a bad thing." Marigold kept her tone light. Though Hadley's comment had been free of judgment, somehow it still stung.

"I didn't mean it that way." Hadley raised her hands in surrender. "I'm a firm believer that a person shouldn't enter into a marriage unless that's what they truly want. Otherwise everyone gets hurt."

"You're so good with Brynn." Marigold deliberately shifted the focus to David. "Do you and Whitney plan to have more children?"

"My mommy can't have a baby in her tummy," Brynn piped up. "The mommy that carried me in her tummy couldn't keep me, so I got adopted."

"That's so special." Marigold put her hand over Brynn's little one. "Isn't it, Hadley?"

"Yes," Hadley said with an odd catch in her voice. "Very special."

The talk quickly turned to sports and the upcoming hockey tournament without David answering her question.

"I used to enjoy skating." David took a sip of his iced tea. "I haven't been on the ice in a couple of years."

Cade leaned forward. "The Ice Holes are always looking for good skaters."

David chuckled. "I didn't say I was good."

Marigold knew all the Chapins were good skaters. You didn't grow up in Good Hope without acquiring a certain level of proficiency on skates and skis.

"You and Whitney should bring Brynn out sometime for Friday Skate Night at Rakes's Pond." Marigold unwrapped the straw for her soda. "Cade and I were there last Friday. It was a lot of fun."

"Whitney isn't much for the cold." David shrugged. "Hence the trip to Boca."

"Please, Daddy, please, can we go skating?" Brynn pleaded.

"I'll think about it." He gave the child a wink and picked up the menu again.

The conversation flowed easily while they ate. They'd just ordered dessert when a woman walked through the door that Marigold recognized immediately.

"I see your grandmother," Marigold told Brynn.

The child's eyes brightened as she spun in her seat. When her gaze settled on her grandmother, Brynn called out in a voice loud enough the deaf could hear, "Grammy."

Lynn Chapin, a pretty woman in her late fifties, lifted her head from the charge ticket she'd been signing. Marigold saw the instant Lynn spotted her granddaughter. Her coral-colored lips widened into a warm smile.

With her silver-blonde hair and classically beautiful features, she resembled her granddaughter more than her dark-haired son.

The hair, Marigold noted with approval, was cut in a shoulder-length bob that flattered her bone structure. Lynn gave a little wave, picked up her boxed-up pie, then made her way to the table.

"What a nice surprise." Her smile was friendly but her gaze was sharp and assessing as she scanned the table. It paused and lingered on Hadley.

Before Lynn could arrive at a very wrong conclusion, Marigold set the record straight. "Hadley, Cade, and I were running the Seedlings' meeting at the Y tonight. We invited David and Brynn to join us for dinner since they're baching it."

"Oh." Lynn's expression gave nothing away as it shifted to her eldest son. "Is Whitney out of town again?"

"Mommy is in Boca with Gina and Tess," Brynn announced before her dad could respond. "The cold makes her grouchy."

The child said the words matter-of-factly, then brightened. "Grammy, I climbed a rock wall tonight, and Daddy is going to, well, maybe, take me ice skating at a pond."

Warmth returned to Lynn's cool blue eyes. "Is that so?"

"May I get you something to drink, Mrs. Chapin?" Flo stopped at the table, a pitcher of tea for refills in one hand.

"Thank you, no. I'm not—"

"Join us," Marigold urged. "We just ordered dessert."

"I really shouldn't—"

"C'mon, Lynn. Take a few minutes. If you do, I will, too."

The masculine voice had Marigold turning in delight. "Dad. I didn't see you come in."

"You were too busy trying to convince this beautiful lady to join you." Steve Bloom flashed a persuasive smile at Lynn. "What do you say? How 'bout we both have a seat, get some coffee, and share a piece of pie?"

The next two weeks sped by with life for Marigold settling into a surprisingly easy rhythm. There was no more talk of her staying in Good Hope from either family or Cade. Everyone seemed to have finally accepted that her time here was limited.

She saw clients most days and Cade most evenings. Activities with her family, as well as Seedling activities, filled the rest of her free hours. Everywhere she went, the upcoming Valentine's dance was all anyone could talk about. Her father and Anita continued to date. Marigold had no doubt he'd be taking the now "reformed" piranha to the dance.

Though Marigold doubted she'd still be around for the event, she told Cade she'd go with him if she was in town.

The job at Angelo's was looking extremely promising. She'd had several conversations with the man himself. He'd been impressed by her experience and had been complimentary about her web page and blog. While he hadn't yet made an offer, Marigold sensed it was coming.

In the meantime, she was determined to ignore the surroundings in the salon and concentrate on practicing her art. She'd even become somewhat desensitized to the poodle wallpaper, which was a feat in itself. Until Loretta Sharkey, the high school choral director, stopped in for a trim after school one Friday afternoon.

"Every time I look at that wallpaper it makes me smile." Loretta gestured widely with one hand, nearly knocking the scissors from Marigold's fingers. "Look at those dogs."

Marigold hesitated. Was Loretta saying the paper was so ridiculous it made her chuckle? Or something else entirely?

"You, ah, you like the wallpaper?" Marigold kept any judgment from her tone. After all, there was no accounting for taste.

"It's so—" The woman appeared to search for the right word. "So Carly."

Unexpectedly, Loretta fixed those steely blue eyes on Marigold, bringing back not-so-pleasant memories of being caught talking when the choral director was giving instructions. "Did you know her?"

"Not at all." Although Carly had graduated from Good Hope High, she'd been a good ten years older.

"She was such a sweet girl and a good student. I never had to reprimand her for talking." Loretta glanced pointedly at Marigold before pursing her lips. "Her husband died when she was in her midtwenties. She used some of the insurance money to go to beauty school, then came back to start this business."

Beauty school. Marigold tried not to shudder. In her mind the term was on par with *hairdresser.*

"This salon became her life. Well, the salon and Vivian."

Marigold paused, a strand of Loretta's dark hair between her fingers. "Carly had a child?"

"Oh, my dear." The sound Loretta emitted sounded more like a bark than a laugh. "Vivian was a standard poodle. A gorgeous animal and incredibly smart."

Loretta continued, lowering her voice to a confidential whisper, although they were the only ones in the shop. "Personally, I think Carly would have done better putting her efforts into grooming dogs. She was great with shears. She could do a buzz cut like nobody's business on the little boys, but she wasn't very skilled with scissors. Which is why I always found the dancing scissors sign a bit ironic."

Marigold kept her expression impassive and only nodded.

"For so many years Carly threw herself into building this business to the exclusion of everything else. Then Vivian died and she was all alone." Loretta's expression softened with sympathy. "A person needs more than a career to be truly happy."

Marigold agreed. Eventually she would make time for a husband and children. She would have a well-balanced life.

But it wouldn't be with Cade. No, not with Cade.

The thought brought a stabbing pain to her heart.

"What about you, dear?" Loretta jerked her head around so abruptly Marigold nearly stabbed her ear. "Have you given any thought to staying?"

"I'm considering a couple of offers, both of them out of state." Marigold kept it vague. "One on the East Coast and one on the West."

"I thought maybe you and the sheriff—"

"Cade and I are good friends. Please sit straight, Loretta, and try not to move." Marigold spoke firmly and reached for the styling razor.

The choral director must have decided that not moving didn't include her mouth. "I saw Sheriff Rallis a couple of days ago with Justin Tooley. The boy is back on leave from the Marines. They were speaking with Katie Ruth at the bake shop."

"Cade mentioned something about doing an interview for the *Gazette*." Marigold slid the razor down the hair. "I don't know Justin."

"He's five, maybe six years younger than you. Nice baritone but always had difficulty reading music." Loretta sighed. "The two men were laughing and appeared to be having a good time. Not surprising, as I've found the sheriff to be extremely charming. I wish I could vote for both him and Travis."

Though Marigold had been counseled to never discuss politics with clients, for now this was her salon. Which meant she could talk about whatever she wanted. "I hope you'll seriously consider voting for Cade. I realize he's not from around here, but he wants to make this his home. He's a good man with strong credentials. I believe he's the right choice for Good Hope."

"I heard he has the Bloom family's support." Loretta's gaze turned assessing. "Is that because of his relationship with you?"

This wasn't the first time someone had posed the question. "He has our support because he's the right man for the job."

While she texturized and made some last adjustments, Marigold found herself extolling Cade's virtues.

Loretta listened, thankfully remaining still. Only when Marigold picked up the hair dryer did she speak, waving a dismissive hand. "Not necessary, my dear. I'm headed straight over to the Y for my water aerobics class. Besides, you'll want to speak with your father. He's been patiently waiting for us to finish gabbing."

Marigold whirled. Only then did she notice her father standing just inside the door. "Daddy, I didn't hear you come in."

"I was enjoying watching you work your magic." Steve's gaze shifted to his fellow educator. "Hello, Loretta."

"Nice to see you, Steve." Loretta touched her hair and sighed happily. "Your youngest is a genius with hair."

"Yes, she is." Steve smiled at Marigold, held up a sack with the Blooms Bake Shop logo. "I don't want to interrupt, but I wondered if you had time for a break."

"A daughter always has time for her father." With that pronouncement, Loretta rose from the chair. She made quick work of paying, then disappeared into the bright sunshine with a cheery wave.

"Do you have time?" Steve asked again.

Marigold glanced at her phone. She had an hour until her next appointment. She smiled at her father. "I do. And I can't wait to see what you have for me in that bag."

Chapter Eighteen

Once she and her father were seated in the back with freshly poured cups of coffee and two red-velvet cake doughnuts between them, Marigold lifted a brow. "To what do I owe the honor of this visit?"

Steve took a long sip of coffee. "There's something I need to tell you before you hear it from someone else."

Marigold's heart froze. She knew her father and Anita had seen each other almost every day since the piranha had promised to turn over a new leaf. It was as if the two were taking a trial run on the marriage train.

If he'd come here to tell her he'd proposed to the woman, she didn't know what she'd say. While Marigold wanted to believe a person could change, it seemed to her that Anita's basic character had been set long ago.

"Anita and I had a long talk last night." When Steve reached across the table and took her hand in his, Marigold held her breath. "Although we'll remain friends, we won't be dating anymore."

The breath she'd been holding came out in a whoosh. Though tempted to jump onto the small table and do a happy dance, Marigold kept her face expressionless and remained seated. "Was she unable to change? Is that why you broke up with her?"

A shadow passed over Steve's face. "It wasn't anything like that. I just realized that there was no real connection between us. Oh, I enjoyed her company, but as a friend, nothing more. I'd eventually like to get married again, share my life with a special someone. I couldn't see that woman being Anita."

There was sorrow in his eyes. "I didn't like hurting her."

Marigold squeezed his hand, kept her gaze focused on him. "This is best for her, too, Dad. This way maybe she can find another person who will be *her* soul mate."

"I hope so." Steve broke off a piece of doughnut, then stared as if wondering what to do with it. Finally, he popped it into his mouth and chewed. "I heard what you said to Loretta about Cade. You think a lot of that young man."

Wrapping her hands around the steaming mug, Marigold inclined her head. "And you seem to think a lot of Lynn Chapin. Are you sure she's not part of the reason you ended things with Anita?"

When her dad began to sputter, Marigold only smiled and took a bite of her doughnut.

"Are those daisies for me?" Marigold beamed when she opened the door and saw what Cade held clutched in one hand.

He leaned forward and kissed her. "Who else?"

All the way to her apartment, he'd worried giving her flowers might be too romantic. He hated second-guessing himself, but after last night he didn't want to spook her.

Cade watched her bustle to the tiny kitchen and pull a red vase from the cupboard. In seconds the pretty arrangement sat in the center of the dinette table. She'd been in high spirits all week thanks to a busy week at the salon and her father's breakup with Anita.

Shrugging out of his coat, he sniffed the air like a retriever. "Something smells good."

"Stroganoff." She pointed to the stovetop, then gestured toward a large bowl. "Accompanied by a mixed green salad with mandarin oranges and almonds."

"Where have you been, woman?" He spun her around and gazed down into her smiling eyes. "I've been looking for you my entire life."

Deliberately, he kept the words light and teasing.

Marigold flashed a smile and preened. "I am quite the catch."

The table was already set with blue-and-white-striped placemats and bright yellow napkins. In the living room area, a fire burned cheerily in the hearth. A warm, welcoming scene. A man would be lucky to end his workday in such a home. And, as his gaze settled on Marigold, casually attired in jeans and a ski sweater, with such a woman.

An image of the two of them discussing their day over a glass of wine in front of a roaring fire flashed before him. There was a little boy with her flaxen hair playing on the rug while he held a gray-eyed baby girl in his arms.

"Cade?"

He jerked his head up and the scene vanished like a puff of smoke.

"Why don't you pour us each a glass of wine?" She smiled. "I've got a nice merlot breathing on the counter."

While he poured, she flipped down the heat on the stovetop and covered the heavenly smelling mixture.

"Do you have time to sit and relax a minute?" Cade gestured with his head toward the sofa.

"The stroganoff has to simmer, so I can sit." She reached out and touched his hair. "You showered."

"After I got off duty, I stopped home to clean up and change."

"I don't think I've asked how things are going at the boarding house." Her gaze was curious.

"It's a room." He shrugged. "The worst part is having the shower down the hall. I share it with two other guys on the second floor."

Marigold wrinkled her nose and plopped down on the sofa. "I'm not much for sharing."

Cade didn't believe that for a second. Oh, he believed she wouldn't like sharing a shower with strangers—who in their right mind would?—but from what he'd observed, Marigold Bloom had a generous spirit.

Dropping down next to her, he took a sip of merlot. He was about to wrap an arm around her when he noticed a set of playing cards on the coffee table. "What are those?"

Following the direction of his gaze, Marigold chuckled. "Those are 'relationship' cards. Max dropped them into my purse this morning."

Relationship cards.

Cade grimaced.

"Max's mother gave them to him." Marigold paused, frowned. "Maybe for his birthday? I'm not sure."

"Relationship cards." His tone said it all. "I'd have burned them."

"Instead he gave them to his single sister-in-law." She lifted the wineglass to her lips, her mouth curving slightly up. "Much less extreme."

"Burning would be better. Then they'd be gone forever."

"I find it interesting that you don't even know what questions are on them, yet you're willing to turn them into a pile of ashes."

"I can guess what's on them."

She appeared to be suppressing a smile. "The cards are intended to help people—couples, primarily—get to know each other better and aid in communication. That's straight off the instruction sheet."

Communication.

According to Alice, Cade sucked at communication. Big-time.

"Want to play?" Challenge filled her blue eyes.

No. Cade absolutely did not want to play. He'd never been comfortable delving deep when superficial was perfectly acceptable. But gazing into Marigold's big blue eyes, something stirred. Though he knew their relationship was temporary, he refused to make the same mistakes with her that he'd made with Alice.

"I still think Max should have burned 'em." Heaving a resigned sigh, Cade held out a hand for the cards.

Marigold inclined her head. "Do you want to pick or should I?"

She was pleased that Cade was willing . . . albeit reluctantly . . . to give the cards a try. But when the timer on the stove dinged, she decided the game could wait until after they'd eaten.

Now their bellies were full, the table had been cleared, and the dishwasher sloshed merrily in the background.

Cade glanced warily at the cards. "How many questions do I have to answer?"

Marigold would have been content if she got him to agree to one. Since he'd left the door open, she stepped through it. "Three."

His gaze sharpened. "Why three?"

"Kind of like Goldilocks and the bears. Not too few where we don't get a feel for how they work, not too many where we might get burned out." Pleased with her quick thinking, Marigold smiled. "Three seems just right."

With a resigned sigh, Cade picked up the cards and shuffled. Then he held the deck out to her.

Slipping one out from the middle, Marigold held it up.

Cade took a gulp of wine. "Lay it on me."

"What comes to mind when you think of your ex?" She looked up, nonplussed. "Doesn't that seem kind of personal?"

"Can you imagine Max and his mom having that discussion?" Marigold snorted out a laugh. "She could give him the skinny on his two stepdads and assorted boyfriends."

Cade visibly shuddered, reminding Marigold of a dog shaking off water. "A horrific thought."

They exchanged smiles.

Cade lifted the hand still holding the wineglass and gestured to her. "Ladies first."

"I read the question." She smiled sweetly, enjoying his obvious discomfort. "Which means you answer first."

He stared into the fire for a long moment, as if thinking back over the time he and Alice had been together. "Regret."

Marigold tightened her fingers around the card, the word like a hard punch to the heart.

"Not regret we're no longer together," he hastened to reassure her. "Regret I didn't care enough at the end to try to work things out."

"Do you think it could have?" It was as if she was in a dark room fumbling for a light, not completely certain she wanted to turn it on. "Worked, I mean?"

"No." Cade rubbed the bridge of his nose. "Neither of us fought for the relationship, which tells me neither of us loved the other enough. I'd say that's a sad commentary on a two-year relationship."

"Either it's there or it's not," Marigold murmured, thinking of Jason.

"What about you?" He gestured with a hand. "What's the word?"

Marigold took a breath. "Superficial. Everything on the surface. We never dirtied the relationship with feelings. We never fought."

He lifted a brow. "Never?"

"Remember, superficial." She shrugged. "My fault as much as his."

Cade's eyes dropped to the deck of cards. "Wow. This is fun. I can see why Max tossed them your way."

"We said we'd do three," she reminded him, though without much enthusiasm. Like Cade, she hadn't expected the questions to probe so deeply.

"Nothing says we have to stick with that." His gray eyes went wicked. "We could move into the dessert part of the evening."

Marigold was oh so tempted. If she hadn't just said that bit about Jason and been reminded of their superficial conversations, she would have dumped the cards aside and jumped Cade's magnificent bod.

Instead she tamped down desire, grabbed the cards, and held them out to him. "One more, then we'll quit."

"Okay." Cade flipped over a card near the top of the deck and read, "When you're ninety years old, what will matter most to you in the world?"

Marigold didn't understand the sudden dryness in her throat. Thankfully, a sip of wine eased the gravel but brought her no closer to the answer. "I don't know what to say."

Cade made a rude buzzer sound. "Not gonna fly."

Marigold decided she'd been premature in rejecting Cade's suggestion to burn the darn cards. "I'm going to drop these off at Prim's house tomorrow. I may even suggest she ask Vanessa over so the three of them can play."

"Totally get that and agree." Cade appeared to be hiding a smile. "Still your turn."

"How 'bout you give me a pass on this one?" She fluttered her lashes and shot him what she considered her most beguiling smile.

"That only works if you're in a vehicle—naked—hoping for a warning rather than a ticket."

Marigold sighed, downed the contents of her wineglass in a single gulp, then blurted out what came to mind first. "When I'm ninety, I'd like to be at peace with the choices I made during my life. I hope I'd have been true to myself."

Marigold could see by the look in Cade's eyes he was trying to decipher that. She'd help him, but she wasn't certain what she meant, either. "Your turn."

Cade's gaze lingered on her. "When I'm ninety, what will matter most to me will be my family: my wife, kids, and grandkids. Maybe even a few great-grands. I enjoy my career. But at the end of my life, family will matter most."

"Your campaign is rockin' and rollin', my boy." Steve rubbed his hands, the look in his eye one of obvious satisfaction.

Cade met Beck and Steve at Muddy Boots bright and early Saturday morning to discuss election strategy. It had been nearly three weeks since Beck had first approached him about mounting an election campaign. Max, in the middle of tax season, had sent his regrets.

"You've been able to compile quite a list of volunteers willing to go door-to-door." Cade scrolled through the list of names displayed on Beck's laptop.

Steve gestured toward the computer with his coffee cup. "You and Marigold did your part adding to this list of supporters. She's always talking you up."

You and Marigold. Everyone spoke about them as if they were a couple. He supposed they were, for now.

"Where is Marigold?" Beck glanced around as if expecting his sister-in-law to magically appear. "I thought she might be joining us."

"She's over at the Bayshore," Cade said absently, his gaze still on the screen. "Something to do with the Hearts and Cherries Fashion Show."

Steve rocked back on his heels. "The fashion show isn't until this evening."

Cade lifted his gaze. "She had to start doing the models' hair this morning. And your daughter is a perfectionist. She wanted to confirm everything she needed was there and ready to go."

"Ami left early this morning, too." Beck took a sip of coffee. "Prim picked her up at seven."

"I like to see my girls getting together, working together." Steve's hazel eyes took on a faraway glow. "Sarah would be so proud. If only Fin could be here . . ."

"Do you hear from her much?" Cade asked.

"We talk once a week. Her job keeps her pretty busy." Steve lifted a hand in greeting, and Cade shifted his gaze to see Jeremy strolling down the sidewalk. "When Fin was young, I swore those two would end up together. But Fin, well, my Delphinium has dreams that can't be realized here."

"Perhaps she'll change her mind, see all that Good Hope has to offer," Cade heard himself say.

"Perhaps." Steve's hazel eyes were now firmly fixed on Cade.

The look in them reminded Cade of his own father when he saw too much.

"When you love someone, you have to let them know how you feel." Steve picked up his coffee cup and peered at Cade over the rim. "That way, if there's a choice to be made, they have all the information."

Though Beck remained at the table, Cade's world seemed to shrink in around him. The noises of the café, the clatter of dishes, the clink of silverware, and the chatter faded.

"Are you saying Fin didn't know Jeremy loved her?"

"I'm not speaking about Jeremy."

No, Cade thought, this wasn't about Jeremy. Or Fin.

"Saying those words too soon can lead to problems."

"Saying them too late can, as well." Steve's eyes once again grew distant with memories. "A true connection between a man and a woman doesn't come along very often. When it does, you have to give it your best shot."

Cade lifted his cup of now lukewarm coffee and took a drink. He lifted a brow. "Meaning?"

"Don't waste an opportunity to let the one you love know how you feel."

Chapter Nineteen

Cade waited until shortly before the fashion show was set to begin to make the trek to the Bayshore. He found Marigold standing with Vanessa Eden at the entrance to Ballroom 1 next to an elaborate red-and-pink balloon arch.

"Sheriff." Vanessa greeted him with a toothy smile. "How nice to see you again."

Max's mother wore some kind of red jumpsuit with heels. Unlike Marigold, who'd twisted her curls up and secured them with a glittery comb, Vanessa's hair spilled to her shoulders.

It was unfair, Cade knew, but when he looked at Max's mother, all he could think of was the cards. He wondered if Vanessa had her own deck. Did she and her boyfriend play the game on cold winter nights?

"Good to see you." Cade shot a glance inside the ballroom. "Does your garden center have a booth?"

"We do." She flashed a smile. "Actually, the Garden of Eden booth is right next to Adam's. He's touting his organic produce. You'll have to stop by. Say hello."

"I'll do that."

"Good luck with the fashion show, Marigold." Vanessa wiggled her fingers and clicked off on her mile-high heels.

"I thought about asking her a couple of questions." Cade lifted a brow. "In order to get better acquainted."

For a second, Marigold looked puzzled. Then a twinkle filled her eyes. "Questions like 'Are you happy with the intimacy you and Adam share?' Or maybe, 'Are you keeping any secrets that you're afraid of letting your partner know?'"

The last one hit a little too close to home for Cade. He had a secret, a big one. What would Marigold say if he took Steve's advice and told her he was in love with her?

Not now, he told himself. *Not the right time.*

"The next time you see Vanessa, ask her one of those." Cade shot her a wink. "Let me know what she has to say."

Marigold simply laughed.

Cade let his gaze linger on Marigold, decked out in a red dress that showed off her curves. Earrings dangled from her ears, three droplets of red encircled by silver. Her shoes with their red soles—they were some designer brand he never could recall—added a good three inches of height to her petite frame. "You look amazing."

She winked. "You're looking pretty spiffy yourself."

He glanced down. Instead of his preferred jeans, he'd changed into charcoal pants and a light gray shirt. "I aim to please."

In response, she slipped her arm through his, gestured to the ballroom. "What do you think?"

His gaze settled on a booth near the end, the colors of the backdrop reminding him of Blooms Bake Shop. "Ami has a booth here?"

"Of course." Marigold smiled. "As does Muddy Boots. They're pushing their catering services."

Cade tried to see who was behind the table chatting with a husband and wife who looked like tourists, but a large floral arrangement blocked his view. "Who's manning the booth?"

"Katie Ruth," Marigold said.

"What about Muddy Boots?"

"Would you believe my dad?"

"No."

"Scout's honor." Marigold gave a little laugh. "Flo was scheduled, but one of her kids got sick. Cory White filled in for my dad until he could come. Beck is, even as we speak, waiting tables at Muddy Boots."

"The Bloom family takes care of their own."

Marigold nodded. "These events help everyone in the business community. If I had a business here, I'd definitely have set up a booth."

Cade thought again about what Steve had said. Should he let Marigold know how he felt? He could say it casually, toss the words out there and then tell her to think about them.

Before he could settle on a course of action, a voice over the loudspeaker boomed a warning.

"The fashion show will begin in ten minutes. Ballroom 2."

Marigold tugged his hand. "Come see the runway."

"Don't you have hair to . . . handle?"

"Already done." She smiled. "My assistant is with the models."

He found himself swept along with a sea of people all headed in the same direction. Instead of finding seats, he and Marigold stepped to the side.

Whoever had decorated this ballroom had gone for romantic. Red Chinese lanterns hung overhead from decorative beams. A center runway, the sides draped in white linen, was edged with red and white flowers.

Rows of chairs surrounded the runway while small, high-topped tables were scattered throughout the rest of the room. The flicker of the tea lights on red linen added to the ambiance.

Tables edged the perimeter of the room, holding an assortment of silent auction offerings.

Cade gestured. "Anything good?"

"Lots of yummy and fun things," she told him. "Wines and chocolates and stained glass. There's even a trip to Iceland."

"Iceland?"

"Don't look that way. I'd die to go there. Swim in the Blue Lagoon. Ah, well." She lifted her shoulders, let them drop. "Someday."

"Marigold." Ami rushed over, gave Cade a slightly harried smile. "Greer messed up her hair. She needs you."

Marigold brushed a kiss on Cade's cheek. "Duty calls."

He watched until she disappeared from sight, then moved to inspect the silent auction donations.

The one with a sign touting the Blue Lagoon caught his eye. He'd like to take Marigold there. Swim with her in the warm waters during the day and make love with her at night.

Someday. Maybe.

The fashion show started right on time. Cade found himself standing beside a couple vacationing from Chicago. His ears perked up when he heard the woman mention Marigold's name.

"I know this should be all about the fashions, but I can't wait to see what she's done with the hair." The woman's voice held an excited edge.

"You say her name is Marigold. Like the flower?" the man asked.

"Yes. She's an absolute marvel, a rare talent. She worked for Steffan Oliver. Everyone familiar with her skills said she was destined to surpass him in popularity."

"What's she doing here?"

"I don't know." The woman's brow furrowed. "I wouldn't think she'd waste her talent on such a small event."

She clutched her husband's sleeve as the first model made her appearance.

Cade paid special attention to the hair. He wasn't sure what he was looking for, but all the styles looked nice.

According to the woman gushing beside him, they were not simply nice, but fabulous. Marigold was übertalented, a genius with hair.

If that were true, Cade thought, the woman he loved really was wasting her time in Good Hope.

Marigold's hands stroked Cade's bare back as she gave him the inside skinny on the fashion show. Though they'd been together since the event concluded, it wasn't until they were back in her apartment that she was able to speak without the risk of being overheard.

Because Cade had looked exhausted and she feared he might head straight home, she'd invited him in for a back rub. No strings attached.

He'd smiled at the comment and now lay facedown on her bed, shirt and shoes off as she rubbed her favorite oil across his well-muscled back.

"Eliza complimented me on the hair." Marigold paused for a second. "It shocked me speechless. Well, nearly speechless. You know me. I can usually find something to say."

"A little to the left."

"I knew you were listening." Marigold returned to the tight knot on the left. Cade hadn't had much to say. She wondered if his mind was on several more incidents of vandalism he'd been investigating.

She didn't mind carrying the bulk of the conversation. The fashion show had been a huge success and her head still spun with all the compliments.

"I love these kinds of events. I was supposed to do the hair for Couture Fashion Week in Chicago, but once he fired me, Steffan got the coordinator to put him back in charge." Marigold paused, then decided it would fester if she didn't tell Cade the whole truth. "I'd feel worse about losing the position if I hadn't edged him out to lead the team in the first place. I hadn't campaigned for it or anything. But I had put a bug in a few ears that I'd be interested, even though I knew it had been Steffan's gig since he moved to Chicago."

It made her feel small now, remembering. It didn't matter that mentioning interest in a position wasn't the same as snatching it out from under him. After all, the final choice had been up to the coordinator.

Marigold tried to assuage her guilt by telling herself it was the way things were done, the way a person got ahead. But did she really want to get ahead by stabbing a friend in the back?

"Do you think I was wrong?" Marigold didn't know why she asked when she already knew the answer.

Still, Cade's opinion of her mattered. She hoped he didn't think too badly of her. She held her breath, awaiting his response.

"Cade?"

Silence.

She thought about poking him, then heard the slow, easy intake of breath. Her lips lifted in a wry smile.

His head was turned to the side, dark lashes fanning his cheek. He looked younger in sleep and somehow vulnerable, though she knew he'd rail at the word.

He'd been letting his hair grow, the military cut no longer quite so pronounced. Marigold resisted the urge to brush back a strand of hair from his forehead, not wanting to take the chance of waking him.

He was a good man, an honorable man. Someone who made her want to be a better woman. But none of that mattered. Cade loved small-town life. He was happy here.

The fashion show had reminded her that her passion was hair. All the compliments and accolades hammered home she was destined for bigger and better. Which meant leaving Good Hope.

"I'll never forget you," she whispered, then gave in to impulse and brushed a kiss across his cheek.

For a second she thought he might wake up, but his lips simply curved into a slight smile.

With great care she pulled the covers up, then eased off the bed. Though it was late enough for her to simply retire for the evening, she wasn't ready to sleep.

In bare feet she padded to the kitchen and considered what to do with herself. She could make a cup of tea. Pull out her phone and check her e-mail. Neither of those options held much appeal.

Then her gaze settled on her art journal. She'd been too busy lately to take time for her art.

She scooped up the book. Within minutes she had it, as well as her favorite supplies, strewn across the dinette table. Excitement replaced some of the melancholy as the pages began to come alive.

Success. Fun. Friends. Family. Hearts and Cherries. She pasted, painted, and got creative with the calligraphy pen.

In one of the magazines in her stash, she found a picture of an immense oak tree with a trunk wide enough to hold a dartboard. She flipped past the page, returned to the page.

Surrendering to the inevitable, Marigold cut out the picture of the massive trunk, leaving a touch of green at the top. In no time at all, the oak stared back at her from a formerly blank page.

She painted the rest of the page in bright splashes of color, careful to avoid the tree. Feeling foolish, she picked up a fine brush, dipped it in red, then carefully drew a heart on the trunk.

It looked good, the bright red against the weathered wood. There was no reason to do more, she told herself.

Yet it wasn't finished.

Picking up her calligraphy pen, she glanced over her shoulder as if to make sure no one was watching, and quickly added CR + MB to the inside of the heart.

Once Cade left her apartment for his shift early Sunday morning, Marigold made the trek to Muddy Boots.

Though she'd been on her own for the past eight years and attended events solo more times than she'd had an escort, it felt strange not having Cade at her side. In the short time they'd been dating, the sheriff had become part of her life.

Pushing open the door to Muddy Boots, Marigold stepped from the quiet into a beehive with full tables and a whole lot of mingling going on. Catching sight of her family clustered at a large table near the back, she began threading her way between tables until a hand on her arm stopped her.

"Got a minute?"

Marigold turned, smiled when she saw the deputy. "Sure. What's up?"

Travis glanced around as if searching for someplace more private, then blew out a breath. "I guess we'll have to talk here."

She cocked her head, concerned by the worry on his face. "What's wrong, Trav?"

"The sheriff is using you." He blurted out the words, the freckles on his face standing out like shiny pennies. "He's using your family, too."

"You need to spell this out for me, because I'm not following."

Travis flinched, obviously hearing the thirty-degree drop in her tone. "He's using you and your family's popularity in this town to further his campaign."

"And that concerns you because he's running against you."

"It bothers me because I like you. Because we're friends," he added, flushing. "I don't want to see you hurt."

"I can look out for myself." Marigold added extra warmth to her smile, knowing the deputy's heart was in the right place. "But I appreciate the concern."

She turned to leave but his hand returned to her arm.

When she glanced down, he immediately released his hold.

"Using a vet to drum up support is low," he blurted, suddenly looking much too young to be wearing a badge. "And not fair."

She merely lifted a brow.

"Did you see the picture in the *Gazette*?" he asked.

"Why don't you tell me about it?"

"It was on the front page. Him and Justin Tooley. Katie Ruth did quite a spread all about this meeting between the two Marines." Travis blew out a breath. "It was like free publicity for his campaign."

"Were you in the Marines, Travis?" Marigold asked, though she already knew the answer.

His face took on the same mulish expression she'd often seen on her nephews' faces. "No."

"Well, I bet if you'd been one, you'd be in the picture and mentioned in the article." She patted his cheek. "Have a nice day."

"He's got you snowed," Travis called out when she walked away.

She ignored the shouted words and kept walking.

"Sorry I didn't make it to church," Marigold said when she reached her family, dropping into one of the empty chairs. "I decided to stay in bed a little while longer this morning."

Max glanced around. "Where's Cade?"

"He's working." Marigold answered so automatically that it took a moment to realize everyone expected to find the two of them together. "It isn't as if Cade Rallis and I spend all our free time together."

Her voice came out sharper than she'd intended.

"What couple does?" Max said good-naturedly. "Though I love spending as much time as I can with this woman."

He snaked a hand around Prim's waist and pulled her to him. "She's my valentine."

Prim's ivory complexion flushed, even as she leaned against her husband's shoulder. "I keep telling him V-Day is still a week away."

"It can't come soon enough for me." Max gave his wife a wink. "Be prepared, Red. I'm going to whirl you across the Valentine's dance floor like—"

Max paused and his blond brows furrowed. "Who's a great ballroom dancer?"

"Don't even go there, Brody." There was a decided twinkle in Beck's dark eyes. "We've seen you dance."

Prim laughed, then mollified her husband by kissing his cheek. "It will be wonderful."

Maybe it was because Marigold had never had anyone spoil her rotten, or maybe it was because she'd always spent Valentine's Day alone, but the holiday held little appeal. She hoped this hearts-and-flowers discussion would end before it affected her appetite.

Ami hurried up. She glanced at Prim. "Did you tell Marigold about the book club?"

"What book club?"

"Well, I—" Ami paused to wave at friends Cory and Jackie White before turning back to Marigold. "I'm starting one."

"Shouldn't you wait until after"—Marigold gestured to her sister's midsection and the barely visible baby bump—"Junior arrives on the scene?"

"My sentiments exactly," Beck piped up, flashed a smile. "Glad you could stop by, Marigold."

"Back to the book club." Ami settled into the seat next to Marigold. "I'm pregnant, not disabled. Hadley's already taken on many of my duties at the bakery, so I have lots of time. Besides, I think a book club sounds like fun, and I don't want to wait."

Her mother and sisters all read for pleasure, but to Marigold's knowledge had never been involved in a club. She quirked a brow. "What made you think of doing it?"

Before her sister could answer, the hairs on the back of Marigold's neck prickled. She turned and there he was. *There he was.* She couldn't stop the smile that blossomed on her lips. "I thought you were working."

When Cade placed his hands on her shoulders, she went warm all over.

"I am working." He glanced at Beck. "I received a report that things might be getting a bit rowdy at this establishment. I decided to personally assess the situation."

"I appreciate a man who's thorough." Beck motioned to the waitress, an older woman with orange hair that matched her lipstick. "Flo, could you get the sheriff a cup of coffee and a cruller?"

"He prefers doughnuts." Marigold spoke without thinking.

The waitress cast Cade a questioning look.

"She knows me and I know her." Cade grinned. "Chocolate cake doughnut with icing, to go. Coffee black, please."

"As I was trying to say." With a determined expression, Ami attempted to wrestle back control of the conversation.

"The hostess for the book club—that's me—will serve dinner. The men come, too, but once the food is taken away, they—"

"—are banished to another part of the house." Beck grinned. "Which is okay by me."

"Sounds like a good time." Cade flashed Ami a supportive smile.

"I'm glad you think so." Ami gazed up at him. "I expect both you and Marigold to be there. It's this Tuesday at six. I'm doing a romance and love theme, both in terms of the food and the book."

"This Tuesday?" Marigold couldn't keep the surprise from her voice. "The Valentine's dance is Saturday. This is a busy week for most people."

"Are *you* busy on Tuesday?" Ami asked.

"No, but that only gives me two days to read the book." Marigold wondered what had gotten into her sister. "Why does it have to be this week?"

"Because I don't know how much longer you'll be in Good Hope." Ami's green eyes held a sheen. "I want you there. At least for the first meeting, if that's all I can have."

Ami shifted her attention to Cade. "I'd like you there, too."

Cade hesitated. When he slanted a glance at Marigold, she knew what he was asking.

Marigold didn't stop to think. "I'd like you there."

He gave a curt nod. "I'll be there."

Still going with impulse, Marigold slipped her arm through his and squeezed. "That makes me happy."

The look that flashed in his eyes was something Marigold couldn't decipher. Which wasn't surprising, as her own emotions were in a turmoil. She should have discouraged him from coming, or at the very least, not *encouraged*. But no, she'd practically made it impossible for him to turn down the invitation.

It was too late to do anything now.

"At least I didn't have to invite Anita." Ami's face brightened at the thought. "I can't tell you how worried I was that Dad would decide to formalize their relationship simply because he and Anita had been dating for so long."

It had been that way, Marigold realized, with her and Jason. Marriage had been something they'd considered on more of an intellectual, rather than romantic, level. They'd dated nearly a year. They enjoyed each other's company and shared many of the same views. When he learned he'd be relocating, marriage seemed a logical next step.

In hindsight, Jason's relocation had been the best thing that could have happened to both of them. The kind of love needed to last a lifetime simply hadn't been there. She never once tingled when he walked into the room. When Jason held her in his arms, she didn't feel warm and safe and cherished.

Heck, she'd never even shared with him what it had been like for her when her mother had been diagnosed with cancer. Not like she had with Cade...

Stop, she told herself. Spilling her guts about something that happened a decade earlier didn't mean a thing, other than Cade was a good listener.

"I think something Cade said about connections really hit home with Dad," Marigold heard herself say. "He realized he and Anita simply didn't have that connection."

"I understand about finding the right one." Beck took his wife's hand, brought it to his lips.

Ami leaned on her husband's shoulder, and he kissed the top of her head.

The scene felt somehow intimate, and Marigold had to look away.

Flo returned with Cade's to-go cup and a small bakery sack.

"On the house," Beck told Flo before Cade could pull the wallet from his pocket. "I appreciate that you made a special stop to check on the rowdies."

"All in a day's work." Cade flashed that easy smile that Marigold had grown to love, er, like.

Marigold rose and took his hand. "I'll walk you to the door."

Once they reached the entrance, Cade leaned over and brushed a kiss against her lips. "I'd best get back to work and let you get back to your family."

Marigold couldn't help herself. She grabbed his face and planted a long, lingering kiss on his lips. It didn't matter that anyone inside the café, or any number of people walking past on the sidewalk, could see them.

When she stepped back, her breath came in ragged puffs. "Be safe."

Then Marigold turned and walked to her waiting family.

Chapter Twenty

"That text was from my dad." Marigold dropped the phone back into her purse before turning to make sure the exterior door to the bakery was tightly closed. "He's watching the twins and asked if I wanted to come over."

Cade noticed her voice held a slight edge. "Did he forget you'd be at Ami's?"

"I think he was surprised I was going to a book club." She gave a little laugh.

When they stepped onto the sidewalk, Cade took her arm. Despite the weather, they'd decided to walk. Cade had to admit to a certain trepidation regarding the evening's events. "I'm not certain I understand how this book club thing will work."

"Your part is easy. All you have to do is eat and hang with the guys." Marigold's fingers, which had been resting lightly on his bicep, tightened. "I had to actually read a book."

"Poor Marigold." His voice oozed faux sympathy.

She shot him a sharp glance. "Reading doesn't come easily to everyone, Rallis."

Something in her tone put Cade on alert.

"Thankfully I was able to get the story on audio." Marigold's gaze remained focused downward as they carefully negotiated the snow-packed sidewalk.

"What is it about reading you find difficult?" Though Cade enjoyed a good spy story or thriller, he knew some had a hard time immersing themselves in a fictional world.

"Just about everything." She was quiet for a moment. "I'm dyslexic."

Cade couldn't believe he'd missed all the signs. *Some trained observer.* Her chin jutted up. "It doesn't mean I'm stupid."

"Never thought it did." Cade kept his tone matter-of-fact. Though she'd announced the diagnosis as if was no biggie, he sensed it *was* a big deal to her. Or had once been.

He wondered if Jason had known. Had Mr. International Attorney made her feel stupid? Could his attitude have been another reason for the breakup and her defensiveness now?

"What did Jason think of you being dyslexic?" Cade casually tossed out the question. This time he paid attention, keeping his gaze on Marigold's face to gauge her reaction.

Surprise had her eyes widening. It was obvious she hadn't expected him to bring up her ex.

"He didn't know." Marigold shrugged. "It never came up."

"You dated him for almost a year."

"Your point?"

"Why didn't you tell him?"

Marigold hesitated for so long Cade wondered if she was going to answer. Then she sighed.

"I don't know why other than it's always seemed like such a private thing." She wrapped her scarf more firmly around her neck as the breeze picked up.

She'd dated Jason for nearly a year yet hadn't mentioned something so important to him. Yet she'd told Cade. Why? Because she trusted him? Or because she knew she'd be leaving soon so having him know scarcely mattered?

"How old were you when were you diagnosed?" A gust of wind from the bay rose up, slapping them in the face with tiny ice pellets. Instead of lowering his head and soldiering the rest of the distance to Beck's home, Cade went with impulse and pulled Marigold into the covered entryway of the nearby Enchanted Florist. The exterior door to the closed shop sat in a protected alcove the size of a phone booth. Though there wasn't much room, it was enough to keep the sleet at bay.

Marigold glanced around. "Why are we here?"

"It's out of the wind. And," he added, "we're not far from Beck's house."

"Ah, I hate to tell you, Sheriff, but you're not making sense. Our ultimate destination is right there." Marigold pointed with one gloved finger. "Why aren't we braving the big, bad wind for one more block instead of cowering in a doorway like a couple of weenies?"

"This is more private." He wrapped his arms loosely around her. "Tell me about the dyslexia."

"Nothing to tell." She averted her gaze, feigning intense interest in the sleet. "It looks like it might be letting up."

He brought her face back to his with the tips of two fingers. Perhaps he should simply let it go and not press. But she'd willingly told him something she'd kept from a guy she was thinking of marrying. There had to be a reason. "You brought it up. Now finish the story. When were you diagnosed?"

"I was ten." The corners of her mouth pulled together.

"I'm surprised it took them so long to make the diagnosis."

"I hid my struggles well." Her lips twisted in a poor semblance of a smile. "I could have gotten help earlier, but I was very good at deception."

Cade could picture her as a little girl, with those big blue eyes and curly blonde hair. Cute and spunky as hell. No doubt she had the same take-no-prisoners attitude back then. The thought made him smile. "I bet the teachers loved you."

"Actually, they didn't know what to think of me and my substandard performance. Most had taught at least one of my sisters. The three older Bloom sisters were excellent students." Marigold's heavy sigh shredded his heart. "I covered by talking excessively and being the class clown. Then, when I was ten, the party came to a crashing halt."

Though the entry walls to the store effectively blocked the wind, she shivered.

Determined not to push her in a direction she wasn't ready to go, Cade didn't say anything. But he kept his arms around her, wanting her to feel his support. He liked the sex they'd shared over the past weeks, liked it a whole lot. But it was these moments of connection that arrowed straight to his heart.

Whenever she let him hold her—as she did now—or reached out to take his hand in a casual display of affection, his heart melted.

Alice hadn't liked being touched, especially in public. It had taken him a while to realize Marigold loved it when he went with impulse and brushed her hair back, or massaged her shoulders. Even when he simply let his fingers linger on her arm.

He liked it, too. It had become increasingly difficult to be close to her and not touch. So he'd been going with impulse more and more frequently. He liked what was blossoming between them.

What he didn't like was wondering how he was going to bear life without her.

"Where was I?" she asked after what seemed an eternity but was likely only a few seconds.

"You were ten." *So young*, he thought, *so innocent and vulnerable.*

"Mrs. Copple, my fourth-grade teacher, saw through the clown act." Marigold's head rested against his chest. "She called my parents to the principal's office to discuss their concerns. They were stunned when she told them what she suspected. As a teacher, my dad felt guilty he hadn't recognized the signs. My mother was so distressed, she cried."

"That must have been difficult." Cade stroked her back.

He would remember what it felt like to hold her close. When she was gone, he would remember—and savor—this moment.

"Although they assured me I hadn't, I knew I'd disappointed them." Marigold inhaled deeply, let the breath out slowly. "That's when I made my vow."

"What vow?" Cade kept his voice soft and soothing.

"I would make them proud. One day I would be more successful than any of my sisters." She jerked back and her blue eyes blazed with determination. "It's a vow I mean to keep."

All the pieces suddenly clicked into place. Cade now understood her drive to be the very best in her field. This also explained why she wasn't interested in staying in Good Hope.

He knew about setting goals and mustering the drive necessary to achieve them. He wouldn't ask her to stay with him, wouldn't encourage her to consider the possibility. If she didn't achieve the goal she'd set at age ten, a goal that undoubtedly had gotten her through some difficult times, she'd never be truly happy. That's what he wanted for her.

Her happiness, even at the expense of his own.

"You're a smart, determined woman, Marigold Bloom." He brushed his lips against her hair. "I know you'll find every success."

The crowd at Bayside Pizza had thinned in the last hour until only a handful of tables held customers. Ever since her talk with Cade before the Book Club meeting two days ago, Marigold had been on edge. She pushed aside the plate holding a half-eaten slice. "I feel as if all I've done is eat this week. I don't even want to think about dessert."

Cade's hand reached across the table and took hers, caressing her palm with his thumb. "Are you sure you don't want to reconsider that statement?"

Before Marigold could respond, she was grabbed from behind.

"I've been looking all over this town for you."

"Fin." Marigold shrieked, then jumped up to give her sister a hug. "What are you doing here?"

Cade rose and watched the two sisters hop up and down, arms still encircling each other.

After a few seconds, Marigold looked around and held out her hand to him. "Say hello to Fin."

"Good to see you again." As his gaze settled on Fin, Cade wondered how Marigold could think anyone would confuse Ami with this woman.

Granted, they had the same nose and lips, the same green eyes and sun-streaked hair. But there was a softness, a gentleness to Ami that her doppelgänger didn't possess.

Fin's smile, while friendly, held a brittleness. There were lines of tension around her eyes. "I heard you've been entertaining my baby sister while she's in Good Hope."

"And doing a bang-up job of it, too." Marigold tucked her arm through Cade's, seemingly oblivious to her sister's narrowed gaze. "I thought you and Xander were in the Caribbean."

"A week in St. John was the plan." Fin's lips thinned. "Unfortunately, Xander has yet to secure a location for this new movie he wants to shoot over Christmas, so he canceled. He's off to God knows where with his cinematographer and production designer to check out some promising site."

"I'm sorry." Marigold's hand went to Fin's arm. "I know how much you were looking forward to the trip."

"Typical man." Fin waved a dismissive hand. "They're all . . ." Her voice trailed off as her gaze focused on something in the distance.

Cade followed the direction. Jeremy stood next to a table by the window, his arm around Eliza's waist. The brunette leaned against him as they chatted with Cory and Jackie White.

"Anyway." Fin's expression gave nothing away. "I'd already put in for the week off, so I thought I'd come see my family."

"I'm so glad you did."

"I also have good news that I wanted to share in person." Fin cast a glance at Cade before refocusing on her sister. "The job with the studio is yours."

"Why, that's . . . surprising."

"Not at all. You're talented, Marigold. You're destined for far more than this little town has to offer." Fin slanted a glance at Cade. "Anyone who thinks differently doesn't have your best interest in mind."

Instead of going back with Marigold and her new temporary roommate to the apartment, Cade paid the bill and gave her a brief kiss.

"Enjoy the rest of the evening with your sister." Conscious of Fin's scrutiny, he kept his voice easy. "Are we still on for the dance tomorrow?"

Marigold's hand remained on his sleeve, as if reluctant to let him go. "Pick me up at seven?"

"It's a plan." Cade turned to Fin and lifted a brow. "If you'd like to come with us, you're welcome."

"I'll think about it."

Though he could tell Fin couldn't wait to get rid of him, Marigold's hand remained on his arm. "Is the hockey tournament at ten?"

"Yes." She'd promised to come and watch, but that was before her sister's unexpected appearance. "If you can't make it, that's okay. Fin is—"

"Always up for ogling a bunch of handsome guys on the ice." Marigold turned to her sister. "They're all great skaters, except maybe for Beck, who—"

"—is getting better with each game," Cade finished the sentence for her. "Seriously, Marigold, don't feel you have to attend."

"I'd love to watch." Fin flashed a bright smile. "We can cheer you guys on to victory, and I can tell Marigold all about the life she's going to have as a supersuccessful hairstylist in LA."

There wasn't much to say after that. The woman had made her point loud and clear.

If you try to keep my sister in this backwater town, you'll have to deal with me.

Fin wouldn't get any fight from him.

Cade shoved his hands into his pockets and hunched his shoulders against the stiff wind as he headed home. Not home, as in the small apartment over the bakery that in the last few weeks had seemed like his, but to the barren room in the boarding house.

Seeing Marigold's talent shine at the Hearts and Cherries Fashion Show had made him see her in a different light. He wouldn't hold her back. He loved her too much to tie her down to a life she didn't want. Even if that meant living his life without her.

Cade's Saturday morning turned ugly when he decided to read the local e-newsletter, the *Open Door*, over a cup of coffee. After reading the front-page article, he wished he'd added a shot of whiskey.

According to a survey taken two weeks earlier, Travis held a commanding lead in the race for sheriff. It appeared not only was Cade going to lose the woman he loved, but he'd likely lose the job he'd come to love, as well.

By the time he reached Rakes's Pond, he was in the mood to skate and skate hard. The ice was filled with fellow Ice Holes as well as members of the opposing team, the Ugly Pucklings. He greeted everyone but kept the conversations brief.

Shortly before the game was to start, Cade scanned the west side of the pond, where temporary bleachers had been set up. He spotted Marigold immediately. Curly blonde hair spilled in all directions from under a bright red hat. As the wind dropped the temperature a good ten degrees, she wore a black parka and thick wool mittens. She'd looped a scarf, the same bright red as her hat, around her neck.

Fin appeared to have gone for style rather than warmth with a green coat better suited to cool California nights than frigid Wisconsin days.

Prim and Ami, as well as the twins, sat with them.

When Beck and Max skated to the side to say hello, Cade joined them.

"You guys look good on the ice." Marigold's gaze narrowed on the other side of the pond, where the other team warmed up, then returned to him. "Do me a favor. Grind those Ugly Pucklings into the ice."

Cade grinned and felt himself relax. "I never knew you had such a mean streak."

"Tim Hornsby, one of their leading scorers, cut off a big chunk of my hair when we were six." Marigold pursed her lips. "He laughed like a hyena."

"He was sweet on you." Ami smiled.

"Funny way to show it," Marigold muttered.

"He was six." Prim glanced at the twins, sighed. "And a boy."

"They're going down." Cade would have kissed her to seal the promise if Fin hadn't been there shooting daggers in his direction.

"Who's all on your team?" Fin asked. "Anyone I know?"

Beck answered the question, rattling off the list of names. He saved Jeremy for last.

"Jeremy's still an excellent skater," Marigold told Fin. "He attends every Friday Skate Night as well as being on the team, so he gets a lot of practice."

"Fin and Jeremy had the best form on the ice." Prim's eyes turned dreamy. "Perfectly in sync. Remember, Max?"

"I remember. I just wish he'd show up. He's late." Max's gaze scanned the crowd. A look of relief crossed his face. "Finally . . ."

Though Jeremy and Eliza weren't touching, it was obvious as they covered the uneven terrain to the pond that they were together. In the morning light, Eliza's face looked softer, Cade thought, and happy.

Until she spotted Fin.

Her lips tightened and the sharp edge to her features returned. She stumbled, and Jeremy immediately reached out to take her arm.

Fin's intense green eyes remained focused on the couple. When she became conscious of Cade's scrutiny, she abruptly shifted her gaze.

"Did you see the survey results?" Beck asked.

Schooling his features, Cade turned to him. "I saw them."

"We'll turn those numbers around." Max's determined gaze met his.

Cade shrugged. "If we don't, I'll be on the hunt for a new job."

His casual tone gave no indication just how much all this mattered. But Marigold obviously knew him too well to be fooled. She placed a hand on his arm.

"I contacted Katie Ruth this morning about doing an interview with you and Travis." Marigold must have seen his look of surprise, because she smiled. "She can't interview you and not Travis without looking as if she's playing favorites, especially since she's agreed to be in charge of your social media strategy. But because your experience is so much stronger, the interview should give you a push."

"You should be getting a text from Jeremy's administrative assistant with dates and times of a couple of public debates," Beck told him. "Going head-to-head with Travis will also boost your numbers."

"Don't forget the door-to-door," Prim added. "I've got quite a list of volunteers ready to spring into action once we give them the go-ahead. Studies show most people make up their minds close to the election, so we'll begin the canvassing ten days out."

"We'll be targeting both undecideds and doing get-out-the-vote canvassing. Dad is putting together a leaflet that he'll be running by you for you and the volunteers to hand out," Ami explained. "It will highlight your experience and include quotes backing you from both Jeremy and Len."

"The leaflet is going to be so compelling a person would have to be a fool to vote for anyone but you." Marigold's earnest face made him smile. "But be warned, it isn't all that long before you'll be spending every free second going door-to-door."

"Good thing you'll be gone by then, Marigold." Fin's cool comment had everyone shifting their gazes. "He won't have any distractions."

A look of distress crossed Ami's face. "Are you leaving soon?"

"I got offered a job in LA with a major studio." Marigold glanced at Fin and smiled. "It's a solid offer, but I haven't decided whether or not to take it. I'm waiting to hear from Angelo's."

"Tiffany, my friend at the studio, told me they need someone to start by March first." Fin slanted a glance at Cade.

He kept his face carefully neutral.

"Not much notice." Prim's strawberry-blonde brows pulled together.

"Most hairstylists would kill for such an opportunity," Fin said firmly.

Ami worried her lower lip. "But to find a place and get settled within two weeks . . ."

"Marigold has a place to stay. My roommate moved out and I haven't taken time to look for a replacement." Fin waved away her sister's concern. "She'll move in with me. I won't even charge her rent until she gets on her feet."

Cade wanted to tell Fin to quit pushing and let Marigold decide what was best for her, but he kept his mouth shut.

Right now, he had some Ugly Pucklings to grind into the ice.

"I don't see why you can't stay for lunch." Marigold's puzzled blue eyes turned the color of Green Bay before a storm.

Jeremy had invited the entire Ice Holes team along with their friends and family up to his house to celebrate the victory over a meal of pulled pork sandwiches and potato salad.

"I've got paperwork I need to catch up on before I launch into all this election stuff." Giving in to impulse, Cade smoothed a hand down her hair and found the simple touch eased some of the rawness inside. "Go, enjoy the time with your family. I'll see you this evening."

There must have been a question in his voice, because she smiled. "I'm planning on it."

Cade had heard all about the Not-on-Valentine's Day Dance. Apparently it was an extremely popular event, not only with locals but with visitors to the community, as well.

Set for the Saturday before Valentine's Day, the dance would be held in the Bayshore Hotel's main ballroom. A band from Milwaukee had been hired to play romantic melodies spanning the last seventy years.

Cade had envisioned spending a romantic evening dancing under dangling red hearts, then coming home and making love until the early hours of the morning. But that was before Fin's unexpected arrival. Now that she was now staying with Marigold, the most Cade could hope for was several passionate kisses at the door.

"Cade."

Be Mine in Good Hope

He looked up to find Marigold's gaze on him, regret in her eyes. His spine stiffened. "What?"

"I'm sorry Fin's unexpected arrival threw a wrench into our plans."

"I'm not sure what you mean."

Her gloved hand slid up his arm. Although hardly skin to skin, he felt the heat through the waterproof jacket sleeve and thermal shirt beneath. "I missed you last night."

Yeah, they had a connection.

"Missed you, too, Goldilocks."

That brought a smile to her lips. "Sure you won't stay for lunch?"

He shook his head, then thought what the hell and leaned over and kissed her. "See you at seven."

Without a backward glance, Cade headed to his Jeep.

By the time he reached the station, he was ready to dig in. Ready to take care of all the mundane tasks in the hopes that the job, the work, would take his mind off Marigold, off the fact that in barely over two weeks she'd be gone.

After finishing his review of several reports completed by a new deputy, Cade went through his e-mail.

A message from the city administrator of Village Green caught his eye. The small community in Illinois, an hour north of Chicago's northernmost suburbs, had once been on his radar.

Filled with streets of beautifully preserved Victorian homes, Village Green was a thriving community that featured carriage rides and historical reenactments as a tourist draw. He'd applied for the job as chief of police around the same time as he applied for the sheriff's position in Good Hope.

Not long after the submission period closed, he'd received a form letter advising him the current chief had decided to stay another year. Cade had scarcely given the matter a second thought. By that time, he'd already accepted the job in Good Hope.

The only advantage to the Village Green position was that he'd have been appointed, no election necessary there.

Regardless of what the Bloom family thought of his chances, Travis was well-liked in Good Hope and was a lifelong resident. In this close-knit community, that counted for a lot.

So what if Travis didn't have all Cade's experience in law enforcement? It wasn't as if Good Hope was a mecca for crime. Since Christmas, the hottest thing on the department's plate was the string of recent vandalisms. Cade had just closed the book on those cases with the arrest of two subjects.

His gaze returned to the e-mail. The city administrator in Village Green wanted to know if he was interested in being considered for the position, which would come open in June. Cade keyed in *no*, then erased it. Saying he was interested didn't guarantee he'd be offered the position. Even if they did offer, it didn't mean he had to accept.

It would be an option. If he lost the election, Village Green would be a good place to settle. In time, he'd return to Good Hope and make his home here.

Cade indicated his interest, asked if they needed an updated resume, and hit Send before turning back to his paperwork.

But Marigold remained on his mind, so he composed another quick message and sent it, this time to her.

Chapter Twenty-One

The ding had Marigold placing the dress back into her closet and snatching the phone from her dresser.

Fin glanced up from Marigold's jewelry box she'd been perusing. "Is it Ami?"

Thinking of you. Can't wait to dance with you tonight.

Marigold's lips curved up as a warm wave of pleasure washed over her. "It's Cade. Just confirming plans for tonight."

If things had been different, Marigold would have told Fin how much she liked the little texts Cade often sent her. Most for no reason other than to say he was thinking of her. She found them sweet and romantic.

In the mood Fin was in right now, her sister would likely label her girlish thoughts lame or foolish.

"You really like him."

Marigold realized with a start that Fin was speaking to her. "What?"

"You like the sheriff."

There was no way to keep from smiling. It was her common response whenever she thought about Cade. "I do. He's a great guy."

"Would he move to California?" Fin's green eyes turned unreadable. "Or to New York?"

Marigold's heart gave a little leap at the thought, until she told herself to be sensible. Heck, to be realistic. "He loves it here. He's a small-town guy."

"I thought he came from Detroit."

"He grew up in a small town. He loves Good Hope and is totally content with his position here."

"Doesn't believe in aiming high, does he?"

"Don't say that about him, not in that smug, dismissive tone." Marigold's voice sliced the air.

Startled surprise skittered across Fin's ivory complexion. Her eyes, enhanced with the expert use of cosmetics to appear wide, widened farther. "I didn't mean it as a slam."

Fin raked a hand through her sun-streaked hair and expelled a heavy breath. "Blame it on Xander. He's been looking for a community about the size of Good Hope to shoot his next movie. For the past couple of months I've found myself defending small-town life to him."

There was a disconnect here, and Marigold wasn't sure where it had occurred. "You don't like small towns. Why would you be defending them to him?"

The lips Fin had covered in a bronze shade similar to the one Whitney Chapin often wore lifted slightly. "You know how it is with me. He says black. I have to say white."

The picture came into sharp focus. "You were compelled to take the opposing side."

"Partly," Fin agreed. "But I love Good Hope. I see the value of small-town life."

"Really?"

"Even if it's not for me," Fin hastily added.

"I imagine it was difficult." Marigold paused. "Seeing Jeremy with Eliza."

Fin lifted a necklace with sparkling amber stones. "I knew they'd been dating off and on for years. I just didn't realize they'd gotten so close."

Her heart ached for her sister's pain. Though Fin showed no outward sign, Marigold could only imagine how it would be when she came back to Good Hope one day and found Cade cozying up to another woman. Even the thought made her knees grow weak.

"The closeness is a fairly recent occurrence." Though Fin's back remained to her, Marigold waved a dismissive hand. "I'm certain you and Xander are far closer than Jeremy and Eliza."

"I thought he was going to propose." Fin turned, her eyes as flat as her voice. "We'd had this trip to St. John planned for months. I had the feeling that this was when he planned to do it. Xander is big on setting the stage. Obviously I was wrong."

"Ohmigod, I didn't realize things had gotten to that point with you and him." In Good Hope time, dating a year exclusively was tantamount to declaring your intentions. In Chicago, and places like LA and NYC, couples dated for years, often with no thought of marrying. "I'm excited for you."

"We'll see what happens." Fin's lips quirked up in a humorless smile. "For now, I'm just happy to know you and I will be in LA together."

"*If* I decide to accept the position." Marigold wasn't sure why her sister looked so startled. She thought she'd been clear she hadn't decided if she wanted the job. "I should hear from Angelo any day. If he makes an offer, then I'll weigh the advantages of both and decide."

"I want you in LA." When Fin's arms wrapped around her for a hug, Marigold didn't know which of them was more surprised. Fin gave a shaky laugh as she released her and stepped back. "Sorry. It's just that being here has made me realize how much I miss my family."

Marigold was oh so tempted to say she'd move to California, because although Angelo's was her dream salon, she had no family in New York. And like Fin, her time in Good Hope had helped her see how very much connections mattered.

"The Cherries outdid themselves this year." Marigold thought the strains of classical music from a trio of musicians outside the entrance to the grand ballroom added just the right romantic touch.

"If you're talking about the chocolate, I'd have to agree." Cade's voice held a hint of awe. "I don't think I've ever seen so much chocolate in one location."

On a table resplendent in Irish linen, a local chocolatier offered samples of Grand Marnier truffles, violet-infused chocolate squares, and raspberry bonbons. To Marigold's mind, not sampling would be tantamount to a sin.

"I'm definitely going to have to pace myself." Seconds later, Marigold wiped a bit of chocolate from her hands with one of the napkins from the table. "That truffle was amazing."

Cade smiled down at her. "You missed a spot."

He dabbed at the corner of her mouth with a napkin. "If we were alone, I'd kiss it away."

"If we were alone," she lowered her voice until it was barely audible, "I'd make sure there was chocolate on every inch of my skin for you to sample."

His eyes darkened with promise. *Later*, they seemed to say.

Cade wrapped an arm protectively around Marigold's shoulder when she was bumped from behind. "We should sample it all."

"I prefer to be selective." Because having him close felt so good, Marigold rested her head against his arm. "I'm going to pick and choose and try several of something new."

"That chocolate cake looks amazing." With his gaze firmly fixed on the multilayer tower, Cade steered them across the room.

He stopped abruptly.

"What the—"

Only then did Marigold see the Crumb and Cake banner.

Anita stood to one side of the display. Her cherry-red dress the perfect foil for dark hair worn in a fashionable twist.

She spotted Marigold the same instant Marigold saw her. For an instant Anita's smile faltered.

"Anita." Marigold kept her own smile in place as she stepped forward.

An unfortunate break in the crowd gave them a semblance of privacy.

"The cake is impressive." Marigold let her gaze linger. The multilayer beauty had been frosted in white icing, then decorated with chocolate swirls. Each layer—as well as the top—held strawberries dipped in chocolate.

"It's a chocolate buttercream." Anita's bright smile didn't quite reach her eyes. "A particular favorite among grooms."

And, Marigold knew, a particular favorite of her father's.

The area surrounding the cake held dozens of mini cupcakes. Dark chocolate ones, ones with peanut butter icing, and a German chocolate that Marigold knew was one of Anita's signature cakes.

"May I?" Marigold's hand wavered above a German chocolate.

"Of course." Picking up a napkin, Anita handed it and the cupcake to Marigold.

"You'll have to try this, Cade." Marigold fought to keep her voice light, though the way Anita looked at her with sad eyes made her uneasy. "This is one of Anita's best."

"Then I'll sample one, too," he said gallantly.

"Is Steve, ah, is your father coming tonight?" Anita might have been striving for casual, but the look of hope in her eyes gave her away.

Marigold's heart twisted. "I believe he's around here someplace."

Anita's smile wobbled. "Well, when you see him, tell him I said hello."

She might have said more, but several other couples stepped to the table, and Cade and Marigold slipped away.

Marigold finished off the cupcake. "That was awkward."

"The woman might be a pain in the ass . . ." Cade paused, licked a bit of chocolate off his lips. "But she makes a damn fine cupcake."

"How did I not know there was a torch singing competition tonight?" Marigold kept hold of Cade's hand as she turned to Ami.

They'd finished their sampling and now stood at the entrance to the large ballroom. Prim and Max had purchased a table for eight and, according to a recent text, were already inside.

"This poster says walk-ons welcome." Cade gave Marigold's fingers a squeeze. "You should give it a try. I'll cheer you on."

"I only sing in church because it would be rude not to participate," Marigold told him.

"Trust me. You don't want to hear her sing solo." Ami's eyes held a teasing glint.

"I'm not *that* bad," Marigold protested automatically, then had to grin. "Okay, I am that bad. Fin is the singer in the family."

"You should sign up." Ami turned to Fin, who'd just walked up.

"For what?" Fin wore a shimmery red dress with ice pick heels that showed off her legs to full advantage.

Marigold gestured to the sign.

Fin studied it along with the list of judges. "Don't tempt me. I might call your bluff and do it."

Her sister's nonchalant attitude didn't fool Marigold. The second Fin had seen Jeremy Rakes's name as a judge, she'd been hooked.

Marigold didn't blame her. Who wouldn't want to stand on a stage in front of a former boyfriend and show him you were as pretty and desirable as you'd been at eighteen?

While Fin left to sign up, Ami and Beck strolled over to visit with Gladys Bertholf and her son, Frank. Marigold and Cade located table fifteen. It was near the edge of the dance floor, close enough to have a good view of the stage but not too close to the band to make conversation impossible.

Prim's purse was on the table, but there was no sign of her or Max. Cade glanced around. "Where do you think they are?"

"Probably on the dance floor." Marigold knew her sister and brother-in-law were out there somewhere, but the shiny hardwood floor that had been brought in for the event was already packed with women in pretty dresses and men in dark suits.

Overhead, a glittery red net held balloons of pink, white, and red. The lights had been dimmed and little lamps at each table surrounded by a dozen tea lights added a golden glow and romantic ambiance to the scene.

Jackie White, looking healthy and strong—despite her cane—stood at the microphone, belting out a bluesy version of "At Last."

The song wrapped around Marigold like a lover's hand. Tonight, it would be Cade's hands that would be on her body. Earlier, Fin had given her a sly wink and informed Marigold she'd be spending tonight at the family home.

Marigold tossed her purse on the table and held out her hand to Cade. "Let's dance."

He didn't move, his gaze fixed on her shiny black clutch. "Should you leave it there? Anyone could take it."

She gave a little laugh and slipped her arm through his. "This is Good Hope, not Detroit. Besides, if someone steals my purse, I'll call the sheriff. He'll track 'em down."

Though still not appearing convinced, Cade let her tug him to the dance floor. She nearly sighed when he pulled her into his arms. "I don't believe I've seen you in a suit since Shannon's wedding."

The tailored cut of the charcoal-gray suit emphasized his broad shoulders and lean, athletic build. The red, paisley-patterned tie against the pristine white shirt provided a nice pop of color.

"What about New Year's?"

"You wore a tux, remember?"

"I remember when you walked into the parlor." His lips lifted in a smile as they moved in perfect sync to the music. "You took my breath away."

Something in the way he said the words had her tightening her hold on him, resting her head against his chest. In the past couple of days, this is what she'd missed.

This closeness. This connection. *Him.*

When she was with Cade, the thought of leaving him behind was heartbreaking. But she would not ruin this night with thoughts of the future. "I remember the night of Shannon's wedding reception."

"When I swept you off your feet?"

She chuckled. "I think we swept each other."

"Agreed." His hold tightened on her. "I know we—"

"Listen." Her head shot up. "That's my sister."

They continued swaying but shifted their attention to the stage. Like a sultry angel in red, Fin stood in the spotlight, microphone in hand. Her alto was as rich and pure as it had been when she'd been the lead in high school musicals.

"What song is that?" Cade asked.

"Cry Me a River." Marigold's smile faded as she listened to the words. It would be that way for her and Cade. There was no chance for them.

To have him she'd have to give up on the dream, the vow she'd made all those years ago. As Fin continued to sing, Marigold thought of her mother. She'd lost her. Soon, she'd lose Cade.

In that moment, Marigold desperately wanted to go back to the apartment, make love to Cade, let herself drown in his taste, his touch. But she knew sex would only be a temporary solution to the ache.

He wanted to stay in Good Hope.

She had a dream to pursue.

Cry me a river . . .

The last note of the song sounded. Marigold added her applause to the rest, knowing she'd be crying a whole ocean in the not-too-distant future.

"I don't care what the judges decided. You were the best." Steve covered Fin's hand with his and gave it a squeeze. "I'd nearly forgotten how beautifully you sing."

"Thank you, Daddy. But I think you might be a little prejudiced." Though Fin demurred, Marigold could see their father's words pleased her.

"You came in second." Prim lifted her glass in a salute. "I'd say that was pretty good, considering you winged it."

"It didn't sound as if you winged it." Steve brought a hand to his heart. "Your rendition brought tears to my eyes. I wish your mother could have been here. She'd have been so proud."

There was a long pause. His misty-eyed gaze encompassed the table. "Proud of all her girls."

Not me, not now, not yet. Marigold lifted her chin. If things went as she planned, very soon she'd make her mother proud.

"I didn't realize you caught Fin's performance." Marigold took a sip of the wine Beck had ordered for the entire table.

"I was on the far side of the dance floor." Steve leaned back in his chair. "You didn't see me. You only had eyes for this guy."

Her father jerked his head in Cade's direction.

Marigold felt her cheeks warm.

"Who were you dancing with, Dad?" Prim lifted a glass of club soda garnished with a thin slice of lime.

This time it was their father's turn to blush. "Lynn Chapin took pity on this old man."

Marigold saw Ami's expression brighten.

"You're not old." Fin rolled her eyes. "If I'm recalling correctly, you and Lynn are around the same age."

"Lynn's husband was a banker. Died about ten years ago." Though Cade spoke confidently, there was just the slightest question in his tone. He'd done a good job of steeping himself in the history of Good Hope's citizenry, but the learning curve was steep.

"Sounds about right." Marigold relaxed, happy to have the focus off of her and Cade. "I've always liked Lynn."

"Who doesn't?" Ami piped up, a ginger ale in her hand. "She's a lovely woman."

Steve lifted a hand, palm out. "Mrs. Chapin and I are simply friends."

"That's what Marigold and Cade said." Ami grinned. "Look at them now."

If Ami would have been sitting closer, Marigold would have given her a swift kick.

An awkward silence settled over the table.

"Oh, look, here comes Eliza and Jeremy." Prim spoke as if that was a good thing instead of something likely to add even more tension to the table.

As usual, Eliza looked stunning. Her glittery black dress hugged her slender frame, while her bright red lipstick popped and drew the eye.

Jeremy's hand-tailored dark suit fit him perfectly. For tonight's festivities he'd combed his blond hair into some semblance of order. Despite the effort, he still managed to look like he should be surfing on a beach in California.

"Sorry about the loss." Jeremy's gaze went immediately to Fin when he reached the table. "The vote was close."

"Performing in front of a crowd was a kick." Somewhat absently Fin ran her finger around the lip of her glass. "I hadn't been on a stage since high school."

"I remember your junior year when you played Maria, and Jeremy was Tony." Prim sighed. "You two brought the house down."

"Weren't you in *West Side Story*, too, Eliza?" Ami asked in what Marigold guessed was a deliberate attempt to pull the other woman into the conversation.

"I played Anita, the one who tries to shield Maria from the dangers of the gang." Eliza slanted a glance at Jeremy. "Mine was more of a dancing role."

"Good times." Jeremy smiled at Eliza, then turned to Cade. "I heard you caught the vandals."

"You're on top of the news." Cade's expression held obvious satisfaction. "Two boys from Egg Harbor just having fun. Their words, not mine."

"The department is doing good work under your leadership, Cade." Jeremy slapped him on the shoulder. "Eliza is on the town board. She tells me they're behind you."

"You fit right in. You've exceeded our expectations. Which is why I'm concerned that—" Eliza suddenly stopped.

Puzzlement filled Cade's eyes. "Concerned about what?"

Eliza waved away the question. "Later. This isn't the time nor the place for that discussion."

Marigold knew Cade wouldn't let it drop. When something piqued his interest, the man could be a bulldog.

Cade made a get-on-with-it gesture with one hand.

Still, Eliza hesitated. She slanted a glance at Jeremy, received a nod.

"I received a disturbing call from my brother several hours ago. Ethan lives in Illinois now, in a little town called Village Green."

"I've heard of the place." It was Beck who spoke first. His dark brows pulled together as if he was searching his memory for more. Then he smiled. "Where history comes alive . . ."

"I believe that's the town slogan." Eliza's serious gray eyes returned to Cade. "Someone on the Village Green town council was aware Ethan grew up here. The councilwoman asked him if he knew you. Ethan didn't, so he called me. I gave you a good recommendation."

Marigold's stomach knotted. "Recommendation?"

"They're seriously considering Cade for a chief of police position that will open up later this spring." Eliza's gaze remained fixed on Cade. "Jeremy and I discussed the matter on the way here. We need to know what it will take to keep you."

Marigold's mind raced as a roaring filled her ears.

Beside her, Cade chuckled. "Helping me win the upcoming election would be a good start."

Everyone laughed. But even when the topic finally switched to the success of the Hearts and Cherries Fashion Show, everything inside Marigold continued to churn. She knew she was being irrational. If Cade lost the election, he couldn't stay. But how many times had he told her he loved Good Hope, insisted this was where he wanted to make his home?

Only here. Nowhere else. Not in a big city. *Certainly not with her.*

Marigold pushed the thought aside as of no consequence. What mattered was that every person in her family had been doing all they could to get him elected. Yet he'd gone behind their backs and applied for another job.

Bubbling fury swelled to full boil.

She'd been a fool.

The hurt, anger, and sense of betrayal Marigold had experienced when she'd discovered her mother had sent her off to school pretending all was well—when it wasn't—slammed into her.

Trust. Without it, a relationship had nothing.

She and Cade Rallis had nothing.

Chapter Twenty-Two

"Let's dance." Pushing back his chair, Cade stood and held out a hand out to Marigold.

He didn't want to talk about the election or about Fin's amazing voice. All he wanted was to take the woman he loved into his arms and whirl her around the dance floor. He wanted to see her eyes shine. He wanted her to hold on to him and never let him go.

Marigold ignored the outstretched hand and made no move to rise. The blue eyes that glittered so brightly at the start of the evening had turned frosty.

"I believe I'll sit this one out." The cool smile she shot him only added to his unease.

When he started to take his seat, she waved a hand. "Go ahead and dance."

Cade had no desire to dance with anyone else. Unfortunately, the person he wanted to hold in his arms was now regarding him as if he were a snake that had slithered out from under a rock.

He had no idea what he'd done to piss Marigold off, but he was determined to find out and make it right.

Offering a pleasant smile, Cade leaned over and took Marigold's arm in a firm grip. "There's something in the lobby I think you'll be interested in seeing. Since you don't want to dance, I'll show it to you now."

Cade caught her sisters exchanging glances. He pretended not to notice.

After a momentary hesitation, Marigold rose with a grace that was as much a part of her as those blonde curls, and smiled brightly at her family. "I won't be long."

No more *we*, the trained observer in him noticed. During the last hour, he and Marigold had gone from being a couple to two singles.

They didn't speak—at least not to each other—while exiting the ballroom. As they threaded their way through the linen-clad tables, they were stopped frequently by friends wanting to say hello.

When they finally reached the lobby, Cade kept moving, continuing down a long hallway that led, well, he wasn't sure where it led. But they needed privacy, and they certainly weren't going to find it in the ballroom or lobby.

The hallway turned, then dead-ended. When they could go no farther, he stopped. Two wingback chairs in a bright floral pattern sat separated by a table holding a vase of red roses.

Marigold looked at the scene, then back at Cade. She arched a brow. "Really? *This* is what you wanted to show me?"

He ignored the disdain woven through the words. "What's going on, Marigold?"

For a second something flickered in those blue eyes, then the shutter dropped.

"I don't know what you're talking about." Avoiding his gaze, Marigold dropped into one of the chairs and took great care straightening the skirt of her dress.

"Everything was fine. We were having a good time." Cade fought to remain calm. "All of a sudden you're freezing me out. I'd like to know why."

"I see why Alice dumped you."

Cade inwardly flinched. He lifted a brow.

"The job in Village Green." She inclined her head, blue eyes narrowed to slits. "When were you going to tell me about that little side plan?"

"It's not a big deal," he began.

"It is to me." She snapped out the words.

The distress on her face told him that, for whatever reason, discussing his Village Green application was important.

"I applied for that position and the one in Good Hope last spring. The current chief of police in Village Green changed his mind and decided to stay until he turned sixty-five. The search for a replacement was halted. I didn't care because I'd already been offered the position here."

Since Cade still hadn't figured out why any of this mattered to Marigold, he continued to talk, making sure not to stint on details. "I got an e-mail from the city administrator advising they were now ready to actively search again. They asked if I was interested in being considered. I said yes."

"You told me you liked Good Hope." A muscle in Marigold's tightly clenched jaw jumped. "You told me you didn't want to live anywhere else."

"I also mentioned if I lose the election in March, I'll be out of a job." He kept his tone matter-of-fact. "It seemed wise to have a backup plan."

"It obviously didn't occur to you to mention this backup plan to me."

The lack of notification appeared to be the stumbling block. "I'd probably have mentioned it."

"Probably?" She surged to her feet and her voice cracked. "*Probably?*"

Her temper ignited his own. Cade slowly stood, clenching and unclenching his hands at his sides.

"What does it matter where I go, where I work?" The anger and the bitterness that rose up every time he thought of her upcoming departure had his voice going hard. "You'll be leaving for Los Angeles. Or New York. Or wherever *you* decide to go. I certainly don't have a say in that decision."

"Why would you?" she shot back.

"You're right. I'm only the man you're having sex with . . . temporarily." His anger disappeared down a dark hole, replaced by profound weariness. "You accuse me of not communicating. You appear to be forgetting that each time I tried to discuss the future, you changed the subject or blew me off."

When her eyes flashed and she opened her mouth as if to protest, he held up a hand.

"You're right. That isn't entirely accurate. What is true is each time I brought up the possibility of you staying in Good Hope, you threatened to end our relationship." Cade gave a humorless laugh. "You've been quite clear from the beginning that we have no future. It took me a while to get that in my head."

"I—I don't like being lied to," she stammered. "I've been nothing but honest with you."

Even as his gut clenched, he had to agree.

Cade resisted the almost overwhelming urge to pull her into his arms. To beg her to . . . what? Stay? Give up her hopes and dreams for him?

No. She was meant to soar and find the success she'd sought since she was ten. He would never try to hold her back. She should know that by now. Should know *him*.

Then it struck him, and those last few puzzle pieces tumbling around in his head fell into place. It was time for her to start wrapping up loose ends. One of those loose ends was him.

Cade hadn't seen this coming, not so soon. He doubted this talk had been on the agenda for tonight. But Eliza's questions had given Marigold the opening she'd likely been searching for . . .

Though Marigold didn't need anything other than the move as a reason to sever ties with him, Cade could only assume she'd wanted something more to add weight. Tonight she'd found a reason—albeit a shaky one—and had clamped on to it with the fervor of a drowning person snatching a life preserver.

He longed for more time but knew, because he loved her, he'd always wish for one more day. Cade let his gaze linger on her face, memorizing each feature.

"Good-bye, Marigold." Cade extended a hand. Immediately realizing how ridiculous that was, he let it fall to his side. "Best of luck in Los Angeles. Or New York. Or wherever your dreams take you."

There was nothing more to say.

No reason to linger any longer.

He turned. With regret for a love that would never be fully realized fueling his steps, Cade walked down the hall and didn't look back.

Marigold wasn't sure how long she remained seated in the chair at the end of the long, deserted hallway. She only knew it was Ami who finally came for her.

"You didn't return," Ami called out from halfway down the hall. "Whatever Cade showed you had to be something spectacular to keep you away this long."

Her sister's smile began to fade the closer she got to Marigold. "Where is he?"

"He's gone." The words seemed to come from far away.

"Gone?" Ami cocked her head. "As in—?"

Marigold surged to her feet. "As in gone forever. As in we broke up. As in I don't want to talk about it."

"But what—"

"I don't want to talk about him. Okay?" It took all of Marigold's control not to snap. She managed a smile, though it felt more like a grimace.

"Sure. Whatever you want." Ami gestured down the hall. "Let's go back to the table. Everyone's . . . concerned."

"What did they think happened?" Even to her own ears, her voice sounded brittle, as if ready to shatter into a million pieces.

Ami said nothing.

Marigold slanted a sideways glance. Two bright patches of color rode high on her eldest sister's cheeks.

"Ami?" Marigold pressed.

"Prim thought Cade may have proposed." Ami lifted her shoulders, let them fall. Her color deepened. "For being so serious most of the time, Prim is quite the romantic."

"Why would she think he proposed?" Marigold demanded. "She knows I'm leaving Good Hope. I've made that very clear."

Ami moistened her lips with the tip of her tongue, hesitated. "Sometimes plans change. You seemed happy here—"

"It's called making the best of a bad situation."

Ami's face blanched as if Marigold had slapped her. She took a deep breath in, clasped her hands together. "I didn't realize being here was such a hardship."

"That's not what I meant." The beginnings of a headache pounded in Marigold's temple. She raked a hand through her hair and tried to think what she did mean.

They'd reached the ballroom. The romantic music made Marigold want to cry. But she wouldn't.

She lifted her chin.

She was Marigold Bloom. She was strong. She was mighty.

She would survive. But it would be without the man she loved.

Chapter Twenty-Three

When Marigold didn't show up for church the next morning or make an appearance at Muddy Boots, the Bloom sisters gathered up all the chocolates they could find, along with a couple of bottles of wine and sparkling grape juice, and showed up at her door.

"No need to wait for an invitation." Marigold muttered the words, but she might as well have been talking to the wind.

Fin pushed past her, with Prim and Ami following.

Marigold swiped at her hair. She hadn't bothered brushing it or applying makeup. The yoga pants and oversize purple shirt she'd gotten as a gag gift for her birthday last year only added to the not-so-pretty picture.

Fin's gaze dropped to read the message dashed across the front of the shirt. She lifted a brow. "*They call me a hairstylist because BADASS isn't a job title. Seriously?*"

Despite her pensive mood, a ghost of a smile touched Marigold's lips. "The tee was a birthday gift from some friends. Their second choice was *Hairstylists Give the Best Blow Jobs*."

Ami brought a hand to her chest. "Oh, my."

"I'll get you that one for your next birthday." Prim gave Marigold a wink. "Before you know it, you'll have a whole drawer of tacky tees."

"If you do, make it another color." Fin narrowed her gaze. "Purple washes her out."

"Keep that in mind, Prim." Marigold's tone held a slight edge. "Fin has decreed no purple."

Prim, looking as pretty as a strawberry parfait in a pink cashmere sweater, lifted her phone and keyed in. "Got it. No purple for Marigold."

Ami hung her jacket on the coat tree just inside the front door. When she turned, Marigold saw her sister had *that* look in her eye. The same one their mother used to give her when she'd tried to keep things from her.

"What's the latest?" Ami asked in a conversational tone.

Marigold lifted a brow. "You mean other than Fin telling me what to do and what to wear?"

Fin swiveled to face her youngest sibling, her eyes boring into Marigold's. "Ditch the attitude, Marigold. It's as unattractive as your shirt."

Marigold gave her an arch look. "Purple doesn't look good on you, either."

"That's why I don't wear it." Fin took a seat in a nearby chair and crossed one long leg over the other.

"We'll get settled, then you'll tell us why you're avoiding us." Ami moved into the kitchen, and from the clinking Marigold heard, she surmised she was grabbing some glasses.

"I hardly think skipping church and breakfast on a Sunday morning constitutes avoiding you," Marigold told her sisters. "Did any of you consider I might just have wanted to sleep late?"

The sisters merely exchanged glances.

Prim cleared the steamer trunk—still masquerading as a coffee table—of magazines, then dumped wrapped, bite-size candy pieces into a white porcelain bowl with yellow stripes.

"Is this foul mood because you broke up with the sheriff?" Fin appeared bored by the thought.

Marigold crossed her arms, ignoring the pang in her heart. "If this is some sort of relationship intervention, you're wasting your time."

"You and Cade broke up last night." Prim's voice went deep with worry.

The words, true as they were, held the force of a hard punch. "Which was the plan from the moment we started dating. It was never—"

Ami held up a hand. A sudden look of tenderness crossed her face. "We understand that, sweetie. Still, you've been dating Cade since you got back in town. The breakup of a relationship that long demands chocolate. It's a takes-a-village kind of thing."

Marigold wearily massaged her brow. Though she was touched by her sisters' concerns, the last thing she wanted was to sit around a steamer trunk and sing "Kumbaya."

"This isn't just about you, Marigold." Prim unwrapped a Snickers Bite and popped it in her mouth, chewed.

"Fin and Xander are on shaky ground, so we need to support her with chocolate." Ami looked up, a bottle in each hand.

"And with wine," Fin added. "Lots and lots of wine."

"Wine," Ami agreed, then glanced down at the bottle of sparkling grape juice and sighed, "for those of you not preggers."

"Plus," Prim reached over and grabbed another chocolate, "we need to celebrate the end of Dad's relationship with Anita. That breakup has been way too long coming and deserves a toast or two."

When her sisters put it that way, how could she refuse to join in? Still, over the next couple of hours Marigold made a concerted effort to keep the focus of the conversation *on* Fin and Anita and *off* her and Cade.

In Chicago, she'd become an expert at keeping her deepest thoughts and feelings to herself. At her level, you never knew when someone might want to use some comment you'd tossed off casually—or told them in confidence—to bring you down.

Marigold trusted her sisters. That wasn't the issue this afternoon. She just couldn't bring herself to talk about Cade. Or about the job offer she'd received just that morning. By the time Ami and Prim rose to leave, the sisters didn't know any more about what was going on in her head than they did when they arrived.

Instead of leaving with the others, Fin merely poured herself another glass of wine and sat back against the plump cushions. It was a relaxed pose, the forest-green cashmere sweater hugging breasts that reminded Marigold of melons.

After pouring herself another glass of wine, Marigold cocked her head. "Did you have a boob job?"

Fin laughed, a full, robust sound that echoed in a room that now seemed too empty. "No. Why?"

Marigold dropped into the chair nearest the sofa. "That sweater makes your breasts look humongous."

Fin glanced down, grinned. "I'll have to wear it more often."

"I imagine lots of women in California have cosmetic surgery." Marigold eyed the candy left behind but shifted her gaze back to her sister without taking a piece.

"People, especially those in the film or television industry, need to look their best. No different than the clientele that frequents the Steffan Oliver Salon." Fin cast her a speculative gaze. "You know we can sit here all day and talk about everything but what's going on in that head of yours. Or you can save us the time, not to mention the calories from these chocolates, and simply be honest with me."

Marigold shifted uncomfortably. Ami's green eyes were always so warm and comforting. The ones trained on hers now were razor-sharp and unbending.

She might be able to . . .

"Don't even think about changing the subject back to me or Anita." Fin rolled her eyes. "Either pregnancy has fogged our sisters' brains or they were too kind to point out your continued evasion. I'm not kind. Or easily fooled. So don't bother."

Marigold's mouth snapped shut. She expelled a breath, felt fresh anger surge.

"Cade didn't say a word to me about the other job." Marigold's voice snapped, then cracked slightly. "Don't you think that's something you should tell the person you're dating?"

"Is it?" Fin sounded slightly bored.

"Of course it is."

Fin took another sip of wine. "Did you two talk much about the future?"

Marigold kept her eyes averted as she filled her wineglass, recalling the accusation Cade had thrown at her. "We talked a lot about campaign strategies."

Fin waved a dismissive hand.

"Cade told me Good Hope is where he wants to live."

"He likes it here." Fin took a drink. "Lots of people do."

"He fits in," Marigold grudgingly conceded. "He's happy here."

"Tell me. What did the happy sheriff have to say when you asked him about the position in Village Green?"

"He said it was a backup in case he loses the election."

"Logical."

"I don't know what's so logical about it. Cade could relocate anywhere, if he was willing."

"Ah." Fin set down her glass of wine, her green eyes glittering. "Now we're getting somewhere."

"No, we're not." Even as panic rose up inside Marigold, she narrowed her gaze on her sister. "How much have you had to drink?"

"Two and a half glasses. Not nearly enough to be steered off track." Fin chuckled. "Anyway, I see it the way you do. There's no reason the sheriff couldn't relocate to wherever you decide to settle."

"He wouldn't do that." The ache in Marigold's chest became a pulsating pain. "He likes small-town life too much."

"More than he likes you?"

"Yes." Marigold pushed the word past frozen lips.

"There are bedroom communities surrounding any large city," Fin continued as if Marigold hadn't spoken, her tone easy and conversational. "He could be a sheriff or a police chief in one of those. You could live in one of those towns and commute. Though, if you decide that's an option, you'd be better off in New York City than LA because of the access to mass transit."

"I got the job," Marigold murmured, wondering why she wasn't shouting the words to the heavens and celebrating. "Angelo called and offered me the position."

Fin's green eyes gave nothing away. "You took it?"

"Not yet."

"What are you waiting for?"

"I don't want to rush into anything."

"It's your dream job," Fin reminded her.

Marigold took a deep breath, let it out slowly. "When I was diagnosed with dyslexia, I made a vow."

Fin inclined her head. "Did you?"

"I vowed I would be more successful than Ami and Prim and you." Marigold twisted her fingers together on her lap, then quickly pulled them apart when she caught her sister's sharp-eyed stare.

"Successful in what way?"

Marigold bristled. "That's a crazy question."

"Humor me."

"In my career, of course. When I reach the top of my profession, everyone would see—" Marigold swallowed hard against the lump trying to form in her throat.

Fin raised a perfectly tweezed brow. "That you aren't stupid?"

Marigold surged to her feet, her heart pounding as if she'd just run a large race. "I'm not stupid."

Her shouted words echoed in the stillness, but the hurled ball of fury merely bounced off her sister.

"Of course you aren't stupid," Fin agreed in a calm voice. "Though at the moment you're not acting particularly brilliant."

Marigold flung out her hands in frustration. "What are you talking about?"

"Cade."

Marigold stiffened as if struck, and when she spoke, she couldn't quite keep the bitterness from her voice. "Cade didn't care enough to look for a solution."

"What about you?" Fin's expression remained carefully blank. "Did you care enough to look for one?"

Marigold waited for Fin to say more, but her sister merely finished off her third glass of wine.

"No. I mean I didn't look for a solution, but it wasn't because I didn't care." Marigold expelled a heavy sigh. "I made it clear to Cade I wouldn't be staying in Good Hope. If he really wanted to discuss a future with me, he should have pressed. Then we could have searched for a solution together."

"Just out of curiosity." Fin set down her empty glass. "What was your response the times he made the attempt?"

"How do you know he tried?"

Fin gave her the fish eye. "You shut him down."

Marigold lifted her chin in a stubborn tilt. "He could have pressed."

"You shut him down," Fin repeated. "You made it clear your plans didn't include him. Why would he?"

Frustration bloomed inside Marigold. She clenched her fists. "Yes, but—"

"Each time he tried, you blew him off," Fin continued despite Marigold's hiss of protest. "You're blaming him for something you have ownership in. Doesn't surprise me. You did the same with Mom."

"Wh-what are you talking about?" Startled, Marigold stumbled over the words.

"Mom knew how much attending cosmetology school in Chicago meant to you. When she'd mention schools closer to home, you didn't want to discuss it. What did you expect her to say when you asked how she was doing? Though her physical appearance said otherwise, you chose to believe she was fine. Why? So you could get on with your life."

Too stunned to speak, Marigold could only stare as Fin succumbed to temptation and popped a chocolate in her mouth.

"That isn't fair."

Based on Fin's unyielding stare, Marigold's protest fell on unsympathetic ears.

"What isn't fair is to blame Mom—or Cade—when you don't communicate your own feelings honestly." Fin's matter-of-fact tone may have come across as harsh, but her eyes had softened to a bottle green. "If you wanted to stay close to Mom in those last days, you should have told her. If you want the job in New York, you need to take it. If you'd like to try to make something work with Cade, you need to tell him. This isn't rocket science, little sister. You can't control what happens next, but at least if you're honest about your feelings, you won't have to live with regret."

Tears stung the backs of Marigold's eyes. This time she didn't blink them back.

Fin leaned over and took her hands. "Figure out what's important to you, decide how far you're willing to bend. This might also be a good time to take another look at your definition of success."

"There's only one definition," Marigold insisted.

Fin's eyes brimmed with sudden amusement before she sobered. "Prim and Ami both have good—what many would consider quite successful—careers, but that isn't where their happiness lies. You and I, no matter how high we go in our chosen fields, can't hope to touch what they have with Max and Beck."

"Cade is my prince," Marigold blurted out.

"All the more reason to be honest with yourself, and with him. A prince often only comes around once." Fin reached for the wine bottle. "Be very sure before you walk away from yours."

"Izzie." Cade pulled to an abrupt stop at the sight of the artist stepping out of the alley. "What are you doing here?"

The day before Valentine's Day had dawned arctic cold. Though a warm front was predicted to be headed their way, Cade wouldn't believe it until the temperature rose above freezing.

"I don't mind the cold." Izzie smiled, a mass of kinky brown hair hanging down her back. "When I'm dressed for it, I barely notice."

Her down-filled puffy coat hit just below the knees. The red-checkered hat she wore, earflaps down, made him think of a lumberjack.

Though he wasn't dressed as warmly and felt the cruel bite of the wind, Cade didn't mind. The rawness kept his mind off Marigold.

"I wanted to review K.T.'s work firsthand. He's so young, and I worried he might not be able to deliver. But," Izzie gestured with her head back to the alley, "his art hits the mark on all counts."

Cade's blood froze. "Are you saying K.T. is responsible for the graffiti?"

Something in his tone must have alerted Izzie. A wary look filled her eyes. "Graffiti?"

"It's a crime." His tone was curt. "Defacing personal property."

Izzie's large, brown eyes went huge. Distress formed a dark cloud over her face. "But that's one of the walls the alley art project will be painting."

Cade paused, considered. In Detroit, it didn't matter how old a perp was or what the circumstances. They broke the law. You hauled them in. It was up to the lawyers, the social workers, and the judges what happened next.

But this wasn't Detroit, and K.T. might stand a chance of having a good future if he didn't have any bumps on his record.

Cade considered, gave a curt nod. "I'll speak with Mr. Potter. He owns the building."

Izzie closed her eyes. "Thank you."

"I'll do my best." Cade couldn't make any promises, but he had no doubt Potter would go along. Neighbors helping neighbors was the Good Hope way.

"You and Marigold have big plans for Valentine's Day?" Izzie smiled as she asked, as if she already knew the answer.

"We went to the dance on Saturday." As the last thing he wanted to talk about was Marigold, he shifted focus. "How about you? Big plans?"

"I'm in a not-seeking-Mr.-Right phase of my life." She grinned. "Right now my priority is building my career."

It was Marigold's priority too, Cade thought bitterly, then immediately felt guilt at the thought. There was nothing wrong with wanting to achieve your potential, nothing wrong with wanting to find your place in the world. He only wished he fit into her plan.

Cade continued his patrol of the business district. He thought about stopping at the bake shop for a doughnut and coffee but kept walking. Marigold could be there, or another of her sisters. He didn't want to make conversation, see the pitying look in their eyes.

He was the poor sap who'd fallen in love with their sister, a woman everyone knew was destined for bigger and better.

At the far edge of the row of Main Street businesses, he paused in front of the Daily Grind, a coffee shop that had opened last fall. As franchises and chains weren't allowed in the community, this was a mom-and-pop operation, begun by guy who'd tired of the big-city rat race and had come home.

Too bad Marigold didn't feel the same way. Too bad she couldn't see all Good Hope had to offer. Too bad she couldn't see all *he* had to offer.

Chilled to the bone and more than a little bitter, Cade stepped inside and let the warmth envelop him. He inhaled the rich scent of coffee and saw, with some relief, there were bakery items in the case. He could go for something sweet.

When he lifted his gaze, Cade blinked at the sight of the woman who straightened behind the counter. "Cassie?"

"Hi, Sheriff." Cassie, dishwater-blonde hair pulled back in a low tail, smiled. "Bet you didn't expect to find me here."

"You're right about that." He gave a little laugh. "How long have you been—?"

"A couple of months. I'm part-time right now, until the season starts. My boss is willing to work around my child care arrangements."

"That's good." Cade hoped this opportunity was just what the woman needed to jump-start her life.

"If you're looking for Mr. Bloom, he's at a table around the corner." Cassie smiled. "I was just telling him how much I appreciated him volunteering to be a Big Brother for K.T. and Braxton. They're getting together next week for the first time."

Neighbors helping neighbors.

"It'll be a good fit." He recalled his conversation with Izzie. "Say, could you have K.T. stop by my office sometime this week?"

Wariness, coupled with a flash of worry, filled Cassie's eyes. "Is there a problem?"

"No problem." He smiled and kept his tone easy. "It has to do with the alley art project."

The tense set to her shoulders eased. "K.T. is very excited about the possibility of participating."

The boy was a minor. Protocol demanded he tell the boy's mother what was going on. But Cassie had dealt with so much and her life appeared to be finally back on track.

As Cade felt certain Potter would go along with his plan, he simply focused on the bake case. "Are those pastries from Blooms Bake Shop?"

"Hadley brings a supply by every morning." Cassie smiled. "They're very popular."

Cade wanted the chocolate cake doughnut, but he needed to stop being so predictable, so boring. "I'll take a cherry Danish with black coffee."

"To stay?"

Cade nodded.

Once he paid, Cade picked up the plate and cup and strolled to where Steve sat reading the newspaper. "I didn't expect to see you here."

Steve looked up and smiled, carefully folded the paper in half, and set it aside.

"Join me." Steve gestured and Cade took a seat. The eyes that met his were kind. "How are you doing?"

Cade glanced down at the pastry and coffee. "I'm out of the cold and wind and about to take a break to enjoy one of your eldest daughter's fine pastries, so I'd say I'm doing okay."

Steve didn't ask about Marigold. Cade knew he wouldn't. That's why he'd come over instead of heading straight for the door.

Cade lifted the pastry to his lips and took a bite. The taste of tart cherries, butter, and sugar came together in a delicious explosion of flavor. "Cassie tells me the Big Brother thing is all set."

"The paperwork is done." Steve's hazel eyes held satisfaction behind the thin silver wire frames of his glasses. "I hope we have a connection. You and I both know that connections are what life is all about."

Connections, Cade thought, like the one he and Marigold had shared. *Correction.* Like the one he *thought* he'd had with Marigold.

Steve lifted the ceramic mug, studied Cade over the rim.

Here it comes, Cade thought. *Daddy bear coming to baby bear's rescue.*

"What'd you think of those cards?"

Cade paused in the act of popping another bite of Danish into his mouth. "Cards?"

Steve grinned full-out. "Max mentioned Prim had given the deck to Marigold."

Oh, *those* cards.

Cade shook his head. "How Vanessa Eden could have thought those were a good gift for her son is beyond me."

"Vanessa is a free spirit kind of woman." Steve shook his head, his smile indulgent. "Women like that kind of stuff."

"But the questions." Cade grimaced, recalling a couple of the ones more focused on sex he'd read when he flipped through the deck before dinner that night. "Brutal."

"I knew Marigold would have shown them to you."

"She not only showed them to me, she made me answer a couple of them." Cade chuckled.

Steve's eyes sparkled with good humor. "That's my girl."

"Yeah, well." Cade took a long sip of coffee.

"Do you recall the questions?"

Cade wasn't really interested in discussing the cards, but what was the alternative? Chatting about Marigold with her father and musing about why she'd dumped him? "One was 'What will matter most to you when you're ninety?'"

"A sound question." Steve nodded. "One obviously designed to get at priorities. How did you answer?"

"Family." Cade wrapped his fingers around the warm mug but made no move to lift it to his lips. "Wife, kids, grandkids, maybe even a few great-grands tossed into the mix."

"Not where you've lived or what you've achieved?" It must have been a rhetorical question, because Steve continued on without giving Cade a chance to answer. "What was the other one?"

"What comes to mind when you think of your ex?" Because he knew Steve was going to want to know how he'd answered, Cade gave it to him without making him ask. "I told Marigold it was regret. That I didn't care enough to fight for my relationship with Alice."

"I suppose that's what you need to think about, then."

Normally, Cade didn't have difficulty following a conversation. In fact, he prided himself on his ability to read between the lines while ferreting out the truth.

"I don't understand," Cade reluctantly admitted.

Steve pushed to his feet, pulled on his coat, and tucked the newspaper under his arm. "You're a smart guy. Think about what you want. Think about what's really important to you and fight for it. I have every faith in you."

With those words, Steve strolled out of the coffee shop, leaving Cade nursing the words and a now lukewarm cup of coffee.

Chapter Twenty-Four

Marigold closed the art journal. For the first time in nearly three days, the path she needed to take, the path she *wanted* to take, was clear.

She started by composing a text.

Steffan,

I sincerely apologize for going behind your back to get the team lead position for Couture Fashion Week. Being in charge of hairstyles for that event was your gig.

I'm very sorry for my actions.

Marigold

She hit Send.

There were a few things she could have mentioned about his less-than-stellar behavior, but this was an apology for *her* actions.

Now she could focus on her and Cade. If there still was a her and Cade.

Marigold knew the wall she'd erected between them couldn't be scaled by an e-mail or a text. Making him see that they belonged together was something that needed to be handled in person.

Today, on Valentine's Day—ah, the irony—she would hunt him down and offer him her heart. She'd tell him how much she loved him and hope he agreed they shared the kind of love that would last a lifetime.

The buzz of the doorbell pulled her from her thoughts. As Ami planned to help Hadley with some last-minute orders, Marigold decided she must have decided to stop in and say hello first.

She'd told Ami it was okay to use her key, but her sister had winked and said she wouldn't want to walk in on anything. But that had been eons ago, when she and Cade had been hot and heavy.

Lately, the only thing her sister was likely to interrupt was a crying jag.

She rose and strolled to the door, reaching it just as the buzzer sounded again. Marigold jerked it open. "I don't know why you don't use the key . . ."

Her voice trailed off. It wasn't Ami standing there, but Cade.

"May I come in?"

Since Marigold was having difficulty finding her voice, she only stepped aside.

He filled the small room, taking up all the oxygen, making it impossible for her to breathe.

"These are for you." He shoved a bouquet of red roses interspersed with baby's breath into her hands.

She hadn't noticed the flowers. Her gaze had been on his face, on those beautiful gray eyes.

"Ah, thank you." Her voice sounded rusty, as if it hadn't been used for a few hundred years, but at least it was steady.

She heard his sigh of relief. It was almost as if he thought she might toss the flowers in his face. But that wasn't her style. She'd never been a drama queen.

Besides, she wasn't angry anymore. Heartsick about the way things had ended between them, but not angry.

While she put the flowers in water, she watched Cade slip off his coat and sling it over a chair. Her heart twisted. How many times over the past few weeks had she watched him do that same thing?

"I've been doing a lot of thinking." He gestured to the sofa. "I'd appreciate if you'd let me say my piece before you toss me out."

"The flowers bought you ten minutes." She'd meant the words to be light and teasing, but he must have taken them literally, because he gave a nod.

He waited until she'd taken a seat on the sofa before settling into the chair holding his coat. Cade leaned forward and rested his forearms on his thighs. "I told you once I regretted that I didn't care enough to fight for Alice. I let her go because she didn't matter enough to me."

Marigold felt a tiny flutter in her chest.

"I love you, Marigold, and I'm here to fight for you. I'm here to fight for us."

She opened her mouth to tell him she wanted to make it work, too. But he continued without giving her a chance to speak.

"You regretted that you and Jason never fought, that you kept things superficial. I regret keeping things superficial with you. I knew I was in love with you for weeks, but I never said the words. I never let you know how I felt. That's on me, and that ends today."

"I—I don't know what to say."

"You don't have to say anything now, just listen." His gaze dropped to the hands she had clenched together in her lap. "Is it okay if I hold your hand? You can have it back anytime you want."

His attempt at a lighthearted chuckle fell flat.

In answer she held out her hand and felt the chill inside her fade when his strong fingers wrapped around hers.

"Somewhere along the way I forgot home isn't a place, it's having people you love in your life." Cade's intense gray eyes never left hers. "When I'm ninety, I want you beside me."

"My career," she began, the words she wanted to stay sticking to her tongue.

"I know how talented you are, and I won't hold you back." His thumb gently caressed her palm. "What's important to you is important to me. I can work anywhere. With your dreams and goals, you can't. Wherever you decide to settle is fine with me. All that matters to me is being with you, building a life with you."

The words wrapped around Marigold's heart like a hug. "You don't like big towns."

His eyes softened. "I can be happy anywhere, as long as I'm with you."

He was speaking from the heart. She could see it in his eyes, hear it in his voice.

It was time she did the same.

"For so many years, I pursued success without really thinking what that word meant to me." She cleared her throat. "I've been doing a lot of thinking, and it seems to me that success is liking what you do and being happy. Fin had to go away to find her success. Ami and Prim found theirs here."

Cade nodded, his gaze firmly fixed on her face. He didn't attempt to rush her. It was as if he realized she needed to spell this all out, not only for him, but for herself.

"I was looking through my art journal entries this morning and I realized something."

"What was it?" His voice was as soft and smooth as freshly whipped cream.

"I've found my happiness here, too. I've been happier and more content in Good Hope than I've ever been in my life. Most of that has to do with you. With us." Marigold paused. "Fin suggested we could move to a bedroom community outside a large city, preferably one with a good transit system. I could work in the city. You could be a sheriff in a small town."

His eyes never left hers. "If that's what you want, that's what we'll do."

"It isn't what I want." Marigold leaned toward him. An urgency filled her tone as she tightened her grip on his hand. "I'm happy here. I like being close to my sisters and my dad. I want to be more than a face on a screen to my nieces and nephews."

Hope flared in the dark depths of his eyes, but his voice was calm. "What are you saying?"

"I can remain cutting-edge. It might take more work, but I'll fly to hair shows and do what's necessary to keep my skills sharp. But I can see clients here. I want to live in Good Hope with you. I love you, Cade. So very much."

In one swift movement, she was in his arms. He held her so close she could feel the wild beat of his heart. "Are you sure?"

"About loving you?"

He gave her hair a tug, laughed. "No, about staying in Good Hope. I don't want you to stay just because of me."

"I'm sure. Now, if you lose the election, we may have to come up with Plan B. But wherever that plan takes us, you and I will be together. That's what matters."

"I want it all, Marigold."

Her heart began to sing. "Yes."

Cade held her at arm's length. "You don't even know what I'm about to ask."

"I do. And yes, I'll marry you. I want that more than anything."

The look of delight that crossed his face emboldened her.

She continued quickly, not giving him a chance to speak. "I know it's tradition for the guy to ask, but there has been nothing traditional about you and me. Starting with when I invited myself back to your motel room after Shannon's wedding reception."

"You didn't ask me, Goldilocks." His husky voice had everything inside her melting. "I asked you."

"Really?" What had stuck with Marigold about that night was the attraction, the desire, and the sense of connection. She shrugged, smiled. "It doesn't really matter who asked whom back then. I'm asking you to be mine now and forever. I'll say the words so there's no misunderstanding. Will you marry me, Cade Rallis? Will you share your life with me, have children with me, grow old with me?"

He didn't hesitate. "I wouldn't have it any other way."

As she gazed into those steady gray eyes and heard the promise in his voice, Marigold made another promise.

They were going to be deliriously happy together.

She wouldn't have *that* any other way.

Epilogue

Marigold flung open the door of the salon and froze. "What the heck happened here?"

"We, ah, got a little jump start while you and the sheriff were honeymooning in Iceland." Ami wrapped her arms around Marigold in welcome, holding her as close as her big belly would allow.

"Shut the door," Beck called out absently from where he stood anchoring a gilt-edged mirror to the wall. "You're letting the cold air inside."

Marigold continued to stare. Where was the poodle wallpaper? The faux marble countertops? This interior was on par with the finest salons in Chicago. It couldn't be hers. She blinked. Then blinked again. Still there.

Max strode in from the back. "The last of the mirrored tile is on the bathroom wall."

Marigold wondered if she could be hallucinating. It had, after all, been a whirlwind couple of months. Once the election—which Cade won handily—was over, Marigold had jumped straight into wedding plans.

At the beginning of June, they'd married in an outdoor ceremony on a piece of land that would one day be the site of the home they would share for the rest of their lives.

The door behind her opened and Cade stepped inside. Like her, he'd changed out of what he'd worn earlier. How anyone could look so sexy in faded jeans and an ancient Detroit PD T-shirt was beyond her.

His gaze was just as puzzled as it slid to her. "I thought we were coming here to paint. This looks like all the work is done."

Relief flooded Marigold. She wasn't going crazy after all. "I'm as surprised as you."

"It's a belated wedding gift." Ami made a sweeping gesture with one hand. "What do you think?"

Marigold did a 360. "What happened to Carly's Cut and Curl?"

"We destroyed all traces of it," Ami said cheerfully.

"The poodle wallpaper is gone." Cade kept glancing at the walls as if expecting the prancing dogs to reappear.

"You sound almost disappointed."

He grinned sheepishly. "It was growing on me."

Marigold moved to the center of the small room and turned in a circle. Beneath her feet the once-scarred dark hardwood gleamed. Above her, the suspended ceiling with stained tiles was gone, exposing a tin ceiling original to the building.

The ceiling gave the room a vintage vibe, as did the exposed brick wall. The dark gray surface of the opposing wall was adorned with several oversize flowers. Marigold recognized Izzie Deshler's work. But the jewel in the room's crown was the chandelier. Marigold struggled to find her breath. "All this is amazing. But the chandelier is . . ."

She struggled to find the right word but came up empty. "Where did you find it?"

"It came from the Sweeney house in Egg Harbor." Beck laid a hand on his wife's shoulder. "They had a tag sale and Ami couldn't resist."

"They priced it crazy low." Ami's gaze lifted to linger on the cylindrical fixture. "It's vintage Capodimonte porcelain from Italy. The ceramic flowers are hand painted. Even though I didn't have a place for it in our home, I had to buy it."

"Of course you did." Beck squeezed his wife's shoulder and smiled indulgently.

"It's unique." The chandelier was unlike anything Marigold had ever seen. Instead of crystals, it held a multitude of flowers in muted tones.

"Unique in a good way?" Worry suddenly filled Ami's green eyes. "If you don't like it, we'll take it down and get something different."

"I love it. I love everything you've done here." Marigold turned to her family. "And I love every single one of you for doing this for me."

"Steve and I refinished the floor the other day." Max gestured. "It turned out even better than we'd hoped."

"Where is Dad?" Marigold had taken stock of the family and realized some were missing. "And Prim and the boys?"

"Prim is getting the champagne so we can toast your new business. The twins are with her." Ami gestured to the champagne flutes on a silver tray. "Dad is picking up a little something extra."

It was all so . . . wonderful. First the lovely ceremony followed by a reception in Beck and Ami's parlor. Then the surprise honeymoon trip to Iceland . . . and now this.

As emotion rose to clog her throat, the door in the back of the salon banged open.

"We're here," Prim called out as she and the boys tumbled into the room. She stopped and smiled with delight when she saw Marigold.

Prim turned to her boys, each cradling a bottle of champagne in his arms. "Give Daddy the bottles. Be careful. Don't drop them."

"This is for you." Connor held his bottle up by the neck. "Because this is your new house."

"It's not her house. It's a salon," Callum corrected his twin before turning toward Marigold. "I got me a bottle, too."

"I told the boys the champagne was a type of housewarming present," Prim explained. "I gave them three choices at the store and they picked this vintage out especially for you."

Though Marigold knew the purchase was at their mother's instigation, love for these two little boys swamped her. "Thank you, Callum and Connor."

"You're welcome." Connor turned to his brother when he didn't respond. "When someone says *thank you*, you're supposed to say *you're welcome*."

Callum shoved the bottle into his father's arms. "You're welcome."

"I can't believe you kept this a secret from us." Marigold crossed the room and gave Prim a squeeze, then turned to Cade. "I'm overwhelmed."

Her husband's arms closed around her, and the light in Marigold's perfect world burned even brighter. When she finally stepped from his embrace, his hand slid down her arm, and his fingers laced with hers.

Using his free hand, Cade pointed to two pink, tufted chairs with a glass-topped wicker basket side table between them. "Pink?"

"What can I say?" Max lifted both hands, palms up. "Prim said it's Marigold's favorite color."

"Forget the chairs." Prim gestured to the window. "Those are hand-sewn curtains."

Marigold realized the white eyelets had been replaced by sheer crushed-voile panels that were not only stylish but let in the light. "You actually made those?"

"Ami and I did." Prim shot her sister a conspiratorial glance. "Pulled out Mom's old Singer and went to town."

Marigold brought a hand to her neck. "I can't believe you went to all that work for me."

Ami's eyes grew luminous. "I believe I speak for both Prim and myself when I say it was a labor of love."

Marigold's heart swelled. Tears stung the backs of her eyes.

"Ami even made Mom's favorite cookies," Prim announced.

"Chocolate chip?" Cade's hopeful look made them all laugh.

"Lavender with rose-water icing." Ami's voice turned husky. "I'm getting closer to her recipe. One day I'll nail it."

"I'm glad you baked them." For as far back as Marigold could recall, Ami and their mother had made the cookies for each special occasion in the family. Marigold swallowed past the lump in her throat. "It's as if Mom is here, celebrating with us."

"Shall I pour the champagne?" Beck broke the emotion-filled silence.

"Let's wait for Dad." Ami glanced at the clock. "He should be here any—"

"I bet you thought I got lost."

Marigold heard her father's voice at the same time the front door opened.

"Did you get it?" Ami's gaze settled on his empty arms.

"You bet I did."

"Where is it?" Ami asked.

"Where is what?" Marigold hated being out of the loop. Right now she felt *very* out of touch.

"In the front." Steve glanced at Beck. "Why don't you pour us each a glass of champagne, then we'll take this outside."

"Do you know what *it* is?" Marigold whispered to Cade.

He shook his head. "Whatever it is, your dad seems jazzed about it."

Once everyone had their glasses of champagne—or sparkling cider—they stepped out into the sunshine.

As they gathered together on the sidewalk, Steve took Marigold's hand. He tugged his daughter free of the group, then pointed upward.

Her mouth dropped open.

Hanging from an ornate iron holder that protruded from the building was a distressed blue wooden sign adorned with painted cabbage roses in salmon and white. Across the front in an eye-catching decorative font was a single name: Marigold's.

The sudden warmth clogging Marigold's throat made speech difficult. "It—it's beautiful."

"Izzie did it." Ami lightly brushed Marigold's hair with the palm of her hand. "She refused to take payment. She said the sign is her gift to you and Cade."

"But—"

Her father stepped forward then, and something in his eyes had the words of protest Marigold had been about to utter sliding back down her throat.

"We love you, Marigold. Your friends love you. And the community of Good Hope loves you." Steve lifted his glass of champagne high. "May your life always be filled with much love and success."

Tears slipped unnoticed down her cheeks as first her father, then the rest of the family, gave her a hug. Then Cade stepped forward and held out a hand.

As her fingers curved around his, the raw emotion and love that surged nearly knocked Marigold to her knees. When her new husband looked into her eyes and smiled, Marigold wanted to pull him tight against her and never let go. Instead, she smiled back.

If success was measured in having the opportunity to do what you loved while being surrounded by people you loved and who loved you, Marigold realized she'd soared higher than she ever dreamed possible.

She didn't realize she was crying until her dad gave her a handkerchief to sop up her tears. As if understanding just what she needed at that moment, he slung an arm around her shoulder and gave Cade a wink. "Let's go inside and have some cookies."

Acknowledgments

To Cindy Hoage, a fabulous hairstylist and friend. An accurate portrayal of life in the hairstyling world must be attributed to her. Any mistakes are my own.

About the Author

Cindy Kirk started writing after taking a class at a local community college. But her interest in words began years earlier, when she was in her teens. At sixteen she wrote in her diary: "I don't know what I would do if I couldn't be a writer." After her daughter went to college, she returned to her passion and jumped straight into composing book-length fiction. She loves reading and writing romance novels because she believes in the undeniable power of love and in the promise of the happily ever after. An incurable romantic and an eternal optimist, Kirk creates characters who grow and learn from their mistakes while achieving happy endings in the process. She lives in Nebraska with her high-school-sweetheart husband and their two dogs.